2/2017

To my friends to
Sunset Ridge.
Thanks for
your support.
All the Best,
Dennis Stephan

Acts of Sedition

By Dennis Stephan

D1302258

ISBN-1537558803

ISBN-13: 978-1537558806

Disclaimer:

This is a work of fiction. Names, characters, places and incidents either are products of the author's imagination or are used fictitiously. Any resemblance to actual events or locales or persons, living or dead, is entirely coincidental.

Acknowledgements:

I dedicate this novel to my wonderful wife of 43 years, Pauline. Without her continued love, devotion, and encouragement I would not be the person I am today.

Thanks to the following people for their help and guidance in the writing of this novel:

Walter Adamek, MD
Joanna Armentani
Anthony Gallo
Frank Morelli
Nancy Morelli
Aubrey Wesser

Prologue

There are times when an innocuous event can serve to chronicle change that history may well view as momentous.

It was a frigid January day; evidence that 2045 would be an exceptionally cold year. Ice covered the west front lawn of the Capitol in DC and there was an ill wind, as they say. Typically, these ceremonies had been held indoors when the weather was this cold, but the president-elect had insisted that today's event be held outdoors, as was the tradition.

The "hand-picked" VIPs were seated up front in a heated section of bleachers. Carol Carson an influential woman and the President of the Power of Women together with her plus one, longtime friend and former sorority sister Angela Maria Mastronardo were relegated to the rear of the seated crowd where they were certain to freeze their asses off. They were so far away from the podium that they could barely see the ceremony. Her outspokenness against the election of the president during the campaign had no doubt cemented her low status among the invitees.

Other excited supporters and onlookers who weren't even allowed into the seated area, braved the wintry 17-degree weather. Some were here to applaud, many were not.

Chief Justice Mark Griffin ceremoniously administered the oath of office to the 50th president of the United States.

While most before him repeated the oath, President Ahmad al-Abbas, which he shortened to just Abbas, insisted that he recite the oath from memory. His voice was loud and clear. "I do solemnly affirm that I will faithfully execute the office of President of the United States, and will to the best of

1

my ability, preserve, protect and defend the Constitution of the United States."

While not unprecedented, the president's use of the word "affirm" instead of the more commonly used "swear," ensured that even his oath of office would be memorable, if not controversial.

Since the election, anti-Abbas sentiments, documented in every major newspaper in the country and on every social media site on the internet, kept law enforcement on edge. Threatening hate letters and email received at the White House over the past few days underscored the gravity of the situation.

The newly elected president, the first Muslim ever to hold the office, smiled and waved to the crowd as he prepared to deliver his inaugural address.

After the usual pleasantries about being a humble man born to immigrant parents who wanted to better their lives in America, the president began by explaining what was wrong with the country. He stressed that he was marshalling in a new era of change that would include drastic measures needed to right the ship, as he often put forth during the campaign.

The president found himself pausing at every mention of Sharia Law, because of a chorus of chants and boos.

Most of the ruckus was coming from the large anti-Muslim and anti-Abbas crowd that surrounded the Capitol area. Thousands displayed signs that told the story of the absolute hatred that many Americans held for this man. A car backfire had people on the edge of their seats.

Unfazed, the president continued his speech by chastising the rich for their greed.

Bottles were hurled in the direction of the podium, forcing the president to duck and be covered by secret service agents.The scattered applause from the guests was quickly drowned out by the protestors chanting "raghead go home".

Carol stood in the aisle, about to take action herself, when she was pushed aside by a middle aged man running toward the stage screaming something that was barely audible over the din of the crowd noise.

"You suck you sand monkey," yelled a young man in the audience who was being escorted away by the Capitol Police. "Go home to live with your towelhead Arab brothers!" he screamed. Secret service agents converged on the man and, fearing that he might have a bomb, tackled him to the ground and covered him with their bodies. Eggs from the rioting crowd joined the bottles and rocks flying overhead. The barricade soon disappeared as the rioters broke through the line of police and raced toward the stage area.

With his speech barely started the president was immediately whisked away by his security detail.

Later that day, Carol and Angela sat in their hotel room in Bethesda, MD just off of I-495, sipping wine and watching news accounts of the day's events. Film footage of the aborted inaugural address showed what Carol and Angela had witnessed first-hand. But the close-ups on the TV left little doubt in their minds that, like themselves, many Americans hated the new president.

As the newscaster began his commentary on the upcoming speech, the final clip showed the president being whisked away from the stage while the sound of gunfire shattered the proceedings. The video showed the intense fighting between the rioters and armed police around The Capitol.

"There is no precedent for this," said the broadcaster. "As a result of the rioting in Washington today, President Abbas was unable to finish his inaugural address marking the first time in US history that an inaugural address will be delivered from the safety of The White House, before millions of television viewers."

The bigger than life image of the president, seated in the oval office filled the screen.

"My fellow citizens, as you are aware, the events at the Capitol Building today created a unique situation, one that brings me into your homes and offices for the completion of my address. Perhaps this unusual situation portends what my time in office promises." The president smiled.

"Earlier I mentioned that we were fighting a desperate war against what I see as the evils of our society. I am well prepared to win this war. My enemies and the scum among us who support the sinful ways of greed, wantonness, and alternative lifestyles have tried to silence me. I will not be silenced!"

The president went on to outline his plan for the country, a plan that involved returning to America's core values that placed the highest value on a love of Allah and country and on restoring the traditional two parent household. In his speech, he stressed the importance of restoring the dignity of the working man and allowing wives to take their rightful roles besides their husbands as the keepers of their houses.

As he spoke, his speech pattern became rapid, and his voice was raised almost to a level of shouting as he raised his arms in praise of Allah and scolded those who opposed his ideas and supported the rights of the haves.

While at times, his 35-minute speech bordered on incoherent and sounded like the ranting of a madman, it was

4

evident that the president's vision of bringing America back to its roots meant something entirely different to him than it did to most Americans.

Angela turned toward her friend several times; surprised to see an utterly relaxed look on her face as though the president's words either hadn't registered with her or had no effect. That seemed strange given Carol's role in organizing today's protests.

Acutely aware of what Abbas stood for, Carol had worked tirelessly to derail his presidential campaign. She believed him to be a tyrant. Oddly enough, Angela thought that Ahmad Abbas was a born leader who was often quoted as saying that he was the right man for America who would right the ship that had wandered from its course. How could she have been so wrong?

At its conclusion, Angela sat teary eyed and in disbelief at what she had just heard. She could do little more than shake her head at the thought of what this man's distorted view of America would mean for the country.

"We were there," she said, at last, proud that she had seen history in the making.

Carol just said, "When democracy ends; war begins."

Chapter 1

I hate my job Angela thought as she walked several blocks to the Broad Street subway train that would drop her off near her office building. There was a time when her posh center city Philadelphia apartment was just a short two block walk to work. She loved going to work back then. She was a respected executive. Now she was a glorified secretary, the result of some severe changes in America since Abbas took over just over three short years ago. The change had been more dramatic than anyone could have imagined and men now held all of the important jobs.

She had spoken to her friend, Carol, a few days ago and felt a particular sadness for her as gay women were treated even worse than most. But Carol was a fighter and someone to be reckoned with. She didn't want pity. Carol wanted results. She was the one who turned Angela's apathy into action.

Tonight they'd be going to a 'by invitation only' event where Carol's good friend, an army general, would be receiving an award. Angela wasn't gay, but she and Carol often went out together. So this was another chance for them to get together over dinner, talk a little shop, and meet Carol's friend, General Josh Redmond. The only negative was that the president would be there. She hoped he wouldn't be asked to speak but guessed he would.

Damn. She was two blocks from home when she realized that she had forgotten her hajib. She would be late again, but she turned back. While not a requirement many women, especially Muslim women, now covered their heads. She remembered reading once about how Catholic women were required to cover the heads, as a sign of respect, when entering a Catholic Church. Because many of her coworkers were Muslim, she did it out of a sign of respect for them. It helped her fit in, and the bonus was that on those days when

6

she didn't want to wash her hair, she could just keep her head covered, a win-win situation all around.

"Screw this," she said out loud as she reached her front step. She was only working a half day as it was because she had to drive down to DC to meet Carol. I'll just take a sick day and work on some of the more important issues in my life before getting ready for tonight's gala affair.

Chapter 2

Maryam admired her husband as he dressed for tonight's black-tie event. He was even more handsome today than he was the day she met him. Of course, she was biased. He was older and the stress of his job had caused a little premature gray hair, but he was still the handsome man for whom she had fallen head over heels.

"I hate going to these things," he said.

"I know Ahmad, but it's one of the obligations that can pay huge dividends for you."

"What is it that I'm attending this evening?"

"It's the '2047 Gala Military Ball' sponsored by the American Veterans Association."

"Yes, I think I've heard of them before."

"You have Ahmad. Last year you also attended. You joked that the acronym AVA was a sissy name for a group of war mongers."

"That was funny, wasn't it?"

"Not to the vets it wasn't. You should have left it out of your speech. In any event, that was last year, and this is an annual affair. This year the group is honoring recently retired General Joshua Redmond. You've never met him, but he's well regarded in military circles ranking right up there with the likes of Washington, Eisenhower, and MacArthur in terms of respectability. People love him."

"Well with all of the changes that I've fostered in the country over the past few years, and considering all of the groups who hate me, it might be good to have the veterans in my corner," he joked.

"That's the spirit."

"And maybe I can get them to support me should I choose to dismantle the ACLU, National Order of Women, NAACP, and the stupid Rainbow Coalition. Who better to join the fight against a bunch of panderers than some war heroes, right?"

"So much for spirit."

"Your limousine is waiting, Mr. President," came a voice in the hall.

The president and first lady left their suite and rode down on the elevator alone, well except for their two secret service shadows. They were seldom really alone.

The state car, or "The Beast" as the Secret Service liked to call it was a large, beautiful, black vehicle, manufactured by General Motors, with all the extras that anyone could imagine. The president loved riding in it because it was a constant reminder to him of how important he was. There was a superior night vision system hidden in the car, and the car was not only bullet proofed, but sealed against biochemical attacks.

The Washington Convention Center was only a few blocks away, and sometimes the president wondered what would happen if he just decided to take a nice stroll instead of riding in the limo. Of course, the Secret Service would have a fit about that.

The limo pulled up to the front of the convention center around 7 pm. The Secret Service agents in the cars in front and the rear were already out on the street heading toward The Beast. Those in the president's car waited for the all clear from the head agent at the door before leaving the vehicle. The driver, who under different circumstances would get out and open the door for his riders, stayed behind the wheel with the engine running when driving the president. This procedure ensured that a quick getaway would be possible.

The president and first lady exited the car on the passenger side to the cheers of hundreds of people who had come out to get a glimpse of the president. The president stayed to the first lady's right. While edging along toward the door, they reached out and shook the hands of their supporters. The president, seeing some of his closest friends and allies, embraced them and kissed them on their cheeks.

Secret Service agents, nervous as usual, pushed him along as they wanted him inside the center where security was much tighter, and the general public would not pose any problems. They had to protect the president who made their jobs even harder by rubbing elbows with his constituents. Abbas enjoyed this part of the evening.

They made their way inside the double doors and onto the plush red carpeting where a doorman took their coats. They were greeted by a few old friends from Congress, who were big supporters of veterans programs, as well as some of the military brass. He shook hands with everyone as he made his way to the main dining hall where the ceremonies would take place. Before entering, they were approached by a few more people.

"Mr. President," said someone to his left. He turned and looked past Maryam to see Carol Carson coming toward them. She reached out her hand as if to shake his when he simultaneously heard her say "why are you screwing up my country" while an agent yelled "weapon."

His trained eye saw a glimmer of pink and shiny metal as a hand reached forward. Instinctively, he grabbed for the

Glock 32 as it exploded, hitting the first lady in the center left chest area, as she turned to shake hands.

Chaos ensued as people ran for cover. Others, with drained faces, stood motionless, unable to move while Secret Service agents leaped into action pouncing on the president of POW who had fired the shot from a mere 5 feet away.

Abbas and the first lady were hurried away as agents yelled "shots fired" over their network followed by the status of the president and first lady using their code names. "Zeus is ok, but Hera has been shot. Repeat Hera has been shot."

Once outside the couple was pushed into the rear of the limo where agents were prepared with four units of blood, two typed for each of them, which were kept in the trunk of the limo. One of the agents applied pressure to the wound on Maryam's blood stained gown using a bandage that was kept in the limo's first aid kit. Another selected the blood that was typed for the first lady and started to run a line.

The agent in the front passenger seat, holding his hand on the ear bud in his right ear, announced that the "carriage" was headed to "Olympus." The limo sped off to George Washington University Hospital.

Chapter 3

The call had come in minutes earlier with the condition of the patient who was in route.

"We have Hera on board with a GSW to the center left chest area. There is no exit wound. The patient's vitals are poor, and she's lost a lot of blood. We've administered one unit of type O blood; a second unit is on standby. Our ETA is 3 minutes."

"Trauma Team One, Code Hera. Repeat Code Hera."

If there had been minor injuries, the state car would have driven directly to the White House where the first family's personal physician would have been waiting. With severe injuries, George Washington University Hospital was the first choice for medical treatment.

"What do we have" asked Dr. Cohen to the head trauma nurse as he exited the elevator?

"GSW to the chest of the first lady."

The ten member team arrived at the rear door of the ER just as the state car sped up to the automatic doors.

Doors flew open, first the front with a secret service agent positioning himself with his gun drawn. It was likely that this was just an incident of one person with a gripe, but the Secret Service had to assume that this could have been part of a terrorist plot, a coup, or even the start of an attack on the US.

The rear doors flew open next with agents jumping out both sides of the vehicle. Two, one still holding pressure on her wound, helped the first lady onto a gurney as the team surrounded her and started moving toward the ER. In fact, when the president got out of the back seat, the gurney was already gone.

To an outsider, the scene at GW might have looked frantic and disorganized but to those working there, the movement of the team was one of exact precision with each person knowing exactly what to do, where to stand for optimum efficiency, and their role as part of the team at any given moment.

The president rushed into the ER screaming "Where is my wife? Somebody tell me what's happening. Where do things stand?" One of the nurses, cutting the first ladies gown, stepped to the side and rather forcefully pushed him toward the door. "I'm sorry Mr. President, but you can't be in here right now. There isn't a lot of room, and you'll only be in the way." The president was ushered into a private room with two of his agents.

"Please wait here, Mr. President, and I'll come to brief you as soon as we know more."

Two other agents were positioned outside the door to the ER and two outside the rear door of the hospital.

Inside ER 1, the first lady was fighting for her life as she was having some trouble breathing. A mask was placed over her nose and mouth to provide oxygen.

"I can't feel a pulse," said one of the trauma residents who had his fingers on the patient's wrist.

The head trauma nurse pushed him aside and with her fingers on the first lady's neck, announced: "I've got a pulse, but it's weak."

Two more units of blood were set up, and a Foley was put in by one of the nurses.

"Vitals."

"BP 78/38, pulse 135, respiration 30."

"Let's put in a chest tube."

Once inserted, the tube was able to suction a substantial amount of blood.

In the ER, the first lady received 900, 1200, and then 1800 ccs of blood. The hole in her chest was slightly left of center, a very dangerous place for a bullet. Despite their best efforts, the trauma team was unable to stop the bleeding. They readied another unit of blood, the tenth.

Dr. Lacey, the head of thoracic surgery, had already been called and was en route so Dr. Cohen had the first lady prepped for surgery.

Inside the OR, the first lady remained critical; moving in and out of consciousness. She continued to struggle as her breathing became fast and irregular and she was losing a lot of blood. Another five units of blood were readied, and the surgeons feared that they would need it.

Time was not on their side as the first lady's breathing was labored and she appeared near death several times. They had to get into her chest, stop the bleeding, remove the bullet, and fix any damage to other organs.

The anesthesiologist administered IV Propofol and a muscle relaxant before putting a breathing tube into the first lady's trachea and connecting it to a mechanical respirator.

Dr. Lacey burst into the OR as the team of two other surgeons, an anesthesiologist, and eight surgical nurses stood ready.

"Scalpel." He made a 6-inch incision in the left central portion of the first lady's chest and used a retractor to spread the ribs.

He pointed. "I can see a couple of blood clots right in this space, and we need to remove them."

"Suction." He needed a better view. With the blood removed, he could see that fortunately the heart, great vessels, and esophagus appeared undamaged but her entire chest cavity was filling with blood.

"I see the entrance wound in the lung, and that's where most of the blood is coming from, but I'm not going to be able to get to it and save her if we can't stop the bleeding."

They used everything at their disposal. Several hands with suction tubes were removing the blood as sponges were inserted to soak it up.

It took about 40 minutes, but they were finally able to get a handle on the bleeding.

"I can't see the bullet from straight on," He called for an X-Ray which showed the bullet angled in the upper part of the lung.

"What do you guys think? Can we go straight in or should we try to get it from the rear? It's lodged in the middle."

One of the doctors suggested not risking other problems with another incision as he believed that they could remove the bullet with minimal risk.

Dr. Lacey concurred.

As he proceeded to remove the bullet, the patient started to shake before stopping cold. The heart monitor sounded a solid beep indicating that there was no heartbeat.

"Shit" was all he could manage to say.

Chapter 4

The president looked up from his chair to see a very somber and tired looking medic coming through the door.

Dr. Lacey was exhausted after almost six hours of surgery. Emergency surgery was a different animal from one that was planned. Sure surgeons held life and death in the balance every time they operated. But the unknowns involved, coupled with the tense nature of emergency surgery, made every hour seem like four.

The president stood to face the doctor.

"Mr. President, your wife is doing as well as can be expected but we have some bad news. We were able to remove the bullet, but the first lady suffered a stroke during the operation. I'm afraid that she's paralyzed on her left side. She's not out of the woods and the next 24 hours will be critical, but I believe that she'll live."

Tears welled up in the president's eyes. Presidents aren't supposed to cry so he fought hard to keep his emotions in check.

"Will she ever be normal again?"

"I'm afraid not, at least not in the sense that you're thinking. I know this is hard to accept, Mr. President, but she's a very tough lady. I think she'll be cognitively ok and with extensive therapy, she may eventually be able to walk with a cane and have some use of her left arm. But I'm afraid that she'll never be as she was. We aren't sure what caused the stroke, but it was most likely the result of a blood clot".

"When can I see her?"

"She's in recovery right now but will be transferred to the ICU within the hour. I'm sure that you have some important things to take care of in the meantime. I'll leave instructions for a nurse to escort you upstairs once she's settled."

As the doctor left, Abbas, still in shock, stood motionless. Then he cried.

Chapter 5

The arraignment of Carol Carson took all of 10 minutes as the prosecutor read the ten charges against her, the most serious being acts of sedition including conspiracy and the attempted assassination of the President of the United States.

The big surprise came when Carol, notifying the judge of her intention to defend herself, entered a not guilty plea.

The actual trial did not take anywhere near the five days that it was expected to take. After hearing the charges read again, Carol Carson again pled not guilty to all counts. The prosecutor in the case, Mr. Jason Pettibone, was one of the best that the city of DC had to offer. His participation was more for show to help his career, as most agreed that a first-year law student could have tried this case.

The jury was made up of 8 men and four women, 2 of whom were from the Middle East; hardly a jury of her peers thought Carol. She was new to this and didn't know the proper use of peremptory challenges, but it didn't matter.

In his opening remarks, Mr. Pettibone told the jury that the prosecution would show beyond reasonable doubt that Carol Carson did knowingly and willfully commit the crimes for which she was charged. He stipulated that, while over 30 witnesses could be called, for the sake of brevity he would be presenting just 3. Also, he would enter into record two pieces of evidence, the security camera footage showing the defendant firing the weapon that wounded the first lady, and the actual revolver that bore the defendant's fingerprints.

In her opening remarks, Carol Carson merely stated that she had lots of respect for the first lady and that she did not assault her with intent or malice. She could have said more but decided to hold her remarks for her closing argument.

Exhibit A, the security camera footage clearly showed Carol Carson aiming a pink Glock 32, marked Exhibit B, in the direction of the president and first lady and while being apprehended, firing the shot that struck the first lady. The three witnesses included the Secret Service agent who engaged the perpetrator, a US Senator, and a Baptist Minister. All corroborated what had been seen on film. The prosecution rested.

Carol, wearing her defense attorney hat, had only two questions for each witness. "Do you believe that the defendant was attempting to overthrow the government?" All three answered that they could not be sure of the defendant's intentions. Then, "Is it your belief that the accused aimed the weapon directly at the first lady and fired it with malice and with the expressed intention of killing her?" All three answered "no." She had no further questions and called no witnesses. The defense rested.

In his closing remarks, Mr. Pettibone merely restated his case as he had presented and proven it. Then going for the jugular, he made certain to point out that a person could be guilty of acts of sedition, even if the intent was not the immediate overthrow of the government. He ended by stating the obvious. "Ladies and gentlemen of the jury, I believe that the prosecution has proven its case beyond all doubt, and I ask that you return with a guilty verdict."

Carol stood before the court and walked toward the jury box.

"Ladies and gentlemen of the jury, while in college, I was a very involved student. I was a leader in my sorority, Student Class President, Head of The Political Science Club, and Head of The Women Studies Club. I was also a National Honor Society member, and a student member of the 'National Organization for Women' and 'Power of Women'. Since those days, 20 some years ago, I have been actively involved in several organizations that fight for human rights, the most recognizable being POW, where I've served as president for the past five years. I've been an involved citizen because I loved my country and hated what I'd seen happening over the last 30 years. I've born witness to the slow erosion of civil rights. Yes, I was a witness to this, and I stood idle. Like all of you, I allowed it to happen. Over the past two plus years, this administration has used the fast track process against the very people who ended filibustering in the Senate and championed streamlining law making to push through their agendas. So, in record time, the president had managed to push through all of his appointees while passing or reversing no less than five laws that spoke directly to the civil rights of women and gays in our country."

"The battle for women's rights started in 1848, so it is approaching its bicentennial. The last three years have shown that the fight for equality is never ending. Sitting idly by, at this point in history, would have been a disservice to brave women like Susan B Anthony, Elizabeth Caty Stanton, Margaret Sanger, and Betty Friedan, who championed the cause of women and fought so hard for what we have in America. I tried to engage in a dialog with the president, but he would not hear of it. I guess it was beneath him. As the leader of a 2 million member organization that has fought hard for women's rights, I was left with no other choice."

"Had it not involved his wife I believe that the president, in his callous manner, would have called the shooting of the first lady collateral damage. I am not so unfeeling that I do not recognize the anguish that I've caused. I am truly sorry for the physical and emotional pain that I've caused the first lady. That was not my intention, and I beg for her forgiveness."

"My intention was to put a stop to this madman and his henchmen who have no compassion for people and were uncompromising in their total dismantling of the civil rights laws of this country. I am using this forum to shout out to women and fair-minded people across this land. Make my actions, and any subsequent consequences, a wake-up call to all. Don't let my fate stop you from achieving greatness. It is your turn to be heard. Rise and act. Take back your country. Your time is now."

Carol stopped and, looking around the courtroom, realized that what she had said was sufficient. An attorney would have told her that she said more than enough and would have stopped her after the first sentence. But Carol cared little for trial strategy. This moment in the spotlight was the reason she had chosen to defend herself.

The jury deliberated for 2 hours, after which the foreman read the verdict, "guilty on all counts."

The judge asked the defendant to stand. "Is there any reason a sentence should not be imposed at this time?"

"No, your honor," she said.

He then asked the defendant if she had anything further to say before sentencing. Carol felt that she had said it all in her closing remarks so she only shook her head with a softly spoken "no."

As was customary in cases of treason, he pronounced her sentence immediately.

"Carol Carson, having been found guilty on all counts, it is my duty to impose the mandatory sentence of death upon you. You will be housed at the Federal Correctional Institute for Political Prisoners in Leavenworth, for one month at which time this sentence will be carried out. By federal law, you will be given the opportunity to select the manner of your execution.

Ladies and gentlemen of the jury, thank you for your service. This court is adjourned."

Thus began the ticking time bomb that, barring some miracle, would result in the execution of Carol Carson and move the country from crisis to calamity.

Chapter 6

Angela, feeling guilty about what had happened to her friend, flew to Kansas to visit Carol. She wasn't sure why she felt the way she did. Carol had not confided in her about any plan to kill the president. She guessed that just knowing that her friend had been sentenced to death was enough to bring out the Italian Catholic guilt in her.

She had never been to a prison before except to visit Alcatraz on a guided tour when she was in San Francisco. That was back in the day when, as an executive, she would travel to her company's west coast offices.

Leavenworth, she thought, didn't look that much different except that there were no nice boat rides, tour guides, gift shops, audio tours, or walking tours. So in reality, Leavenworth was nothing like Alcatraz.

Angela signed in at the front office where a female guard patted her down, and her purse was dumped out for inspection. She was then immediately escorted to a heavily guarded visitor's room. She was a little disappointed as she half expected to see Carol on the other side of a glass partition where she would have to speak to her by phone. Must have watched too many old movies, she thought.

Guards brought a shackled Carol into the room. She looked dreadfully ordinary, as a drab and shabby orange jumpsuit replaced her stylish Ralph Lauren business attire.

When Angela reached out to give her friend a hug, a guard immediately stepped up and said "no touching."

Wow get a grip, she thought.

"Thanks for coming," said Carol.

"No problem. How're they treating you?"

"Like someone who tried to kill the president." They both laughed. "But the other inmates love me. I'm like a hero to them. They give me some of their desserts when they don't want it. Sort of like a thank you for trying something they all wished they could do."

"You're going to make me cry."

"Ah, it's nothing. Being here is better than being outside and putting up with that dirtbag president and all the shit that's going down with him. Here it doesn't matter anymore to me. If the news mentions something that could happen in a few months, I know that I won't be around for it."

She paused.

"So how are you and what's going on?"

"Well I was called in for questioning right after your arrest, but they let me go. I told them that I didn't know anything. Did you plan that or was it just something you felt at the last minute?"

"I had it planned. I didn't tell you because I didn't want you to get into trouble. In fact, I suggested that you stay home, but you seemed excited to come. I had originally planned to shoot him after dinner but then at the last minute, I thought that he might leave early, and I wouldn't get my shot. So I took it when I could."

"I wish you had told me."

"Why? If I had told you, you'd be in here with me waiting to die. I need you on the outside to carry on."

"I understand. I still have the notes from what we talked about before. I'm working on it."

"Good. How's work?"

"I'm not working any longer. Even though the police let me go, it was common knowledge that you and I were friends

25

and that we were together that night. So I guess I'm guilty by association."

"I'm sorry."

"Yeah well when I went back to work after your arrest my boss called me into his office to tell me that they had to let me go. He said there was too much bad publicity about me being linked with the assassination attempt. It's ok. I hated that job. It used to be a good job, but after Abbas had changed the laws to give hiring and promotion preference to family men, I was demoted to being a glorified secretary, which sucked. So, I took a part-time job at Mrs. DiMaggio's gift shop in my neighborhood. It pays the rent and puts food on the table. And now I have the time for more important things."

"Well, you should make some new friends in your neighborhood then. Having a lot of friends is good. You never know when you might need some help with something."

"Yes, that's what I figured. I'm going to be reaching out to people when I get back."

"Great. No more talk of that here, though, you know?"

Angela could tell that Carol was nervous. It didn't matter for her own safety as she was going to die. She wanted to keep her safe now that Angela was an extension of Carol on the outside. There was a lot to accomplish, and Carol was protecting her protégé.

They had chatted for another 15 minutes before the guard told them that visiting time was over.

"I have a big favor to ask, Angela."

"Sure, what is it?"

"I want you to come back to witness my execution. I need to see a friendly face in the crowd. Will you do that for me?"

Angela wanted to scream no. She nodded her assent.

Chapter 7

With shades drawn, a somber Angela Marie Mastronardo sat alone in the dark.

Between going to Carol's trial and then her visit to Leavenworth, she was drained. And, she had mixed emotions. On the one hand, she felt invigorated by Carol's call for action and her prison visit. It felt good to be important and to have goals.   And yet the loneliness she felt, weighed on her. She would miss her dear friend.

But Carol had always talked about how action was the only way to stop tyranny, and she put her money where her mouth was, so to speak.   She was a leader, and she was admired.   And, she had passed the baton on to Angela, who had given her word that she would not let her die in vain.

She could not believe that she had once been an Abbas supporter, considering how much she hated him now. It had been almost three years since the inauguration, and yet it felt like twenty.   Catastrophic mistakes had a way of slowing time and dragging out the subsequent tortured feelings.

As she tidied up her apartment, she thought about the many changes that had occurred in her life; in the lives of women; in the lives of most Americans. Her once flourishing career was now over.   Her posh bachelorette pad on Rittenhouse Square in Center City Philadelphia had been replaced by new digs that were a marked contrast to the old; and a stark reminder of what the New America was really like.

Abbas, in just three short years, had set the women's movement back a hundred.   And it could have been worse. Had he listened to his spiritual advisors, there would have been attempts to stop women from working. But Abbas realized that reforms like these could not be successfully implemented in this country.   Even so, not since the 1950s had women been relegated to such a low status.   What was it that her great grandmother had written in her diary about those times past? Oh yeah. *A woman's place was in the kitchen. Keep her barefoot and pregnant.*

But thinking about what her life used to be like, especially compared to this sad state, usually made her cry, so she blotted that out of her memory. It was much more relaxing to remember the family she loved and what life was like when they were alive before the world was turned upside down. And it was both therapeutic and motivational to remember their "way of life" that had been lost.

She looked around her tiny apartment, a far cry from how she once lived. Even a minimalist might call this place "distraught." The yellowing walls had not been painted in years. There were very few photos; mostly of nothing special. Those were just store bought pictures that she had purchased at the long out of business discount retailer; HandyMart. The kitchen cabinets were cracked, and the barely working appliances looked like holdovers from the longest recession in US history, this one in the early 2000s. The kitchen table sat on the fraying carpet near the living room. She called that area a breakfast nook to make it sound much nicer than it was. Gives it a touch of class, she laughed to herself.

Her bedroom wasn't any better than the rest of the house. Angela liked to joke that she wouldn't want to be caught dead in there.

For someone raised as a devout Catholic, to find no crucifixes or religious paraphernalia anywhere was an oddity especially given that her mother gave her the middle name Marie in honor of The Blessed Mother. The lines of separation between church and state were now blurred, and while there was no official religion in the US, Islam was the fastest growing. Mosques far outnumbered synagogues and the ornate and ostentatious churches of old. Most Christians, opting not to stand out, preferred to worship at home or in small chapels.

It was hard for her to imagine even what life could have been like had she been able to stay in her posh condo. But as dark and dank as this place seemed, it was now operation central for Angela and her friends. She picked up a book "Understanding Islam" and began to read. She was only mildly interested in the book but felt that understanding an enemy was crucial to defeating him.

Her little alarm went off reminding her that she had a little over an hour before the guests would arrive so she figured she might as well take advantage of the time by taking a nice hot shower. After putting on a pot of coffee for her guests, she stripped naked in front of her bedroom mirror and admired her figure.

Once inside the shower, she closed her eyes and allowed the hot water to soak her hair and back before turning to her body. This was the most relaxed she had been in ages. Letting her hands glide over her wet body, always made her a little horny. While she hoped to have sex sometime soon, the sad reality of her life was that no one was likely to see her naked for quite some time.

Chapter 8

Angela, feeling rejuvenated after her shower, sat with a towel wrapped around her as she put on makeup.

Born a Roman Catholic in Philadelphia at Christmastime in 2003, Angela was a strikingly beautiful forty-something woman. She had a fabulous figure but because of the extremely modest religious rules and customs in force around the world today, she was compelled to dress very conservatively, literally keeping her body under wraps. She worked out at home when she had the time. Doing pushups, sit-ups, squats, and yoga helped her keep her body toned, breasts perky, and her butt firm. At one time she worked out regularly at the gym but of course, women didn't go to the gym anymore. Gyms were for men. She smiled, thinking about the absurdity of trying to get in a good workout while wearing a Khimar. But still, she was proud of her 5'5," 115-pound frame; that and her 36, 25, 36 measurements.

Her long flowing locks weren't as nice as they once were. She started to gray prematurely a couple of years ago and began dying it the same chestnut brown color as it had been in her early adult years. Looking beautiful and professional was important back then. If she were alive her grandmother Concetta, more commonly Connie to her friends, would say, "Notta so much." In fact, since she covered with a Hijab while outdoors, touching up wasn't quite the priority it once was.

Every couple of months, she would use what she called youth in a bottle if only for vanity's sake and to tease a few of her male friends.   Remembering what the boys called her in high school brought a smile to Angela's face because, at 44, she was still a cock teaser. Although with life seemingly getting shorter by the day, she'd like some action. Maybe Tony DiPietro would be the one. She laughed out loud. He'd had the hots for her since she was a sophomore and he was a junior at Neumann-Goretti High School in South Philly. Back then he would drive by her house and whistle while she hung out with friends. Everyone knew it was meant for her so Angela would just say in what was her typical South Philly accent back then "you wish, jack off." Tony would smile, wave, and drive off.

More recently, at their weekly prayer meetings at her house, Tony had been paying much more attention to her. Seeing her in shorts and a skimpy top must have something to do with that. The bulge in the front of his pants suggested it did. How sacrilegious, Angela thought, part of the reason for the get together was to pray, and all she could think about was giving Tony a boner. She laughed aloud. She paid much more attention to how she looked on days when she was going to see Tony. She wanted to give him the hots again, and then let nature takes its course. Of course, that's not all Angela thought about, especially on days like today when some of her new friends would be joining her shortly.

In mid thought, she heard the doorbell. Who could that be she wondered? There were still 45 minutes before the scheduled meeting. She didn't have time to dress entirely as the visitor kept ringing the bell over and over. "Ok for Christ's sake. I'm coming."

She opened the door to find Tony grinning from ear to ear. "What are you doing here and why that silly grin?" she said feigning annoyance. She was glad to see him and happy that he came early.

"I'm here for the meeting. It is today, isn't it?" He ignored the second part of her question as he stood there staring, trying to picture her without the towel.

"The meeting's today but you're 45 minutes early."

"Well I was in the neighborhood, so I thought I'd just come a little early."

"Ok, Tone, grab a cup of coffee while I finish getting dressed." Angela knew why Tony came first. He was in the neighborhood? Right. Tony lived in the neighborhood. He was always in the neighborhood.

She finished getting dressed and then joined him in the living room.

"Can I help you with anything?" he said.

"No, I have everything ready for the meeting. I took a shower and figured I'd just sit and relax for a while."

Tony sat on the couch. She sensed that he wanted her to sit next to him, so she purposely took a seat in her favorite chair instead.

"Well, this is nice. It'll give us a chance to talk. We don't get to do that very often."

"So Tone, I just realized that while we've been acquainted for some time, I don't know much about you. Who is the real Tony DePietro?"

Tony smiled. "Well, there isn't much to tell. You know I was born and raised here in South Philly. My dad was a postal worker, and my mom worked in the school cafeteria for years before she retired. They both hated the winters, so they're living down in Sarasota Florida now. I go down once in a while to see them, and I talk to them every chance I get, at least, a few times a week. I'm a 6th generation Italian, you know".

He said that like it was something unusual, but the fact was that most people who lived in South Philly were 6th generation Italians.

"How about you, though?" said Angela. "What are you like?"

"Well, I'm a pretty simple guy. I like my life I guess. I wish there was someone special to share it with but that someone special hasn't quite found me yet". He looked to see if she had picked up on his not so subtle hint. She didn't let on that she had. "We went to high school together, so you know about that. I was a pretty average guy. After high school, I went into the service and learned to command as an NCO in charge of one of the battlefield platoons. When I got out, I went to business school, and I'm working as a middle manager at EatMore Supermarket. I don't think I'll stay there long though as it's a pretty dead end job but it pays the bills".

"What would you like to do then?"

"Oh, I don't know. I just take it a day at a time, you know? How about you? What is Angela all about?"

Too much time alone gave her too much time to think. All of her friends agreed that drastic measures were needed to "take back" the country as they put it. By "take back" they were referring to the times of their parents and grandparents.

She sat back, relaxed, as she told Tony about her past and especially about her family. To Angela, a large part of her makeup and the person she turned out to be was the result of her family.

She turned on the light, pulled out her family photo album, and sat next to Tony on the couch. The album was a mere five pages.

"This is my great grandmother. She was part of The Greatest Generation. I'm guessing that she was probably middle aged in this picture although the haggard look about her made her look 30 years older. I suppose that growing up during the Great Depression and living the hardships of World War II did that to people. I didn't know her, of course, but I've read her diary that was handed down to me. In many ways I feel like I know her better than I knew my own mother."

"Now who is that gorgeous woman with the love beads" he laughed, as he pointed to a photo of a hippie with long straight black hair, a headband, multicolored midriff top, bell bottom jeans, sandals, and a ring on every finger.

"That was my grandmother. I didn't know her either. She was pretty much a free spirit, part of the Woodstock Generation of loud music, drugs, and free love that resulted in her pregnancy with my mother. She was only 17 when she had my mom. My mom told me that even as a little girl, she remembered granny being high most of the time. Like my mom, she was big into protesting, especially against war. They were anti-nuclear and fought for clean air, rights for blacks, gays, and women, including abortion, or free choice as it later became known."

"So, the apple didn't fall far, so they say, huh."

Angela laughed. "Nah, I'm nothing like them. I guess they thought that they were fighting for good causes, but they really messed up with that anything goes approach to living".

The next photo was one of her mother dressed in business attire. She was strikingly beautiful.

"Is that you?"

"That's my mom."

"Well, I can see where you get your good looks."

Angela smiled. It was incredible that her mother had been so brilliant and so successful, given the conditions under which she was born. But, like her grandmother, Angela's mom was dead at an early age, the result of an auto accident while driving under the influence.

"Yeah she was attractive, but she was pretty messed up too. We can thank people like her who were greedy and wanted more and more for a lot of what's wrong with our country today. Between the greedy rich and people who wanted more and more entitlements, it's no wonder that a guy like Abbas and other Islamist extremists were able to rise to power."

Once again their light-hearted stroll down memory lane had brought them back to the politics of today. The real America was gone, replaced with one that was taking on the shape of a third world Middle Eastern country. Some of the rights guaranteed under the original constitution were gone. Many great traditions and holidays had gone by the wayside too.

Tony had wanted a more personal view of Angela, not a political commentary, but that is how the conversation evolved. It was almost as if the fight did define Angela now. The two were inseparable. Not that it mattered all that much. He loved her and just having her sitting very close to him on the couch made him feel good, not to mention a little randy.

"I'm sorry."

"That's ok Ange. I just love being alone with you, even if just for a short time. And I loved hearing your stories. You have such passion. But I would like to get to know the real Angela a little better."

She gave him a flirtatious wink that made his heart melt. "I think we can arrange that," she said as she rose to put the photo album away. "Maybe we can get together later; after the meeting. That is if you don't have any plans."

If he had, Tony would have canceled those plans in a heartbeat. "Sure."

Soon her friends would arrive to discuss the many problems they faced. Tony was the only long term friend. The rest were people who had come together to share their pain. Most were Christian leaders in the Philly area including a Roman Catholic priest, a deacon or two, a Methodist minister, and a few friends and former congregants that they brought with them to the meeting. The eight, who would be joining her shortly, were once respected community leaders with the ears of thousands.

They all claimed to be disgusted by the new direction in America and itching for a change. But Angela knew in her heart what was needed to bring about lasting change, and she feared that these were not the kind of people who could make it happen.

Chapter 9

President Abbas displayed the physical attributes that made him look like a leader. That and his reputation as a great orator helped him get where he was today. He stood 6'3" tall and was in great shape at 180 lbs. He ran at least 2 miles a day and walked at other times. Plus, of course, he had the White House gym. He had a rugged chin and dark brown eyes. His hair was short and dark and his skin was a dark olive color that was typical of middle easterners. He had a neatly trimmed beard that while mostly black, had a little salt and pepper look about it. The president looked like he could have been a movie star. He was good looking in a Ben Affleck sort of way. Of course not the aging 76-year-old director but more like the suave 40 something movie star that he once was.

But the president was a changed man, a man filled with hate. It had been just three weeks since his wife, Maryam, had been shot by that crazy bitch from POW. Mental replays of the shooting and the sight of Maryam in a wheelchair were constant reminders to Ahmad that his wife took a bullet that was meant for him. It weighed heavily on him and every time he saw those small custom made pink "L-shaped" lapel pins, symbolic of the pink Glock used by the assassin it was like salt in an old wound. Those pins, worn sideways to resemble a gun by POW members and Carol Carson supporters, were yet another reminder of the hatred that his heart held for them all.

Fittingly, in a week, that bitch Carson would be executed; a just end for someone who was so unjust. But that would not end the torment that the president felt. And it would not stop the pain that Maryam dealt with every day. Killing Carson twice over was about the only thing that would satisfy his rage.

For now, throwing darts at the photo of her face taped to the door of the oval office would have to do. This was his new pastime as he awaited the endless number of meetings that were an important part of his daily life.

As he prepared his notes, he reflected on his seemingly meteoric rise to power. It had been so easy and yet it took a considerable amount of time, patience, and planning. He remembered an old proverb that his grandfather had told him "sit long enough by the river and the corpse of your enemy will float by."

The intercom buzzed.

"Mr. President", Mr. Khalid is here to see you."

"Tell Omar to come in."

Chief of Staff, Omar Khalid, was a Syrian-born naturalized citizen. He came to the US as a teen with his parents, sister, and two cousins and had been Ahmad's best friend since childhood.

He entered the oval office and sat across from the president. When it was just the two of them, they dispensed with formal greetings.

"The big vote is tomorrow morning, Ahmad."

"Yes, it is. I'm excited. I think it will go our way. Most senators recognize how screwed up America was with its self-indulgence, greed, drugs, and sexual permissiveness that had ruined this country. They see the good work we've done over the past few years, and I think they'll want me to continue."

"Maybe Ahmad but I have my concerns."

"What concerns?

"The vote is likely to go along party lines. The three independents are the big problem. We need two of their votes to get this passed."

"Well, I know that Virgilio from Pennsylvania has been very outspoken against the change."

"He has, and he's almost sure to be a no vote. I've spoken to him personally, and his position remains unchanged, Ahmad."

"I know that you weren't much for science, Omar, but do you remember Newton's laws, specifically the first law concerning inertia?"

"Yes, I do but...."

"No buts. You have three men who are set in their opinions, and you need to exert some greater force to get them to change – to move off of their positions. What do we know about them? Is there a weakness that we can exploit? Is there something that any of them want that we can use in a trade?"

"Well, Virgilio is a widower with no kids. When not in town, he leads a pretty simple life on a farm outside of Harrisburg. He's been against everything you stand for since day one. He's your harshest critic, and it's been speculated that he will run for president in the next election. I don't think we can get him to change, but I'll try again. Tom Flannery is married to a high profile lawyer. He has a teenage daughter who is the apple of his eye. He posts pictures of his family all of the time on his website. His daughter is an honor student headed to college with the hope of being a surgeon someday. Flannery has agreed with you on many issues involving family values and the need for high moral standards. I would think that he would be on our side, but so far he's been an active opponent against us on this measure."

"And what do you think of my friend from Montana?"

"Senator Eastwick is a strange bird. On the one hand, he's sided with you on many of your most significant achievements. He's been very conservative except when it comes to gay rights. On every measure that you enacted that limited LGBT rights, he's been on the opposite side of the fence. He voted against you when you overturned the equal rights for gays legislation, and he's been a proponent of marriage equality laws."

"So he's for gay rights but isn't gay? What does that tell you?"

"It has been rumored, but no one knows for sure. And if I were elected in Montana, I don't think I'd want to come out. I can't figure out what he'd want."

"Well, I can. He's gay, and he's in the closet. There will come a time when he will prefer being a married gay man over being in the Senate. For him that legislation is necessary. What if we let him know that we're willing to support the new gay rights bill in Congress?"

"I'm not 100% sure but it would get his attention. And if he's as he seems, it should help get his vote."

"Ok. Make it happen. But I want more than his vote. If I'm going to flip-flop on gay rights, he needs to step up and somehow actively support my agenda. Is that clear?"

"Yes, it is Ahmad."

"Good. And figure out a way to get either Virgilio or Flannery on board with their vote before I make this commitment to Eastwick. I don't care what you have to do to get it but get it."

"Do you want me to report back to you, Ahmad?"

"No." He stood with his back to his friend and looked out the window. "I don't need to know details. I just want results. I'll see you tomorrow afternoon at the group meeting. We'll find out if you've succeeded by then."

Ahmad used to be even less subtle in the old days when he'd have just said I'm done you can leave now.

After Omar had left, Ahmad thought back to how America became ruled by a Muslim like himself.

Throughout history, strong leaders had risen to power during times of chaos and uncertainty. Arguably great men like Napoleon, Roosevelt, Lenin, Hitler, and Hussein, had risen to power when times looked darkest, and the people were restless.

His seemingly meteoric rise to power had been decades in the making taking its roots all the way back to the Tea Party Movement of the early 2000s. The Tea Party was a term that its leaders hoped would conjure up images of the American Revolution and the fight for freedom. To Ahmad, the term better described a group of old people sitting around drinking tea and expecting change. Stupid people, he mockingly spits. Change doesn't just happen. People make change. And the real change agents in America at the time were Ahmad's grandfather Rabah Amin and those, like Ahmad, who followed him.

There were so many things that happened that made it like the perfect storm for him. One scandal after another; one financial crisis after another; and one war after another kept people on edge. But then a wealthy real estate mogul ran for the presidency and sounded the alarm against do-nothing career politicians and the overwhelmingly liberal views that had gripped and weakened America. People who were fed up with the problems caused by illegal immigration and government subsidies for those with no ambition took notice. That started a trend toward electing more conservative right-wing leaders that would eventually lead to Ahmad's rise to power.

Ahmad laughed at the old America. As a boy, he was told stories about his parents' homeland. In Jordan, this behavior was not tolerated. Hungry people would be allowed to starve in the old country. Someone who had stolen even a loaf of bread to feed his family was dealt with harshly. The King did not coddle anyone back in the old country. Those who were strong found work. Those who were weak or had no skills had to find a way for themselves. The government didn't provide for the disadvantaged. That is how it should be.

The Muslims' plan to rule, set in motion in 2001, was simple. Distract America; make it spend itself into bankruptcy through its overindulgence and its propensity to police the world. Ruin the economy; feed its thirst for cheap oil and easy money thereby exploiting its greed. While this was happening, cells would form and their recruits would wreak havoc on the world in the name of Jihad. Millions of refugees from the war torn countries of the Middle East would immigrate, first throughout Europe and then the US. Identities and cover would be provided for those chosen. While some would carry out acts of terror, many would attend its universities, become law abiding and respected citizens, have children who would be raised under the traditional and strict laws of Islam and move them into positions of power within government, business, and education.

The plan was born out of the early 2000s when his parents, along with others, emigrated from the Middle East, had children in the US and taught the Quran, and the proper way to lead their lives. His parents were filled with hate back then.

But, the real implementation began around 2020 when Ahmad, while attending Michigan State's undergrad business program, decided that, rather than attend the school's MBA program, he would attend law school at Yale University in Connecticut. It was at Yale where he would meet Syed Rashad, his future Vice President. He graduated at the top of his law school class, a necessary prerequisite for his many job offers and future opportunities resulting in him being a power broker that allowed his principal associates to rise with him.

Ahmad's thoughts were interrupted by a knock on the door. "Enter," said Ahmad. "Mr. President, don't forget that you have a luncheon meeting with the Business Leaders of America" replied his secretary, Julia Garner, a 30 something who was not only a beautiful woman but a great gatekeeper. Nothing and no one ever got past her. "Thanks, Julia, I'm on my way."

Chapter 10

After most of the guests had left, Angela took little time to unload on Tony. "Well this sure isn't working," she said through a few tears. These were tears of frustration. These were tears of anger.

"I know. These people are only gripers, Ange. They want to sit around and debate, quote scripture, and talk about the way things used to be instead of coming up with a plan and acting to make a difference."

She couldn't disagree. "What can we do, Tone. While her actions may have been extreme at least Carol had the guts to do something. She gave her life trying to make this place better and what do we have; a bunch of whiners? I expected religious leaders who were loved by their people and who hated the creeps who turned them into sheep to be motivated to act, to bring down the twerps who had belittled them and stripped away their respectability."

"Well Ange, they may be former leaders, but sometimes a beaten man is just a beaten man. Sure they're angry, but there's no fire in any of these men any longer, and I can't come to another meeting and listen to this bullshit. We need new blood. We need people who are outraged. We need people who will act. Did you see 'The Face of the Nation' last night on TV?"

Angela admitted that she had not.

"It was really unbelievable. All they did was give a recap of the changes to our laws under Abbas. On the next show, they're going to have someone on who may run for president. I don't remember his name, but I'm anxious to see it. I know that the changes have screwed up your life big time, Ange, but for many of us, the changes came about gradually, so we didn't feel the full impact. But holy shit Ange this president is not the guy you thought he was when he was running for office."

"Tell me about it. I feel so stupid."

"He conned a lot of people. And now there's a chance that he might be able to run for a third term. It's like he wants to be king or something. Worse yet, I fear that he's just a puppet for some friggin religious kook."

It was comical to hear Tony speak like this. In high school, he had been almost non-existent. He wasn't involved in any clubs or student government, and he didn't play sports. Hell, Tony didn't even attend any sporting events to support the school's teams. He was a good looking guy back then but not a very happening guy. Tony was one of those young men who just "put in his time" as if he was serving a prison sentence. That was the Tony that Angela knew and a big reason she didn't have much to do with him in high school. But things changed later in his life. After serving several years in the Marines and fighting in one of the many wars in the Middle East, Tony was a new man. Serving in the military gave him a new perspective on life. Serving forced him to grow up, as he put it.

So after his military stint was over, Tony went to junior college and then earned a degree in business. He was a manager in several industries and learned how to be a leader. Apparently, he learned how to spot weak links in short order as well.

"Of course, you're right Tone. I know a lot of guys who would have the balls to take on this fight. I just never saw them as leaders. You were a platoon leader in the Marines, weren't you?

Tony knew where this was going so he chose his words carefully. "Ange, I'm not the right guy for the job. Sure I was a platoon leader, but that was easy. When I gave an order, my troops had to listen, or I would have their asses handed to them. I could force them to do what I wanted. This situation calls for some element of diplomacy. How about you? You've been running the meetings and put some goals down on paper. People listened to you. Well, they did until they started their weekly pity party. These are just the wrong people, but I think you're the right leader. Don't get me wrong, they can be useful to us in rallying more people, but maybe we don't need this bunch to lead. Maybe we just need some good, headstrong, flag waving Americans who will come to meetings, contribute, follow you, and then act. Hey, maybe a few Sicilians would do the trick?"

"That's not a bad idea," she chuckled. "But you want me to be the leader? I've never thought of myself as a leader."

"I know." "But when I look at you, I see a brilliant, strong-willed former executive who people respect. People will follow you."

"Hell and I thought you only wanted me for my body."

"Think about it, Ange. Just think about it. We have to do something." Then it finally registered with him.

"You know I do want your body too," Tony half-joked.

They sat in silence for a while and then Angela felt Tony's hand on hers. She turned her hand over so that they clasped and held hands like they were teenagers again. She turned toward him and kissed him lightly on the cheek, and then on the lips. Tony returned her kiss with one that was much more passionate. As he felt her mouth give a little, he slipped his tongue between her lips and let his hand move up over her breasts.

Angela let out a slight moan.

"I want you," he said as he kissed her neck and began unbuttoning her blouse.

She remained quiet as she purposefully ran her hands between his legs, feeling a bulge straining against the inside of his pants.

With her blouse unbuttoned, Tony lifted her bra revealing her firm breasts. As he bent to suckle one, she whispered: "not here."

They got up off of the couch and made their way into her bedroom.   Angela thought about hiding the statues of Jesus, Mary, and St Joseph but then thought that with all that they've seen in their lives, watching two people having sex wouldn't be so terrible.

They quickly removed the rest of their clothing and fell onto the bed. I'm glad I shaved this morning thought Angela.

Tony had to notice as he moved his hands down her body, over and then between her legs. He worshiped her and was treating her body as if it were a rare treasure. Angela was no longer the teenage girl that Tony first loved, but when he looked at her, his eyes were blinded to the changes in her age and body over the years. She was still that same teenage girl.

She was happy that he took his time running his hands all over her, kissing her and then moving his mouth down from her neck.

Yes, she thought, *lower. Yes, lower.* His tongue flicked over her nipples before moving downward.

She closed her eyes as her mind tried to communicate with him.

Lower Tony. You're getting warmer. It was like she was playing the old warmer-colder game. She opened her eyes to watch. *You're getting hot, hotter. Oh God yes* her mind screamed as he finally found his mark.

His tongue flicked quickly over her most private area. She closed her eyes, letting the problems of the country recess in her mind. All she could think about now was Tony's delicious tongue and the pleasure she was feeling, and it wasn't long before she felt the tension in her body rising until she couldn't help but scream aloud with delight "Yes, yes, Oh God. I'm coming. Come with me."

Tony climbed on top of her, bracing himself with his hands. He was inside of her in one swift motion. His slow rhythmic pace gave way to a frantic flailing as he climaxed with her within minutes. It had been a long time of no sex for both of them.

After lying naked in each other's arms for several minutes, Angela said: "Do you want to get together again tomorrow morning?"

"Hell, I can go again today; just give me a little more time."

"No silly, I mean should we meet tomorrow to talk about what guys we can get to join the group and what the next step will be."

"Sure Ange, but does that mean that we don't get to go again today."

She giggled and then kissed him hard on the lips.

Chapter 11

The Senate delayed its scheduled 10 AM session for two hours.

The purpose of this hastily called special meeting was to discuss and vote on the proposal that was approved by 310 members of the House calling for the repeal of the Twenty-Second Amendment to the Constitution.

There was a lot of chatter in the room as the senators waited patiently. All 100 senators were expected to attend, but Senator Flannery's office called with an urgent message asking for a brief delay so that the senator could deal with a family crisis. Some of the talk was about the vote, but most of it surrounded around speculation about why Flannery was late.

A frazzled and obviously distraught Flannery arrived at 11:30 AM and with all 100 senators present for this all important vote; the meeting was called to order. Given that they themselves had no term limits, some felt that it was a fait accompli that they would send a joint resolution to repeal the Twenty-Second Amendment to The National Archives and Records Administration's Office of the Federal Register. The folks there would process the publication and subsequently, send to the governors of each state for ratification by that State's Legislature. While only a simple majority was now required for an appointment confirmation, ratification vote by three-fourths, or 38 of the 50 states, was needed for the amendment to be repealed. But many hated the president enough that they had vowed to stop this change at all costs.

As was routine now, there was a limit of two speakers before the vote; one in support of the proposal and one against it. This process was instituted years ago when it was customary to drag proceedings out for days as Congressman after Congressman stood and repeated the same arguments as his predecessors for the sole purpose of being seen "doing their jobs" by the press and their constituents.

The first speaker, Rashad Amin, of California, a staunch supporter of President Abbas began. "Members of Congress, I know that I was slated to speak on behalf of this issue, but I'm feeling a little under the weather and wish to relinquish my time to the good senator from Montana, Senator Barry Eastwick.

"Members of Congress," Eastwick began. "This should be an easy vote. Everyone in this chamber understands that in a democracy, the people get to vote for their elected officials. As you all know, I was against this at first. But when I stopped to think about it, I realized that term limits are anti-democratic in that they deprive the American people of their right to select the best-qualified candidate just because he has served two terms. How many of you who are sitting here have already served more than two terms? How many outstanding presidents like Ronald Reagan, Bill Clinton, and most recently Justin DuPont were denied the ability to carry out essential programs simply because of this amendment?

The Twenty-Second Amendment robs the country of its most experienced leaders. Like most, there is a learning curve to this job. Just when the president has mastered the job and built up strategic alliances both here and abroad, he is forced to leave office, and the training of his successor must begin again. We lose continuity by doing this.

For those who would argue that term limits ensure that the country can rid itself of a badly performing president, I give you two instances. Consider cases where we've had mediocre to bad presidents like Herbert Hoover and Jimmy Carter, who were voted out of office by the American people, who through their right to vote, actually do set terms limits on each and every one of us. If you don't do a good job, the people will remove you from office.

Lastly, term limits by their very nature limit the ability of the president to carry out programs. No sooner has he started his second term when he's faced with the reality that he is a lame duck president who will face stiff opposition in the implementation of any of his programs during his second term. The tendency of us all is not to work with the current chief executive but to look forward to the next administration thereby rendering the current president impotent.

My dear colleagues, our forefathers and the framers of the original document had the foresight to reject the notion of the president serving but one term. Let us follow their wisdom by example. Let us repeal the Twenty-Second Amendment. Thank You."

Senator Franklin Wallace from Alabama followed.

"Thank you for stating your case so eloquently, Senator Eastwick, but I could not disagree more. My fellow Senators, The Twenty-Second Amendment was ratified to prevent the office of the president from becoming more like the reign of King George of England. While my distinguished colleague pointed out that the citizens can surely prevent re-election by voting for a new president, we all know for a fact that many people vote based on name recognition. The president is very visible, and he has the power of the presidency behind him. As commander in chief of our military, he can stand before our nation and command respect. Along with this comes the ability to raise large sums of money for his reelection bid. Potential challengers cannot even imagine raising comparable funds. Should we expect the best and brightest among us to go up against such daunting odds?

Lastly, the presidency sometimes calls for new ideas and a new way of looking at past problems. When we re-elect a president, we are also giving him the power to name his key advisors and key members of the cabinet. In a third term, stagnancy could result as he and the key members of his staff look at the problems they face with the same biases as in the past. Doesn't our country need a fresh pair of eyes on what are sometimes very complex matters?

Our founding fathers with all of their wisdom and knowledge could not have foreseen the complexities of the world in which we currently live. Had they been able to do so, they surely would have realized the strain that our complex society would place on a mortal man, and they would have limited the terms of future presidents. We have the ability to view the world of today. Let's not make the mistake of repealing this amendment. Thank You."

Senator Aamir Nazari of Virginia, the sponsor of this proposal, asked for a roll call vote. As expected, the roll call vote ran along party lines but there were two exceptions. Despite their recent and very vocal objections to the measure, Senators Eastwick, who surprised everyone by speaking out in favor of the measure, and Flannery voted for it.

The chamber was abuzz.

The roll call vote was completed, and the clerk handed the tabulation to the president pro tem who announced the results. "Ladies and gentlemen of the Senate, the yeas have it. The proposal has passed by a vote of 67 yeas; 33 nays. The joint resolution will be sent on for subsequent forwarding to the 50 States for ratification."

As they left the chamber, both Eastwick and Flannery were surrounded by their colleagues demanding an explanation for their change of heart.

Both men rushed out saying "I have no comment. My vote stands".

Chapter 12

Ahmad had the next day's staff meeting, originally called for 1 pm, pushed back to 2. Following lunch, he had decided to take a walk in the park, a practice that riled the secret service, but one that allowed Ahmad to digest his meal and clear his head.

As his team of six key advisers filed in and took their designated seats, the president's mind raced across a lot of what has been happening and what this meeting would be about.

This meeting was not going to include the full cabinet. It was more of a preliminary strategy meeting that Ahmad had adopted. His most trusted and loyal followers attended this meeting and then set about ensuring that the agreed upon agenda was followed by the rest of the cabinet. It usually was, because these six men were the White House movers and shakers. The remaining cabinet members, especially the mild mannered Interior Secretary Larry Richter, were mere minions who followed their directions.

These were the people who shared Ahmad's vision of "The New America." Ahmad was not what one would call a "Radical Islamist." He was not as extreme in his views as radical groups like ISIS. He thought of himself as more of a "Modern Islamist." But America needed a jolt, and while he would allow freedom of religion as promised by the US Constitution, Ahmad would make sure that the laws of Sharia would guide him and his administration. Initially, he had to take a very hard line approach because Americans were like lost sheep. He had eased his harsh policies in recent months and how was he repaid? Someone tried to kill him, doing irreparable harm to his lovely wife.

So he now needed to be their shepherd, but one with a heavy hand; tough love is what was needed. To Ahmad, what was foremost in his mind was that the members of his inner circle supported his views. In a general sense, they would be guided by the Five Pillars of Islam. The outward behaviors like prayer and fasting were necessary, but these actions were simply a natural progression from Shahada, the first pillar and the belief that there was no deity but Allah and that Mohammed was his prophet. Their actions in their social and political lives would be in keeping with tradition.

"Salam wa aleikum, Mr. President," they all said as they entered and bowed before sitting.

The first to enter was his Vice President Syed Rashad, followed by the rest of his most trusted advisors and Ayatollah Mohammad Khatami, a descendent of the great Ayatollah Khomeini of Iran. Being a Shiite, it was important to Ahmad to have an Ayatollah as his spiritual leader and to include him in all important decisions and matters of public policy. Ahmad wanted the hand of Allah guiding his every decision. He had to admit that the Ayatollah was a little too old world for his tastes. After all, Ahmad was not born in Iran but the US. But as recent events showed, America needed a very harsh dose of medicine if it was to return to greatness.

Each of the men that Ahmad selected for his inner circle believed in what Ahmad wanted for the country, and each behaved in accordance with how Ahmad wanted them to act. They were the leaders of the cabinet and the rest of America. But to Ahmad, these men were his closest friends and advocates. These were the people who he put in the most important positions because they could be trusted, they could control others, and because he had confidence that these were the people who could stamp out the vermin who were trying to infest his presidency.

As he looked around at the men, Ahmad couldn't help but marvel at the greatness of this team he had assembled. Each was dedicated to Ahmad and an expert in their particular area.

The Ayatollah was his spiritual leader. While not the power broker that he would be in his native Iran, he ensured that any decisions being made by the administration were in keeping with the will of Allah and the writings in the Quran. He didn't say much during the meetings, but he helped shape policy nonetheless. It was the Ayatollah who had helped the president with his initial reforms, and it was he who told the president of the importance of distancing himself from some of the wayward ways of the West and toward the teachings of Islam and the traditions of the past.

Ahmad's Vice President, Syed Rashad, was born in the US of Jordanian descent. He was a top Harvard B-school grad and among the top 5% at Yale Law School. He worked for five years at one of the top law firms in international law in the country. Syed's strength was that his language fluency enabled him to interact with the heads of foreign countries like a native. He was very aggressive in his approach and had the uncanny ability to predict a country's position and potential actions before even it knew.

His Secretary of State, another US born and raised Muslim, was thirty-one-year-old, Saeed al-Bashir. His father, originally from Saudi Arabia, had been a principal advisor to King Badr, the youngest son of King Ahmad, before migrating to the the DC area in 2014. Saeed studied foreign languages at Georgetown and attended Georgetown Law. He spoke seven languages fluently including English, Arabic, Russian, German, Modern Hebrew, Spanish, and Italian which him the perfect choice to represent the country worldwide.

Defense Secretary Colonel Hakim Bahar, born Tucker Matthews, was an African American raised in a strict upper middle-class household in Raleigh NC. He was the son of a Baptist Minister who converted to Islam in his late 40s after an illustrious career in the military. At 63 years of age, he was the oldest member of the cabinet but also the most traveled having lived in the Middle East. He was also one of the foremost military strategists.

Secretary of the Treasury, Thomas Hilton, is a former Tea Party leader. His education and expertise were in finance. Hilton was the one who came up with the new simplified tax code. Many hailed it as revolutionary, but all it did was eliminate a lot of paperwork, give large tax breaks to businesses and individuals based on their tithing and the amount of time they spent working for their respective churches, and increase the tax burden on everyday Americans. No one complained since the result was a surplus.

Ahmad's White House Chief of Staff, Omar Khalid did an outstanding job managing the White House staff. But his primary value to Ahmad was that of a trusted advisor and friend. He was more important to Ahmad than the VP or any other member of his cabinet because Omar was not only the president's speech writer and first point of contact with the outside world but also the eyes and ears of the administration. He had an extensive network of people across the country that kept him informed of the mood and actions of the people, especially potential foes of the president.

This was quite a team that Ahmad had put together, and he was proud of all of these men and what they have been able to accomplish in just three short years.

There was one additional person at this meeting who was important to Ahmad and that was his deputy chief of staff. While not in this inner circle Tarif Mansour was another boyhood friend of Ahmad. Because he had studied Geology at the University of Arizona, the leading college for Geological Studies, Tarif asked the president to appoint him to the position of Secretary of the Interior. Ahmad wanted to help his friend fulfill his dream but he wanted more for him, and he needed to keep him close. Ahmad in private called the Department of the Interior the Department of the Inferior as he had little respect for their work. No, Tarif was a brilliant man and Ahmad valued his judgment too much, so he appointed him deputy chief of staff. That would ensure that Tarif was close by should Ahmad need advice and would also prepare him for a future position in the administration. While he usually attended to the White House staff during meetings like this, Ahmad wanted him to attend this particular session.

"Gentlemen," Ahmad began. "First off, I would like a moment of silence for us all to say a short prayer to Allah for the safe return of Senator Flannery's daughter who was apparently abducted in a carjacking early this morning in Nashville."

After a few moments of silence, The President continued.

"We've done it." It was a very close vote but thanks to Omar's hard work wheeling and dealing behind the scenes, the Senate this morning agreed to repeal the 22nd Amendment."

Everyone applauded.

"Now if we can get the leaders of every state to get out the vote in our favor, we'll be able to stay in office to complete the many improvements that we've proposed."

They again applauded.

The president mockingly took a bow.

With that out of the way, the president proceeded to brief everyone on the agenda for this meeting; namely to reaffirm their purpose, discuss other upcoming votes in Congress, and to develop a strategy to deal with the growing unrest in the country.

"We had to make a few promises to pull this off. Omar made a promise that I would change my position on the gay rights legislation that is up for a vote in Congress in a few months. I intend to ask for a delay in that vote. I'll say that I'd like more time to re-evaluate the bill. That will send a signal that I'm leaning toward supporting the bill."

"Is that wise, Mr. President?" said the Vice President. "Your position against gay rights helped you get elected. To change now will hurt your chances for re-election."

"I understand, and I have no intention of changing my position on this legislation. I'll only send the signal that I'm open to discussing it further. During the delay, we need to get the votes lined up to ensure that this legislation never reaches my desk. That way I can keep my promise but not have to deal with it."

"And if the bill passes, then what?"

"Well it will be unfortunate, but I'll use the veto. I know we had to promise this to Eastwick but as president, I have to weigh what is good for all of America, not just the fringe element. So there is no way that I'm going to sign new gay rights legislation."

"Now, what is the word on the street? "

One by one, the advisors told of what they had heard from friends, business leaders, and others outside of Washington. And all agreed that the president's approval rating had been slowly declining over the years. The last to speak was Omar. "Mr. President, at its height, your approval rating was 52%. That was shortly after you took office. Last month it dipped to just under 20%. People are very frustrated, Mr. President, and frustrated people do irrational things. Look what that Carol Carson did out of frustration." Everyone mumbled and nodded." And we have been witnessing more and more unrest, especially in our large cities."

Ahmad nervously made a gesture with his hands mocking the idea that Americans would do anything in the way of trying to get him out of office. "I know there have been a few protests, but that is good. It makes people think that they matter. But let's be honest, gentlemen. Have we not seen how simplistic and apathetic Americans are? Given the chance of being active and making a difference, most prefer to sit at home and watch TV or play video games. Given a choice between living in the real world or the fantasy of reality TV, most choose the fantasy. Most of them have the attention span of a flea, a lazy flea at that" said Ahmad.

They all laughed

"But gentlemen I do share your concern about some of the dissenters in our country who have taken up the hatred for us. They too have been inspired by Iblis just as Carol Carson was when she shot the First Lady. During her trial, Carol promoted violence by telling Americans to stand against what she called my tyranny. She'll be dead soon, and I'm hoping that her cause dies with her. But we need to make sure that happens. And, we need to smoke out any leaders and bring them to swift justice. Do you understand?"

They all nodded.

"Good. Keep vigilant so that we can be aware of any rumors of intifada."

Tarif was still locked in thought over the timing of the disappearance of Senator Flannery's daughter and his subsequent changed vote. How convenient he thought. His thoughts then shifted to Carol Carson's actions and what the others had reported about how people were forming secret prayer clubs as a cover for meetings to discuss Ahmad and who knew what else. He had heard that some were outraged and were prepared to mobilize for change. Despite what Ahmad has just said, Tarif believed that he was taking the notion of another Carol Carson or these congregations forming too lightly. Tarif had inside information about these meetings and knew that they were more than rumors. This was serious business and something of grave importance. He would take it upon himself to keep his ears open so that he could learn more. After all, that was one of his primary responsibilities and the reason that Ahmad wanted him nearby. That was what made Tarif valuable.

Chapter 13

Executions at the Federal Correctional Institution at Leavenworth were not that unusual. There was a time when only a few per year were carried out but over the past 15 years or so the rampant increase in murders that were considered federal offenses, coupled with the softened stance on imposing capital punishment resulted, on average, in several executions per month.

Everyone at Leavenworth knew the drill, and no one gave it much thought.

Today's execution of Carol Carson was front-page news though and the fact that the witness gallery was expected to be packed, added to the nervousness of the staff. But what made this execution even more significant and newsworthy was the presence of the President of the United States.

Late yesterday afternoon, the warden had received a call informing him that the president had decided that he wanted to see the person who tried to kill him fry. He knew what the president meant, despite the fact that there would be no frying in this instance. Carol Carson had selected lethal injection as her preferred method of execution.

The Secret Service advance team arrived at 2 pm CST, about a half hour before the president. The execution was scheduled for 3:30 pm, so the president toured the facility for a short time after meeting with the warden and then took his seat in the front row of the witness gallery. The rest of the area was to be made up of family and friends, members of POW, and the press.

This would be the first execution President Abbas ever witnessed, and he felt hatred in his heart for this woman who almost killed his beloved. This would be the first execution Angela Marie Mastronardo had ever witnessed as well. She felt nothing but love for her friend and sadness for her country as she sat motionless awaiting the condemned.

At 3:15 pm, Carol Carson was brought into the execution chamber and strapped to a gurney that for the time being was tilted forward to allow her to see her friends and relatives one last time.

Carol, facing the gallery, scanned the roughly 40 faces, most of whom she didn't recognize. Her family visited her two days ago and told her that they would be there to claim her body for burial but that they could not bear to watch. They would have taken the remaining ten seats in the gallery.

She tried not to look at the president, a difficulty given that he was front and center. When she looked to his right and toward the rear, she noticed her sorority sister and gave her a short wave of a few fingers on her left hand. Angela gave a halfhearted wave as tears streamed down her face.

The Chemical room, next door, contained storage cabinets and a work bench, plus the chemical mixing pots, pipes, and valves used for executions by lethal gas.

The anteroom was reserved for last minute calls from the governor, attorney general, or the Supreme Court.

The warden sat waiting for a phone call that he hoped would never come.

At 3:25 pm, the phone rang. He answered the call from the attorney general.

"Yes sir, I understand."

He made his way into the execution chamber saying something to his deputy who, with an astonished look on his face, backed away as the warden left to go back into the anteroom to await a final call.

The president, seeing this, excused himself from the room and made his way into the anteroom to speak to the warden.

"What's going on here?" said a very agitated President Abbas.

"I'm sorry Mr. President but apparently there is one last review of the case being conducted at the request of the ACLU acting on Ms. Carson's behalf, and the attorney general has ordered me to stand down until I hear back from him".

"Bullshit! You will not stand down!"

"But Mr. President, I have my orders."

"You have your orders? I'm the president. The attorney general works for me, and I'm overriding his directions. If you know what's right for you and your career, you will proceed with this execution. Do you understand?"

"Yes sir, Mr. President."

The president returned to his seat as the warden entered the execution chamber, nodding to his deputy.

The gurney was lowered into its reclined position. Two IVs, one in each arm, were inserted; one for the execution, one as a backup. The dose of drugs selected in this case all had long, difficult to pronounce names, but was merely a lethal combination of a barbiturate, paralytic, and potassium solution.

At 3:40 pm, ten minutes after the scheduled execution time, the warden gave a nod, the signal to administer the lethal cocktail. After each drug had been administered, the line was flushed with a saline solution until the final drug entered the tubes. Carol closed her eyes. Shortly after that, she stopped breathing; entering into her eternal sleep. A physician on hand pronounced her dead at 3:44 pm.

As Angela turned to leave the room, tears streaming down her face, the president gave a sympathetic nod in her direction as if to say "I'm sorry for your loss."

Angela turned toward the president; revealing the pink pin that she had placed on the lapel of her jacket. She cordially nodded back and under her breath said: "Up yours."

The faint sound of a phone ringing went unheard

Chapter 14

Friday morning newspapers, generally just fodder for weekend fun, had two blockbuster stories.

The first was the story that Senator Flannery's daughter had been found. She was mysteriously abducted a few days earlier and then just as mysteriously, had been released unharmed. To the best of everyone's knowledge, there had been no ransom demands.

The second was about Carol Carson's execution. Executing Carol Carson was like detonating a briefcase of C4, but the story was made juicier with the news that the president had overridden the attorney general's stay order. Every major newspaper across the country called for an investigation into what was being dubbed misconduct by the president. And of course, as they did with all conspiracy stories, the press gave it a name, Carsongate.

Protest marches that started early the next day in Washington, DC made their way across the country with the worst being in the major cities on the east coast. While at first peaceful, many of these protests in response to Carol's execution and the president's actions, turned violent as some only wanted to loot for looting's sake.

The president, seeing what was happening in the nation's Capital, had called for riot police and had his staff call the governors of every state to warn them to be on the lookout for what he termed un-American activities. They were told to use the full powers of their offices, including a National Guard call-up, to ensure that riots were squashed quickly and that rioters were dealt with harshly.

While freedom of speech and assembly were guaranteed under the first amendment, Abbas was not going to allow any further dissension in his country. He called Kyle Simpson, the Director of Homeland Security to see what his office had heard about these protests. Convinced that this was more than just a few acts of civil disobedience, Abbas invoked the enforcement of a law that was signed by President Obama in 2011. Under his interpretation of that law, Secret Service agents could designate any place they wished as a place where free speech, association, and petition for the government were prohibited. And it permitted the Secret Service to make those determinations based on the content. His next call was to Sadeem Ali, Director of the Secret Service.

The protests were worse in New York City where anti-Abbas protesters, blaming Islam for the president's policies, turned up at a local Mosque to disrupt midday prayer that was a part of Jum'ah, The Day of Assembly. What started out as taunting, turned into rock throwing and ended with the burning of the Mosque. The subversives hurled beer bottles into the crowd injuring several Muslims.

Police in riot gear tossed teargas to disperse the crowd and, of course, that resulted in injuries to both Muslims and the protesters.

After an hour of fighting, hundreds of demonstrators had been arrested. The most notable of these was Aaron Rudzinsky, son of noted Rabbi Saul Rudzinsky.

Aaron demanded an attorney and then called his father.

Chapter 15

Once home, a tired, bewildered, and angry Saul Rudzinsky, sat across the kitchen table from his son.

Saul Rudzinsky was the stereotypical rabbi with long graying hair and a beard down to his chest.

"How could you do this, Aaron? You've always been a good boy. You never got into any trouble. Are you planning to give me more gray hair as I get older? Is that what you're doing?

"I'm sorry father. I know you don't want trouble. But I felt that someone had to speak out."

"Speak out? Is that what you call hurting people with bricks, burning buildings, getting arrested?

"I didn't mean to do any of that, and technically I didn't do that. I didn't throw anything or set anything on fire. I was just part of a peaceful protest."

"Oh, I see. You were part of a peaceful protest. So technically you didn't do anything that would get you arrested and make me have to go to the police station to bail you out of jail?"

"I don't know what to say, father. I'm sorry. But these are troubling times. The attempted assassination seemed to have empowered people. My friends and I had been talking about the changing face of America that led Carol Carson to do something so out of character."

Aaron spoke softly but with conviction to his dad. He had been on the debate team in school, so his speech pattern often switched from everyday chat to oration.

"But when we heard that the president countermanded the stay of execution so that he could avenge his wife's shooting, well that was beyond belief. Someone had to do something."

"Oh and you had to be the one. The son of one of the most well-known rabbis in New York City had to get himself arrested for burning down a place of worship no less. Do you not see how you have humiliated me, Aaron?"

"I do. But we might as well be living in Israel surrounded by the Arabs. At least, everyone would know they hated us, and we hated them. We would be enemies, and there would be no pretentions. But here father, we have to act like we're all on the same side, and we all want the same things in life. Or, we have to turn to drastic measures to make our wishes known. What are we to do, father? How can we continue to live like this?"

Saul now just sat stoically and listened to his son. He was so young, so full of life, and so naïve. When he was passionate about something, Aaron took on the role of a filibuster and he was prone to prattle on.

Saul knew of what his son was speaking, though. A tragedy in his life led Saul to his vocation. As a religious leader for over 30 years, it was not only Rabbi Saul Rudzinky's job to teach and lead but to keep his fingers on the pulse of what was happening to the Jews around the world and to do everything and anything to stop atrocities before they occurred. It was Saul's job to know *thy enemy* and, outside of the leaders of Israel, Saul and others in Jewish communities around the world were failing miserably.

Something went very wrong in the world. It began when allies of Israel started making deals with Iran, Syria, and other sworn enemies. Then somehow enemies of Judaism were able to become dominant players and seize control of many of the major institutions and even governments without so much as a shot being fired; a coup d'état with no bloodshed. This happened first in Europe and then in America while the country was distracted by wars overseas and its self-indulgence. By enemies, Saul did not mean all Islamists. Of course, he disagreed with the fundamental teachings and beliefs of Sharia. But like Christians, there were many Muslims who were content to worship as they pleased and left the Jews alone. Those were the Muslims that Saul could tolerate. What scared Saul, and the people of Israel, was the shift to more radical views by many Islamists who had come to America and raised their children here as they would have been raised back in their countries of origin. The Jewish leaders back home had warned of such. Sadly their warnings were ignored by a populace who, for some reason, believed that these Muslims were good, God-fearing men who were true Americans and that the evil doers were only members of ISIS, al-Qaeda, The Taliban, and The Egyptian Islamic Jihad living in the Middle East and Northern Africa. Well, thought Saul, America was duped. He knew now that those making noise in the US and most of Europe were not peace loving peoples of Islam but Islamist extremists who were out to gain control or engage in a jihad. From what he had seen so far, there was now an American Taliban every bit as dangerous as those in the Middle East. Saul knew this, and he was aware that he, and religious leaders of all faiths, had failed America.

"And we've heard of others, like us, in Philly," Aaron said. "They meet and talk about the same stuff. People are finally waking up. Sure, they're scared – I'm scared, we're all terrified but they're just like us, and they've had enough."

"What people?" said Saul, "Other Jews?" He hoped that the answer would be yes and that there was a movement among Jews to rise and be heard. This was the one thing that had been missing in Germany in the 1930s.

"No father," said Aaron, "I don't think. From what I've heard, it's mostly Christians. There's even some speculation that they are plotting in secret to take back the country."

His father pondered this for a minute and then dejectedly said: "Ok, tell me more about what you know."

"Well, there is not much more to tell, Father," Aaron explained to his dad that he heard that there were both Catholics and Protestants meeting weekly in Philadelphia at someone's house and that several religious and community leaders had joined the group, each claiming to have a following.

"And, I've heard that Philly isn't the only place this is happening. My friend, Jed, told me that he heard about similar groups in Baltimore and Boston too. And there might even be another group like that here in New York."

Aaron said that the Jewish friends with whom he had been meeting in similar fashion now numbered in the 50s, and continued to grow. "A month ago we had 20 people or so, father, and now there are over 50 with more expected at the next meeting. I know it's small, father, but it's just the start."

"Whoever's leading the group here is doing a lousy job from what I saw today." Who is leading the group?" asked Saul.

"Well father, that's the problem. Except for today, little was getting done because there is no leadership. Everyone complains about how they believe their 1st Amendment rights have been violated. There are stories, father, of people trying to worship in their homes over Yom Kippur, who faced grave consequences. In one instance, an Arab landlord called the police to break up the meeting after hinting that something illicit might be going on. These are very real situations. Many have similar stories, but no one knows what to do."

"What can I do about that?" said Saul, with a shrug.

"You're very well respected, father. You're a recognized leader. Come to this week's meeting and see for yourself. Maybe you can offer some suggestions on how to better organize and get started. It's time father. For years, our ancestors have fought to protect our right to worship and what are we doing to protect that right; to stop it from being taken from us, father? We must act."

"Such dramatics. You should have been an actor. Look, first off I'm a religious leader, Aaron, a spiritual guide, a teacher; and certainly not some revolutionary. And if what you did today is any indication, the only change will be that you will all be put in prison."

They sat silently. Saul hoped that what he had just said would sink into his son's thick skull.

Saul noticed the look of disappointment on his son's face. "I'll tell you what. I'll stop by just to see what is going on but I can't promise that I'll be able to help. We'll see. We'll see. In the meantime, see if you can learn more about the groups meeting down in Philadelphia. I would be interested in knowing if there are Jews organizing and whether we're talking about a few people griping or an organized effort with some chance to radically but peacefully change things."

"I will, father, thank you and I'll let you know what I learn."

"Don't thank me. Just stay out of trouble."

After his son left, Rabbi Saul Rudzinsky, deep in thought, rubbed his long beard. He started doing that many years ago to get attention and to make people think that he was wise. Now he did it out of habit. Maybe he's right, Saul thought as he sat in his office gazing out of the window. "Maybe it is time to act," Saul whispered to himself. "Maybe if our ancestors had taken action, there would have been no Shoal and six million Jews would have lived."

With that thought, he picked up the phone and dialed his longtime friend, retired Major General Joshua Redmond.

Chapter 16

The doors to the Hassan III Mosque were heavy and having one arm made it difficult for the young Arab to navigate the crowds entering for Jum'ah, the noon time Friday prayers. As he pushed his body against the door, he felt the weight lifted as a man in a stylish suit held the door for him. He nodded a thank you.

They removed their shoes, entered, and sat beside one another throughout the entire prayer service. He thought he recognized the man from newspaper photos but wasn't quite sure it was him. If it was, he knew that he hated him.

Following the sermon, they knelt in silent prayer before exiting the same doors they had entered 40 minutes earlier.

Curious about the man's identity, he followed him down the street and watched as he entered City Hall. He heard the security guard greet him "Good afternoon Mr. Mayor".

It *was* him. This man is President Abbas' henchman in Boston, the man who has declared war on the poor and the less fortunate people in the city. Everyone he knew hated him and wished him dead. Now that he was sure, he would act. He went to his car and took a knife from the glove box. Using some Teflon tape that his brother had asked him to pick up at the hardware store, he wrapped the knife. *That should do it,* he thought.

He entered city hall and asked one of the guards for the office of vital statistics. He passed easily through the metal detectors and stood before the elevators looking for the floor which housed the mayor's office.

On the elevator someone asked him what floor. "Fourth", he said, nervously.

As the doors opened, he turned right to see that the Mayor's office was at the end of the hall. He stood outside the rest room for almost a half hour. The palms of his hands were sweaty. *I should just go home*, he thought.

As he was about to leave the door to the mayor's office opened. Mayor Kamel walked down the hall toward the elevator pausing for a moment before entering the men's room. The young Arab pulled the knife from his pocket and followed him. As the mayor turned toward the sink to wash his hands, the young man stabbed him. Blood gushed forth from the victim's chest as he fell face down on the floor.

The young Arab smirked as he quickly washed his hands and the knife. He threw the knife in the trash and poked his head out of the bathroom door to make sure that the coast was clear. Assured that no one was watching, he turned to his left and walked down the stairway at the end of the hall to the first floor. He exited the building unnoticed.

I did it. I finally did something that will make my brother proud.

As he walked to his car he got a nervous feeling in the pit of this stomach. He bent over and threw up his breakfast. *What have I done?*

In a panic, he called his brother but got the answering machine. "Are you home? Pick up if you're there. I'm on my way home and I need to talk to you right away. It's important."

Chapter 17

"Assalamu 'Alaikum."

"Wa'alaikum Assalam"

The two brothers exchanged warm greetings and a hug before sitting to discuss what Makim had called urgent matters.

Qasim Amin Khalid was a chemical engineer by trade. He was born in Syria in 2008 at the start of a long civil war. His father, Dr. Ulfat Khalid was a surgeon, working for the military hospital before resigning his commission and taking a stand against President Bashar Hafez al-Assad over his use of chemical weapons against his people. Of course, the president had denied using chemical weapons, instead blaming the rebels. But, after pressure from the International community, he admitted that he had ordered the limited use of chemical warfare on the rebels. It was sad that there had to be some fallout among the people, but that's what war is really like. The regime slaughtered thousands of innocents, many women and children. Qasim's mother, Sehrish and his sister Mahveen were among those killed by sarin gas. A short time later, his father was shot dead in Maaloula, a small town north of Damascus. Qasim Amin, and his younger brother Makim Wafi, who at 12 years of age lost an arm during the civil war which claimed the rest of the family, became orphans. They were forced to move into the home of their Uncle Hassan and Aunt Ishtar.

The brothers hated living with their uncle because, unlike their father, he was an extremist and a hard-line backer of President al-Assad. And, he was a miserable human being. He would withhold food from the brothers as punishment for even a minor transgression. And he would beat his family simply because things didn't go well for him that day at work or because the sun didn't shine that morning. He was very unpredictable. At times he seemed to be a nice person and then he'd lash out at someone and belittle them or worse yet, hurt them. His son, Omar, followed right in his father's footsteps. He was always getting Qasim and Makim in trouble over silly things. After watching Omar psychologically and physically abuse his sister, Qasim vowed that one day he would repay his uncle and cousin for the wretched lives that they forced upon them all.

Unexpectedly, when they were 15 and 13, respectively, their uncle decided to move the family to Tewkesbury, a northern suburb of Boston where the brothers still reside. Their uncle began working for a large pharmaceutical company as an engineering manager while his wife stayed at home raising the four children. Qasim liked his aunt and his female cousin, but he and Makim were always at odds with their cousin Omar who, like his father, held unyielding extremist views when it came to relations with the Western World. While not all Muslims in the US shared their opinions, Qasim and Makim hated President Ahmad Abbas, his cabinet, and especially their cousin Omar. And they loathed all that they stood for. But the president was a very charismatic person who easily duped an unsuspecting people to get elected to Congress and eventually the presidency.

"I got your message. What is it that you want, brother?" Qasim asked his younger sibling.

Makim spoke excitedly. "Some of my friends and I had lunch a few weeks ago, and they were all steamed at the government. I told them that if they were that upset, then they should do something about it like many would have done had they been back in their countries. They joked and laughed at me saying that there wasn't anything anyone could do let alone a one-armed man."

"I can see why that has upset you but don't pay any attention to them, Makim. Even with one arm, you're better than most of them. Is that all you wanted to talk to me about?"

"You don't understand, Qasim. Nobody likes Abbas' rules, so I asked them if they would be willing to follow me if I could prove to them that I'm a leader who could bring about changes they wanted."

"And did they agree."

"Yes. We agreed to meet to discuss what we could do but I was kneeling at noontime prayers at the mosque near City Hall Square and the man kneeling next to me was Mayor Kamel. He's pro-Abbas and helped the president get elected. Lately, he's been making some changes in the city and from what I've heard, he's been lining his pockets at the expense of the poor and working people of Boston. I hated him."

"Well, I don't care much for the man either. He reminds me of our old neighbor Anas. Do you remember him? He was....."

"I killed him."

Qasim laughed.

"Don't laugh at me. I mean it. I went to city hall, and when that asshole left his office to take a leak, I stabbed him in the heart."

Qasim stared at his brother in disbelief.

"Say something!"

"I don't know what to say. I'm stunned. How did you get a knife through City Hall security? Did anyone see you in the bathroom or leaving the bathroom or city hall?"

"I wrapped the knife with your Teflon tape so it wouldn't be picked up by the scanners. I was able to leave unnoticed. No one saw me. I'm sure of that. But I'm scared. I'm afraid I acted hastily. I don't think that I can lead these men, and I'm also afraid that it is hard for a Muslim to rise against another

Muslim. Will they follow me when they learn of my deed or will they...."

"Stop talking. What's done is done. You can't change your mind now."

"I know I can't, but I realize that I can't fix the problems in the country either. Many of the president's rules, like the ways of the old country, are already in place."

"Is that so bad, Makim?" asked Qasim playing devil's advocate. "After all, we've seen what has happened in America just since we've been here. Is it so bad to return to some of the ways of our jadda?"

"In some respects, it's not. Family ties and our faith were always strong. But many came here to escape the rigid rules of home and to prosper in America. It isn't happening, especially here in Boston, so I took it upon myself to do something about it."

"Ah, so your concern is that you took action to change the 'hard line, return to the ways of the old country approach' that you feared would drag America down to the level of our homelands, but now you realize that what you did was stupid and won't change a thing. "

"Yes."

Qasim laughed. "Well it was stupid, and your one act won't change a thing."

Makim, looking dejected, stared at the floor. "Father would demand that we rise up, Qasim. You know that he would."

As if suddenly realizing what he had just said, Makim felt empowered again. "Disadvantaged people like me, who at one time received help, are shunned as outcasts. There are still poor people but instead of receiving help they, like in the old country, must turn to crime just to eat. America was once a world power that other countries could count on for aid, if not protection. But look at this country now, brother. Our leaders now support the very people we hated back home. The strongest allies of the US are now Russia, Syria, Iran and Libya, while its once strong allies, like Egypt, England, Germany, and France are on the outside with Israel. Brother, this country's leaders are acting more like the leaders back home. Our father hated, condemned, and died trying to change that country."

Qasim stared at this brother. He said nothing. Makim has not had it easy. He never liked school because learning was never easy for him. He's not a professional. He hadn't seen much future in being a tradesman either as it's not easy to be a plumber or an electrician with only one arm. Of course, Qasim made good money as an engineer and he took care of his younger brother, letting him live with him and paying him to do small jobs around the house. But Makim hated feeling helpless so he had a passion like no other when it came to wanting to help those who might be a little weak.

"Qasim, are you not listening to me?" He said impatiently.

His seeming indecisive at times bothered his brother, but Qasim was brilliant and made good decisions. Makim knew that. What was most important was that he never shied away from a fight. Once back in Syria when Qasim was 11 years old, 5 or 6 of the older boys started picking on him on the walk home from school. He fought back, but there were too many. Over the next two days, he managed to corner each boy and beat him to a pulp. No one ever bothered him again.

"Yes, brother, I'm listening. And I'm thinking."

"I'm scared and confused. I felt that I had to act, but now that I've started this, I don't know what to do next. "

Makim had passion, but he was a rash person who did things without much thought. Passion without common sense could get him into trouble. And it undoubtedly made for a lousy leader.

"Don't do anything that might call attention to you. Stop acting impetuously and foolishly. Go about your life as you have been. We have to be patient and see what happens. This is not like our homeland, Makim. People do not rise up here. Call your friends and set up a meeting. It would not be prudent of us to act beyond that at this time. I will attend the meeting with you. Then we will decide what to do."

Chapter 18

"Josh, thanks for coming," said Saul

"No problem. I figured if you thought it vital enough to interrupt my retirement, it must be really important."

Saul shook his friend's hand. "A lot of people are very concerned about what has happened to our country."

"I am too, Saul. Hell, I figured that I'd be resting on a beach part of the time. Then I'd be golfing part of the time, and getting laid the rest of the time. Unfortunately, the way the new tax code was written, I have to work part time in order to golf, and that leaves me too little time for screwing." They both laughed.

Few would use such vulgarity when talking to a rabbi, but Josh and Saul went back to a time when neither had any idea of what they wanted to do in life.

"You're laughing but doesn't it make you angry that you aren't living the life you worked so hard for," said Saul.

"You're damned right it does. I wake up angry every morning asking how I can get in to see the president so that I can cut off his balls."

Saul laughed as he pictured his friend neutering Abbas.

"My son was arrested the other day."

"Aaron? What did he do?"

"He took part in what he called a peaceful protest but what the police called a riot. I bailed him out but that got us talking. He's very angry at Abbas and you know Aaron when he's upset. He's got that Rudzinsky, excuse my expression, 'piss and vinegar' attitude about him. He's always had an activist streak in him."

Saul explained everything that Aaron had told him about what seemed to be the start of an underground movement to possibly overthrow the government.

"You understand that what they're talking about could be treason," he told Saul.

"I guess so but, to be honest, I'm not sure. Aaron complained that the people here lack leadership, so I'm not sure what has been discussed. According to him, it's mostly griping about how things are and some fantasies about the world that they would like. But apparently, other than some spontaneous protests and few small ruckuses, like the other day, there haven't been any real plans formulated because no one has stepped forward as the leader."

"And Aaron wants you to be that leader."

"How'd you guess?" said Saul laughing. I think he sees me in a different light, but I am not what this country needs and I can't be the person he wants me to be."

Saul's father, Caleb, was killed on September 11, 2001. He was a financial advisor for Centaurus Partners working in the World Trade Center. Saul was a young boy back then, and all of the TVs in the school had been shut off once school officials understood what was happening. The building was on lockdown for a short time before it was decided to dismiss the children early. At home, he was greeted by his grieving mother who gave him the bad news.

For years, Saul had a burning hatred for Arabs. His mother told him that there was good and bad in every nationality, race, and religion and that he should not have a blackened heart over this. Saul understood, but he also knew that there were heroes and superheroes; villains and super villains. Hitler he believed was a super villain. Osama bin Laden was a super villain. But watching TV in the aftermath of 9/11 and seeing the Arab world rejoicing over the fall of the twin towers, convinced Saul that Arabs were, at least, villains, if not of the super variety. It took him many years to get passed that, growing up without his father during his formative teen years didn't help but following his calling to the religious did.

"I'm torn, Josh. I'm a shepherd now. I lead my flock. I'm not supposed to hate anyone and yet I hate Abbas. I'd love to see him impeached, but I don't see that happening. So violence may be the only means to bring about lasting change. Don't get me wrong, if he were dead, I would not feel any remorse. But I can't be the one to cause his death."

The general laughed. "So you want me to have that job?"

"I'm sorry. I didn't mean it quite that way and to be honest, Josh, I'm not sure what is going on or where it will lead. All I'm asking is if you would join me at this week's meeting so that we can see for ourselves."

"No problem. I'm free all week. Just let me know when and where the meeting will be, and I'll be there."

"Great, Josh. Now how about we step out for a bite to eat and I promise no talk about politics or revolution," said Saul.

The two left for Saul's favorite Jewish deli. He felt in his heart that this was going to be the start of something big. He just hoped that they were both up to the challenges they faced.

Chapter 19

Saul and Josh reminisced over lunch about the good old days when they were young boys getting into trouble for what were silly pranks. Despite his promise, Saul then steered the conversation to the more serious discussion about what they were about to do. *Look at the two of us now,* thought Saul; an obscure rabbi and, although retired, a legendary general nonetheless.

Josh Redmond's military career started at an early age when his father, also a career military officer, thought a military school would be good for his somewhat devilish son. Even in grade school, Josh had been a leader. Of course, being a hero to a bunch of young boys who thought placing a "kick me" sign on the back of a student or a mouse in a teacher's desk drawer was cool was not something that made his father particularly proud.

Despite all of his shenanigans, Josh was an outstanding straight "A" student. Schoolwork came naturally to him, especially math, science and courses that dealt with logic and how the world worked.

The same outstanding academic record followed Josh throughout the remainder of his student life. Since the family traveled so much, the location of his high school was irrelevant. His father selected Valley Forge Military Academy outside of Philadelphia for his son; figuring that a tough-minded high school would knock the chip off his son's shoulder and force him to grow up a little.

Valley Forge proved an excellent choice for Josh. Cadets were required to live on campus and, like most military schools; students are a part of a corps of cadets that must abide by a strict, no-nonsense honor code of conduct. Cheating was grounds for immediate expulsion and the playing of pranks, Josh's specialty, could result in severe consequences. As was the case in the military, life was extremely structured so that students, apt to get into trouble in the past, found little time or opportunity for such nonsense.

The key to Valley Forge for Josh was the fact that since the corps of cadets was almost entirely autonomous, the student leaders within the Corps were responsible for the day-to-day administration, discipline, and training of the other students. Since the school was small, with a total of only about 800 students, someone who had a strong work ethic, was smart, and was well liked, had a greater chance of being seen as a leader by his peers.

Josh was the top student in the school, and that earned him the rank of First Captain, Regimental Commander, the highest rank possible, making him responsible for the entire student body.

Upon graduation, Josh could have easily enrolled in the military college at Valley Forge. However, since taking the easy road was never something Josh preferred, he decided that he'd rather attend the US Military Academy at West Point. Armed with recommendations by two senators and a congressman from PA where he was living, along with the vice president, Josh would have had little trouble getting into West Point. To play it safe, though, Josh sealed the deal by obtaining the recommendations of President Barack Obama and the Secretary of Defense Chuck Hagel.

At West Point, Josh majored in Defense and Strategic Studies. In 2019, Josh graduated as a distinguished cadet and was commissioned a 2nd lieutenant in the U. S. Army. His career accomplishments in the Army were no less outstanding than his scholastic achievements. At every turn, Josh made the next rank within the shortest possible 'time in grade' required for eligibility. He was a major within his first eight years and a full bird colonel in 18 years. Contributing to his rise in the ranks was the fact that Josh served well in every assigned combat mission.

As an Army major in the war against Syria in 2029, Josh was the leader of several missions that required a great deal of detailed planning and joint services coordination. He was awarded The Distinguished Service Medal, The Bronze Star, and a Purple Heart for his service in that war. In other campaigns, Josh received The Silver Star, two oak leaf clusters for the Bronze Star, The Meritorious Service Award, and The Joint Service Commendation Medal to go along with a host of other military awards and decorations.

The highlight of the Syrian campaign was the liberation of the town of Azmarin. Azmarin, while a small town of roughly 4,200 people, was of significance to the US military because of its location along the Turkish border and it being considered home to the rebels who had families living there. Syrian rebels set up their headquarters there because it afforded them the opportunity to escape capture by effortlessly traveling unnoticed across the border into Turkey. Josh's command needed to support these forces because they not only supported coalition missions by wreaking havoc on the Syrian Army with their quick strikes but also because of the ability of the rebels to infiltrate the army, thereby providing valuable intelligence to the US forces. Recapturing the town from the Syrian Army, which had taken control, would give Josh credibility with the rebels and make them feel that the US was their friend. In the long run, this would help win the war but even in the short term, this was a great public relations maneuver.

The key to victory in Azmarin was the ability to obtain detailed information about the number of ground forces and a map of the fortification positions of the Syrian Army throughout the city and neighboring 'Ayn Hamzah. A young lieutenant in the Syrian Army, who was a rebel sympathizer with family in the city, provided those. Armed with this vital information Josh developed a daring set of plans that involved a great deal of cunning, deception, and misdirection.

With the support of US Air Force air strikes out of Incirlik Air Base in neighboring Turkey, US Forces under Josh's command were able to infiltrate and take the city of 'Ayn Hamzah from the Syrian Army, thereby cutting off all supply and escape routes to and from Azmarin. They also captured Azmarin in just three days and nights of fighting. Syrian soldiers killed totaled one hundred and fifty plus. Another 30 or so had been wounded, and hundreds had been captured trying to flee. United States casualties had been minimal with five dead and 13 wounded, only two seriously. The rebels, who supported the fighting, lost ten men. But they were so re-energized by the victory that they were easily able to regroup for the move south to assist the coalition forces who overtook the towns of Hamah and Homs. A major assault on the city of Damascus ultimately resulted in the surrender of the city and a treaty being signed between Syria and the coalition or Joint Multinational Task Force as it was formally known.

The real feather in his cap came when, as the young 47-year-old Colonel Redmond directed the joint US military command in Libya. Commandeering the end of a war that was projected to last four years, but ended within two, made Josh a cult hero of sorts and three years later earned him the promotion to brigadier general.

By the time he was ready to call it quits after almost thirty years in the military, Josh Redmond had achieved the rank of major general, been credited with leading 13 campaigns, and received over 60 medals and commendations.

After a more detailed discussion over lunch, Josh found himself itching for a fight. He was excited about the possibility of leading a campaign that promised to have greater significance in US history than anything he had undertaken to date. What he hoped would be his greatest triumph was the liberation of the country he loved from the man who represented everything that he hated.

As they stood to leave, the two friends realized that their handshake was more than a goodbye gesture. It signified their joint resolve in moving forward.

Chapter 20

In the southwest corner of The White House, President Abbas relaxed in his second floor private sitting area just outside of the master bedroom. The president loved this room. It was the one room that did not get redecorated when he took office. He stood his ground while his wife Maryam seemed determined to redo every other part of their residence without any concern for cost.

Much of the furniture was old, from the 19th and 20th centuries, and it was comfortable. He had asked to have some photos moved to other areas of the residence so that he could have the exact photos that he wanted hanging in this room. There were a few presidential portraits including one of George Washington, the very first president, John F. Kennedy, the only Catholic president, and Barack Hussein Obama, the first black president. He hoped that his portrait would someday hang in this room as the first Muslim president, although there were a few holdover Tea Party members who still believed that Barack Obama was a Muslim. His favorites though were gorgeous photos of the World Trade Center in New York hanging side by side. One was taken at night, not more than a month before the al-Queda attack. The second was taken just as the first tower had begun to crash to the ground. There is a small brass nameplate with the words "Never Forget." Ahmad would not.

It had been a long day that continued at 7 pm with a small private dinner party for a few of his largest donors. He had tried to cancel the party altogether, even using the excuse that his wife was still weak after her ordeal and needed her rest. But it was his wife who insisted that they host the dinner because she needed to see some "real people" and he needed to cajole the moneymen. Assuming that the 22nd amendment would be repealed, and barring any changes in election financing, he was going to need their contributions for a third term run.

The president and the first lady were an odd couple of sorts.

The president was born and raised in Naperville, IL. His parents were immigrants from Jordan and were very devout Muslims. They were extreme in their views while living in the old country. From what Ahmad gathered when talking to his aunts and uncles, both of his parents had hated America and Americans. Given these attitudes, it took Ahmad years to fully understand why they had moved to the United States. Of course once here, some of their views were tempered a bit, but Ahmad heard his parent's criticism of the people here regularly. So while he no longer hated all Americans, his father certainly had little respect for the way Americans conducted their lives. The one thing that never wavered was his father's faith and the way he went about the business of being the head of the family. Salat, the mandatory prayers that were said five times daily, was obligatory in their family's lives. And his two children, Ahmad and his sister Daniyah, were raised to be great physically, morally, and mentally. Ahmad lived his life to make his father proud, and he vowed to raise his family in the traditions of Islam as he had been taught.

On the other hand, Maryam was a Coptic Christian. Her parents were Copts, an Arabic-speaking Egyptian ethno religious community of about 11million people. When she was eight years old, her family emigrated from Egypt, settling in Jersey City, and later living in Bayonne, New Jersey. While it might seem odd that a Copt would marry into a devout Islamic family, Maryam was an ultra-conservative who strongly believed that people should live their lives by what was morally right. Their religious differences had never been a problem for her, though. She wasn't what one would call a devout and practicing Christian. She believed in a supreme being but cared little whether that was God, Jehovah, or Allah. She understood Islam and was ok with her future children being raised in the ways of Islam.

Maryam received a Ph.D. in Forensic Anthropology from Michigan State after graduating from Mercyhurst University in Erie, PA. It was at Michigan State that she met her future husband. Before becoming the first lady, she was one of the foremost Forensic Anthropologists in the country, working for the NYPD and often serving as a guest lecturer at her alma mater as well as for some of the top Forensic Anthropology programs in the country at The Universities of Florida and Tennessee.

She was well respected in her field, and her work became an important part of who she was. Sadly, Maryam miscarried several times and was not able to bear children. The one area that had been a contentious one early in their marriage was the place a woman held in society. Ahmad held strongly, at first, that unless she was a teacher, nurse, or in other traditionally female roles, a woman's place was in the home raising her family and being there for her husband. His attitude changed somewhat because of his wife's circumstances. He conveniently, some thought, altered his thinking about women in the workplace to include those, like Maryam, who worked in science and technology.

There was little doubt that his personal situation affected his views. It wasn't just his wife's occupation but also her analytical ability and powers of persuasion that impacted some of his policies as president. He not only loved her but he admired her. Ahmad discussed almost everything with his wife and like it or not; she always had an opinion. The thought that not long ago he had nearly lost her still gave him pause. Where would he be without his loving wife? And yet, many women were still held in low esteem in Ahmad's America.

"I had another meeting with my cabinet today. We discussed my low approval rating and the rumors of more violence by people who want me out of office," Ahmad said to his wife while rifling through some on-line news feeds and VAPTs, the newest and just as misguided social media app, on his tablet. "I just don't get it. Everyone was clamoring for change because they were disgusted with the direction in which the country was heading. Polls showed that the people thought that the morals had declined and that the value of the family as a thriving entity was totally eroded. There were equally strong feelings about drug abuse with 90% of the people polled believing that drastic measures were needed. This is the reason I ran for office, Maryam, and I've fixed a lot of the problems in a very short time. And yet I'm not liked, and people want me out of office. What do they want, another tax and spend liberal who thinks there is nothing wrong with gays or that hard-working people should take care of people who won't work as if they were their family?"

As was usually the case, his wife mostly listened, especially when Ahmad gave one of his soliloquies. She could sense his frustration and she knew that he was a good man at heart. She also knew that he was a very stubborn man who thought he always knew best and listened to very few people. In fact, it was his stubbornness, and his desire to keep women at home leading the simple life of a homemaker, while sacrificing their careers, that gave her pause when it came to voting for Ahmad. She'd always snicker to herself at the thought of the president's wife voting for his opponent. In the end, though, Maryam could not betray her husband.

"Ahmad, I can sense your frustration but things take time. You've made a lot of changes and people do not like change. Even when the change is good for them, they like to be spoon fed like taking their harsh tasting medicine in small doses."

"In this country, Maryam, there is no time to do things slowly as you suggest. Assuming that I'm reelected, I will only have five years to turn things around unless I can get enough support to do away with term limits."

"Be patient, Ahmad. People will come around. And have you asked me about these term limits? No, you haven't. Well, I like term limits. A term limit for you means that in 5 years, we get to live a more simple life, and I can go back to work full time and not just lecture once in a while."

"I know you miss your job, but there is so much work to do. And the rumors about people gathering and talking about me are awful. Sources tell me that there's even been talk of violence in some places. I cannot and will not tolerate violent acts against my administration. You know that."

"Yes, my husband," she said with a touch of sarcasm in her voice. "I do know that. What I don't know is what you think you can do about people talking. There is a first amendment you know."

"Don't remind me," said Ahmad. "I'll bet things are a lot easier in Libya and Iran where there is no free speech unless it's approved by the dictators who are running the country. There are times when I think I should govern the United States in a similar fashion. Then you give the people some freedoms but not too many, and you strike a good balance that will keep everyone in line."

"Then you wouldn't have to worry about any rumors or talk of further violence or term limits or anything but doing whatever you want, whenever you want. Right?"

"That's right, Maryam. That's like my Jannah."

"I'm tired, Ahmad, and you're giving me a headache. We can talk about your ideas about repealing the Constitution tomorrow."

Ahmad looked at his wife as he helped her to bed. He guessed that whenever he looked at her, he would remember the night of her shooting. But she was still so stunning. In fact, many have told him that she was the most beautiful first lady in history. Brains and beauty, what else could he ask for? *No one will ever harm my Maryam again,* he thought. *And no one will take away my presidency. No one.*

To calm his mind, he retired to his adjoining room where he could read without disturbing his wife.

"Sanjay" the president yelled. "Sanjay", he called again.

The valet came running. "Yes, Mr. President."

"Do you like working here?"

"Yes Sir, Mr. President."

"Look at my bed. It's all crumpled. My sheets were supposed to be changed today".

"I'm sorry Mr. President. I was called away and left appropriate instructions. I should have checked when I returned. I'll straighten the sheets for you".

"Don't bother now. What's the point? I'm going to bed anyway. Just make sure it's done first thing in the morning."

"Yes Sir, I will Sir."

Ahmad didn't know why he yelled or why he was so upset over something so trivial. He had just been so on edge lately. As he pulled down the covers to slide into bed he heard a growling, hissing noise and went white at the sight of a coiled snake; head raised, ready to strike. The president jumped back just in time to avoid the attack of a striped snake which had been hiding under the covers.

Slowly backing out of the room, he shouted "Sanjay, come quickly. Hurry!"

The valet turned to see the large menacing snake slithering toward the edge of the bed. Sanjay grabbed a spare blanket and threw it on top of the snake. He was then able to wrap it in the blanket and carry it from the room.

A visibly shaken Ahmad left with him. He wasn't taking any chances. Only Allah knew if there were other dangers lurking. No sooner had his heartbeat slowed when his thoughts jumped to Maryam. He dashed into her room to find her sleeping soundly, Allah be praised.

Secret Service Agents, who had rushed into the room, combed the area to ensure that both bedrooms were secure. "Everything is in order now, Mr. President," assured lead agent Russ Walcott, "I've called for animal control and they'll be here shortly. I can have them do another sweep if you'd like but I'm certain there is no further threat."

"Thank you, Russ. I'd appreciate that."

The Animal Control Officer identified the coral snake as not particularly aggressive by nature. But, anti-venin is no longer made so its bite could easily have resulted in a fatal injury.

An hour later all was quiet. The sweep by Animal Control had given the president some peace of mind and relaxed him enough so that he was able to retire to a freshly made bed. But as he laid there he wondered who on his staff had done this. Someone wanted him dead.

Chapter 21

With last night's brush with death fresh on his mind, an edgy Abbas barged into Omar's office, closed the door, took a seat, and asked him flat out "which one of your people, you know the White House staff, wants me dead?"

"Calm down, Ahmad, what's this all about?"

The president told Omar what had happened the night before.

"I can certainly look into it Ahmad. These people have been with us for years though. They are loyal to you and I do not think any member of our staff would do this."

"Well how else can you explain what happened? Who else could have gotten into my bedroom?"

"There are other people who come to The White House; visitors, delivery people, outside service providers and contractors."

"There must be some way that we can see who was here yesterday?"

"We require all of our vendors to issue photo IDs. Every person who comes into The White House is photographed, and must sign into our electronic log. We record every image and every ID number. I'll be sure that we look at our staff, Ahmad, but if I were betting on this, I would bet that someone brought the snake in from the outside. We scan for guns, Ahmad, but not for snakes."

Getting up to leave, "Ok I need you to handle this for me. It's your top priority today."

"I'll get right on it Ahmad."

Chapter 22

Smithtown, on Long Island, was much more than a town. It was made up of three incorporated villages; Head of the Harbor, Village of the Branch, and Village of Nissequoque. When he and his wife, Karen, moved there after his retirement, Josh Redmond loved the Village of Nissequoque but said "We can't move here. I'll never be able to pronounce that, let alone ever spell it correctly."

That seemed to Karen like a pretty stupid reason to not move somewhere, so she told her husband just that. In the military, Josh was used to being in authority, and while some men respected him enough to tell him when something didn't make sense, most under his command merely said "Yes Sir" or "Yes General." At home, though, things were different. Karen had no qualms about telling her husband when he was thinking or doing something that made no sense.

But when all was said and done, they ended up moving to Head of the Harbor, along Long Island's North Shore. Josh was happy to get his way. Karen was thrilled to live "exactly" where she wanted to live in the first place while letting Josh think it was all about what he wanted.

Head of the Harbor hadn't grown much over the years. The 2040 census put the population at around 1,520 and 535 homes. When asked to describe where they lived, quaint was the first word on everyone's lips.

Their ranch home was on Mill Pond and had just a gorgeous picturesque view. Josh loved to sit outside on the porch and read, especially in the spring. He could see the lighthouse and the small sail and fishing boats coming and going. At night he'd listen to nature's symphony created by the owls, frogs, and whip-poor-wills. Even winter didn't stop him from enjoying his home as he'd go out on the porch in frigid weather with a winter coat. He'd freeze his ass off, but he never let on that he was cold. Karen suspected as much when he came inside after a half hour or so and asked for some hot chocolate.

He was stubborn like that; which made him a difficult person to live with at times but it made him a great general.

Karen was a very lovely woman of 44, seven years younger than Josh. She wasn't model gorgeous, but she was cute and had a petite yet very sexy figure. And her smile could light up a room. Despite her small frame, whenever Karen walked into a room, people could not help but stare. She had a certain air about her that ensured that she never went unnoticed.

They first met when she was an 18-year-old freshman at the University of Alabama and Josh was a newly minted Army first lieutenant stationed at Fort Rucker. She had gone out with some friends to a local restaurant and was sipping a Shirley Temple while Josh was on a three day pass in Birmingham celebrating his silver bars with some of his friends. They didn't hit it off at first. In fact, they were like the odd couple. To this day she couldn't tell you how a wholesome, Shirley Temple drinking, co-ed from Birmingham, AL ended up dating, let alone marrying, a *stuck on himself* Army lieutenant from White Plains, New York. But Josh had a great sense of humor and her grandmother always told her "Karen if you find a man who can make you laugh, you hog tie him and marry him 'cause he's a keeper." Her grandmother was right. He wasn't very experienced in the bedroom and, truth be told; he was a little clumsy. Oddly enough, though, he was always able to get her off every time starting with the very first lovemaking session. But after twenty-four years of marriage, Josh could still make her laugh. And that was what she cherished most.

Over dinner, Josh talked at length to his wife about the possibility of his running for president. He knew she didn't like the idea, but she always gave in to him when he was sure about something. She would this time too. The problem was that this time he wasn't sure himself. If he thought that his running would bring about the necessary changes in the country, he would run. But Josh knew better.

He finally changed the subject to his lunch meeting with Saul.

"You know Karen, when we were kids I never thought much of Saul. He was a nice enough guy alright but he seemed like someone who would never amount to anything. And over the years, I was not the least bit surprised that he never became a successful businessman or anything. Seeing him today gave me a new perspective on the man."

"What in heavens do you mean?" she replied in her charming southern drawl.

"Well, he still doesn't look like much. Hell, he looks even worse than that, Karen. I swear to God he looks like Moses. "

"You mean he's thousands of years old," Karen egged him on.

"No, we're about the same age, although I have to admit I look a hell of a lot younger than he does. He has this long gray beard and long gray hair. And he dresses like a homeless person from skid row."

"Did you give him a dollar to help him out," Karen laughed out loud.

He smiled. It was obvious that her husband still loved her. He made her feel so beautiful, and no matter how bleak things looked at times, they had this knack for making light of everything.

"You're a goofball; you know that. It's hard to have a serious conversation with you."

"Me? You're talking about this old, gray-bearded rabbi who looks like a street bum but is your best friend from your childhood, and you want me to take you seriously. Could there be any bigger mismatch between two friends?"

"Ok, you got me there. But we had an interesting conversation, and then I treated him to a corned beef on rye."

"How is his darling wife, Beth?"

"Dead."

"Dead? You mean dead as in not alive?"

"Is there another dead?"

"No, but you never told me that she died. When did she die? How did she die?"

"It slipped my mind. She was about 40 I guess. She died of cancer about five years ago."

"Five years ago? I spoke to Saul since then. You mean that she died five years ago, and y'all never told me about that. I feel downright awful."

"Why should you feel awful, you didn't even know about it, and before I told you, you were fine."

"I can't believe you didn't tell me. I could have done something."

"What could you have done? Cured her cancer?"

"You know what I mean. I could have baked something special for the family or something."

"They don't eat ham."

"Ugh, you're impossible sometimes."

"Ok, I'm sorry. Something must have come up at the time, and it slipped my mind and then over the years, I just didn't think about it again. Send him a ham now," joked Josh.

"You know he doesn't eat pork, but I'm going to send him a note regardless. I didn't know her that well but she seemed like such a lovely person. Do you remember that time when you were stationed at Fort Dix, and they joined us for a night on the town in the city? That was a fun night."

"I barely remember that but I do recall that Saul was a rabbi who liked scripture, the New York Giants, and my picking up the tab; and seeing him today made me realize that he hasn't changed one bit."

"I swear you're a nut case. My grandma was right. She told me that you'd always be a clown."

"I said I was sorry. Why are we fighting over a person who died five years ago?"

"I give up. Go ahead and tell me about your lunch with Saul."

She listened as he told her about his meeting with Saul and about their plans to meet with a group of anti-Abbas people. He said that Saul had intimated that there was some talk of uprising, and since Saul is a peace loving rabbi, he had called Josh. Josh assumed that he was called to do the dirty work.

"Josh, it sounds like you want to lead this group but have you considered how leading a group like this would impact your running for office, should you decide to run?"

"Yeah, that's the tricky part but can you imagine how hard it would be for Abbas to get a beat on what I'm doing while I'm right in front of his nose?"

She hadn't seen him this animated in years. "I just want you to be careful. You've spoken about running for congress and eventually even the presidency. If this group is viewed as unpatriotic or worse yet, un-American, it could ruin any chance of you winning an election."

"Karen I've gone over this in my mind so many times I'm getting nauseous. I just feel that this is something that's more important than my ambitions."

"So the North is seceding from the Union? And you are going to work for Saul?" she joked.

"Yeah right. Me and the rabbi. I guess I'd be his altar boy."

"Rabbi's don't have altar boys. If I didn't know better, I'd swear that you'd led a sheltered life. But I love you just the same," she said as she bent down to kiss him. Three glasses of Chablis was all it took to loosen her up. It had been a few weeks since they had made love and for some reason, all this talk about a rabbi and his dead wife hadn't completely turned her off. In fact, talk of an uprising must have subliminally turned her on.

She wanted him and let him know with another long passionate kiss and a few undone buttons on her blouse.

His rebellion could wait until tomorrow. Her libido couldn't.

Chapter 23

"Tarif, it's so good to hear from you," said Qasim after answering the phone. "What can I do for my old friend?"

"Well, I'm not sure if I'm calling to see if you can help me or if I can help you."

"I don't understand. Do I need help?"

"I met with the president and his key people this morning," Tarif began.

After listening to Tarif tell about the meeting and the concern of some of the president's inner circle about the possibility of some action to remove the president from office, he was asked: "Have you heard anything about this?"

He hesitated before responding, a sure tell. "I've heard talk no different than what you've heard, nothing more. As far as I know they're just rumors."

"Well, what does your gut tell you, Qasim?

"My friend, my gut has been out of practice for quite some time, but I'll ask my brother when I see him. In the meantime, when will you be back in Boston? I'd like to get together for lunch or dinner to just catch up. It's been a long time since we've done that. I almost feel as if my old friend has left me."

Qasim had heard through the grapevine that Tarif had been poking around asking questions about him. At first, he dismissed any notion of Tarif being a spy for the president, but couldn't help but wonder what he was up to. He almost called to confront him but decided to wait in the hopes of finding out more. No doubt Tarif was up to something, and he needed to find out what it was. How much did he know? Could he be on his team or was he solidly in the president's corner on some covert mission?

On the one hand, he wanted to meet him face to face but at the same time, it bothered him that Tarif had jumped at the chance to get together.

"That sounds great," said Tarif. I'll be back in Boston later tonight. Let's do lunch tomorrow."

"I can make that work. But how about we make it dinner instead? Come to my house around six tomorrow evening so that we can have an early dinner and then sit and talk without either of us having to worry about work? And, that will give me more time to catch up with Makim to see if he's heard anything.

"Very well, I'll see you then," said Tarif

"Sounds good."

After hanging up the phone, Qasim continued to wonder about his friend. Tariff rarely called out of the blue like this. Had they been in touch more often, maybe Quasim would feel more certain that his friend would be someone in whom he could confide. But he hesitated for good reason. Tarif was close to Abbas. And Qasim was more than a member of an anti-Abbas group. He was now their leader in Boston. Did Tarif know this? Did he have a real and personal interest in what he was doing or was he merely on a recon mission? He hoped that a face to face meeting might reveal the truth.

Chapter 24

General Redmond knew as soon as he spoke to Saul that, if there was going to be a resistance movement, he wanted to be a part of it. Saul was hoping to bring up the idea once more and to finally convince the general to run for president. The argument was the same as had been made for Eisenhower and other former high-ranking military officers. The general was well known and respected; having served as the commander of the coalition forces in the Middle East during the last two wars. But Josh had already spoken to his wife and some trusted friends. He had thought long and hard about it and the answer was a resounding *no*. He had no stomach for politics right now, and he didn't see himself running for office as a solution to the problems in the country.

The two had attended a meeting at the Temple Beth Shalom Community Center in New York City and after speaking with various members of what he started calling the Nationalists, Josh had agreed to join the group.

During the second meeting, Josh was promoted to commander of the group. The general knew that Saul wanted to stay connected, but he also knew that having the rabbi actively involved in this group was ill advised and not conducive to the type of planning and action that was likely to be needed. Saul still believed that actions through the democratic process were viable but Josh knew better. Yet Josh knew that he would need Saul's help so he convinced him that he was needed to keep the meetings straight and be the liaison to the group in Philly.

Josh always found it interesting that the CIA, FBI, and NSA all claimed to know everything that was going on in the intelligence community, if not the world, and didn't even know that he had retained his secure cell phone when he retired. It was supposed to be turned in, but Josh figured that, with a maniac running the country, he might have to use a secure line sometime. He didn't realize that the time would come as soon as it had. He'd only been retired eight months now and used it to call some of the greatest soldiers with whom a man could have served.

The hard part was figuring out who were friends and who were foes. Which members of the military were loyal to the US and which were loyal to the president? When he was a second lieutenant, they were one and the same because the president was the face of the country. He was more than that, though. As the commander in chief, the president held the lives of every serviceman in the palms of his hands. Josh knew that all too well as one minute he was home having dinner with his wife and children and the next minute he was packing for an all-expense paid trip to Libya or Turkey to fight yet another war.

Times sure had changed, and two years ago Josh began privately reviewing the records of each colleague, each key officer under his command, and the key members of the joint chiefs, and the president's cabinet. Despite the government's intelligence capabilities, Josh felt confident that he had been able to vet them all in a way that would not raise suspicion. There could be no mistakes, or he would be arrested for treason and executed. So the tricky part in all of this was figuring out who to call and who not to call. Josh created a special list of people whom he felt he could trust and who he hoped would be willing to support him.

Josh called his old friend, Kyle Simpson, who had served as a Colonel under Josh during his Military Intelligence days. Over the past two years, Josh and Kyle had many conversations about what was happening in the country. Like Josh, Kyle was one of those "loyal to his country, not his president." Kyle was now the department head for homeland security. He jokingly told Josh that with that fancy title came all of the privileges of the position which were namely taking shit from everyone in the government, working long hours to protect the country, and possibly getting blamed for every stinking little thing that could go wrong with national security.

After some small talk about his TV appearance later that night on *The Face of The Nation*, Josh got to the real purpose of his call. He explained to Kyle that most of the military personnel who had secured phones were in their corner but that there were a few who were loyal to the president.

"If what you're doing is discovered, Kyle, you'll be tried for treason. I need you to understand that because you'll be taking an enormous risk," said Josh.

"Roger that." was Kyle's only response.

So from Josh's call list, Kyle developed a secured channel with real-time voice and data encryption and decryption. It had taken Kyle a couple of weeks to coordinate, but he managed to call the nine key leaders in the DOD and the head of the Secret Service with the excuse that he had to update the crypto software and settings on each of their secured cell phones. All came in with their phones, and all phones were adjusted, according to Josh's instructions.

There were nine people who Josh wanted referred to as The Assembly of Nine or simply Assembly during the conversation. Josh, of course, was the head of the group. The others included Kyle, Deputy Secretary of Defense Demetri Kotsopoulos, Deputy Chairman of the Joint Chiefs Admiral John Barrington, Secretary of the Army General Raymond Rivera, Secretary of the Navy Admiral Terrance Combers, Secretary of the Marine Corps General Bradley Gallant, Secretary of the Air Force General Richard O'Meara, and Commandant of the Coast Guard Admiral Jesse Happ.

Josh had spoken to each of the nine on the secured phone that he had, taking a chance that no one else was listening. At various times over the years, Josh had spoken to each of these men about national security issues. They were all of like minds in almost every way. Unlike the pansies in Washington who thought that being a career Congressman with a fat paycheck and cushy benefits was serving their country, each of these men loved his country, and each would be willing to die for it. More importantly, during his last year in the Army, Josh had spoken to these men about the president and what was going on. Each hated everything that President Abbas stood for and told Josh that if he ever wanted to compete for the big throne, as they called it, they were with him. Last week when he called them, each expressed a willingness to back Josh no matter the plan, no matter the consequence. They were willing to risk everything so it was mission critical to Josh that everyone had "eyes and ears" on the White House.

To prove that he had a sense of humor, Kyle set up a distinct channel 69. The symbolism was lost on the general, who seemed all business at this point. Even after Kyle explained something about getting a lot of pleasure by turning things completely upside down, Josh still didn't crack a smile.

Each of the Assembly's phones was programmed to hear everything that was going on within the group via channel 69 and everything transmitted between Defense Secretary Bahar, the president, and those loyal to him via their secured channel. Those left off of channel 69 were Bahar, General Elway Bishop Chairman of the Joint Chiefs, and Sadeem Ali, the Director of the Secret Service. Their phones were set up so that every conversation they had was heard by the Assembly of Nine. However, their phones did not have access to channel 69.

When finished, Kyle called Josh to let him know what he had done and that all systems were a go.

"Thanks Kyle, welcome to the club." He and Kyle were officially co-conspirators.

Chapter 25

Josh Redmond showed up just in time for the taping of a news show hosted by his longtime friend, Bob McCrimmon.

"Hey Josh, how have you been?"

"I'm well Bob, and you?"

"I'm great. I'm glad to have you on, Josh, but are you sure you want to do this? I'm afraid that this will throw you into the limelight and from what you've told me, you might be better off hiding in the shadows for a while. "

"I've heard similar concerns, but I figure what better place to hide from your enemy than right under his nose."

And, 5-4-3-2-1 On Air

"Good evening. Tonight's guest on 'The Face of the Nation' is retired Army General Joshua Redmond. Welcome to the show General Redmond."

"Thanks for having me on, Bob."

"Let's get right to the heart of this, General. While you have not officially announced your candidacy for president, there has been a lot of talk and speculation that you may run. Is there any truth to this?"

Laughing, "I'm flattered that there are people who think I would make a good president. The fact is Bob that when I retired from the military, I expected to relax and take it easy. But I didn't come on your TV show to dodge questions so I'll be honest. I am considering it."

"Do you have a set date to announce or is that a little premature?"

"Well, Bob, I'm testing the waters, so to speak. A big factor in my decision will be whether the president runs for a second term or not. I have some people working on some polling numbers to see how I would fare should I run against him."

"So I take it that you're not a supporter of the president."

"Hardly Bob. You know, I've spent my entire adult life in the military defending the freedoms that we share and protecting our country from people like him. The president has made a mockery of those very rights and freedoms."

"Many of us are upset but is there anything in particular that President Abbas has done that is making you consider this giant step?"

"To me, the most drastic changes to laws were influenced by the president's key religious advisor, namely The Ayatollah. These are the changes that have reversed some of the hard earned civil rights laws regarding women and gays and that impact our daily lives. Things like the 'Women's Modesty and Dignity Act' which has its basis in religion. Under this law, women must dress modestly in public. They are restricted from working outside the home without their husband's permission, and of course their wages are comparatively low."

"So you're considering a run based on the president's restrictions on women?"

"Not just that. There is so much wrong with this administration."

General Redmond went on to discuss how the liberals, especially the Democrats in Congress, wanted swift enactment of federal laws that legalized marijuana use, euthanasia, and gay marriage. To accomplish that, he argued, they streamlined the way laws were passed such that a process that once took years, was completed in a matter of months. This new process enabled the president, using that same process, to push through his agenda.

He highlighted the new law that defines homosexuality and other gender preferences as being a disease subject to mandatory treatment through the Sexual Identity Care (SIC) treatment programs until such time that the person was cured.

"Most people can see what is happening to women because it's very visible," said the General," but regarding homosexuals, most people are oblivious to what they are going through."

"Now you mentioned the changes to the criminal justice system earlier. What can you tell us about that?"

"The Patriot Act of 2038 certainly tightened security in our country, even more than the 2001 version. But the 'Capital Offense Sentencing Law' has had an even more profound impact on our criminal justice system. Under this law, offenders convicted of first-degree murder or any other capital offense that once carried the possibility of a death sentence, now automatically receive a mandatory death sentence upon conviction. The capital offenses include espionage, treason, and death resulting from aircraft hijacking, but mostly consist of various forms of murder such as murder. The sentence is to be carried out within one month of their conviction and comes with a restriction on appeals. The only appeal heard is one in which the defense provides new and irrefutable evidence as to the convicted person's innocence in a written summary to the judge. This law eliminated the sentencing phase in all capital offense cases. The only decision is how the sentence will be carried out, and that decision now rests with the convicted person. The one positive that has come out of this law is that it has dramatically decreased both legal costs and the costs involved with providing food and clothing, for those convicted. As you might suspect, the American Bar Association and the Trial Lawyers Associations fought hard to stop this but to no avail.

A second, closely related law is the 'Treason Sentencing Law'. Under this law, any person convicted of treason will receive the same sentence, with the same processes and restrictions, as someone convicted of first-degree murder; except there is absolutely no appealing a treason sentence. That in itself is bad but what constitutes treason is very ambiguous and open to interpretation under the new law. Someone who is protesting against the government is no longer protected by the first amendment if their activities are in any way deemed to be of a subversive nature or putting the general public at risk. So anyone taking part in a peaceful protest might be charged with treason."

"And that brings us to the last topic, namely election reform," said the host.

"Thanks, Bob. Okay, nothing has been finalized yet, but two key pieces of legislation have been proposed by Congress, no doubt by the supporters of President Abbas."

"The first of course is the joint resolution to repeal the 22nd Amendment that was recently passed by both houses and sent on to the Archivist of the United States. I don't want to get into too much detail on this, but this person heads the National Archives and Records Administration (NARA). NARA has the responsibility for administering the ratification process under the provisions of Title 1 of the United States Code, Sec 106b for Amendments to the Constitution. That repeal resolution will be packaged and sent on to each State for ratification. Ratification would remove the term limit placed on the presidency and open the door for President Abbas, if re-elected, to seek a third term after his next term is up."

"The second is a proposed law that would put restrictions on how candidates can conduct their campaigns. This proposal is complicated, and we're running short on time, but briefly, the purpose of this law is to stop campaign advertising as a means of disseminating any negative information. Under this law, paid advertisements would be limited to three infomercials during a campaign. The purpose of these would be to disseminate positive information about the candidate running for office. There could be no negative content regarding the opposition. Other than some buttons and signs, this is the only area where candidates could spend money on campaign communication. The only other ways to communicate a candidate's position would be through a series of three debates in which each party would be able to make claims and counterclaims about the records of their opponents and through information provided to the press that is deemed newsworthy." As you can see both of these pieces of legislation substantially help the president and all of the incumbents who are well known and have a record on which to stand."

Bob McCrimmon interrupted. "Thank you, General Redmond. We're running out of time, so I need to wrap this up in a hurry. Do you have any final words for our audience?"

"Thanks for having me on Bob. I love America, and I'm ready to lead. I hope that everyone watching tonight understands exactly where our president has led us and what his administration has done to the freedoms they once enjoyed. This is a fight for the survival of America and it's not one that can wait. I can no longer sit on the sidelines while Americans are forced to give up the freedoms that I spent my entire career protecting. It's time for new leadership in the White House. Please, join me in my fight to end this president's reign."

Chapter 26

Angela and Tony had made plans to meet alone the following day, but Tony was anxious to get more people involved in what they were doing so he called a neighborhood guy he'd met in a bar named Nicky Gervasi. He thought he could help with their community outreach efforts. Nicky was a small time gangster; a bit player in the Gangemi Crime Family. There was a Gangemi funeral home nearby. The two were not connected except that Nicky liked to say "we pump em, they dump em" when asked. Nicky had a reputation as someone who took no shit from anyone and who was as likely to shoot your ass as to look at you twice. He had a nickname that suggested as much but, not wanting to scare Angela, Tony kept that to himself. Nicky was the kind of guy who could help, though. The key was not only that Nicky had street smarts but that he was well known and well liked.

A robust Nicky showed up at Angela's door with some coffee and donuts, raring to get started. The one thing that became apparent at the last meeting was that the people who were attending just weren't the *action* people that were needed to bring about change. After two cups of coffee and three cream donuts, Nicky was hyped and ready to go.

"C'mon let's get started."

He picked up a fourth cream donut as he stood to leave. One for the road, Angela guessed. She wasn't sure if he was on drugs or if sugar and caffeine had that effect on Nicky but he was very hyper this morning.

They strolled through the neighborhood, and Angela saw these streets and her neighbors in a whole new light. If you had asked her yesterday what it was like living in South Philly, she'd have said: "Oh you know, it's nice and fairly quiet. People are a little boring, but everyone gets along." After talking to 4 of her neighbors, Angela realized that there was more to this place than she had realized.

First they stopped to talk to Giani, the local numbers guy. Angela thought running numbers ended when the state-sponsored lottery came into vogue decades earlier. Apparently not though since many people trusted the local bookmakers more than The State of Pennsylvania.

Then they met Vito and Johnny Fingers outside of Buddy's Bar & Grill, on the corner of Tony's street. Johnny had been a driver for one of the biggest Italian crime figures in Philadelphia history. He got his nickname when the head of a rival gang kidnapped him and cut off his two index fingers to send a message to his boss. It worked. The boss realized that war was brewing and had the guy killed. Vito was the local pipe fitters union boss. His life hadn't changed much under Abbas. He was a roll up your sleeves, blue collar guy and most of the trade guys still had their jobs, still made good money, but hated Abbas nonetheless because he was a Muslim. When asked about why he hated Abbas, Vito said "What, ya gotta have a reason? Isn't being a raghead good enough reason?"

Inside the bar, they met Buddy Riley, the owner. His bar was one of the few cash businesses that weren't owned by the Greeks or Turks. Buddy was a blue collar Irishman with a temper. There was a time when he would have lived in a mostly Irish neighborhood. Back then people segregated themselves based on race and ethnicity. Now all Americans lived as one with common enemies; the many Asians and Middle Easterners who were taking over the city.

Buddy had a rep as a headbanger; a moniker earned because he kept a baseball bat behind the bar. When guys were getting rowdy, he'd bring it out and slam it on the bar or a table. Oddly enough, he never hit anyone with it, but no one doubted that, if pushed far enough, he'd split a few heads. They talked to Buddy in general terms, like they had with the others on the street and Buddy agreed to attend the meeting.

So walking across the street to the opposite corner, they all felt pretty good about what they had accomplished so far. They were four for four in the recruiting department.

"This is Connie Sapienza's house, yous guys know her?" asked Nicky.

Tony said he didn't.

"I know her to see, say hello to, but that's about it," said Angela.

"Yeah well she likes to keep a low profile, ya know." They didn't.

Nicky banged on her door. "Yo Con. It's me, Nicky. Open up."

Connie was a very pretty but plain looking 50-year-old woman who just a few weeks ago started worked at Nunzio's bakery a few blocks away. She opened the door with an expression of surprise on her face. Apparently she didn't get much company.

"Hey Con, how they hangin?"

"Hey Nick, you know gravity but what's the use of complain'?"

"How's it feel bein' back in the real world?"

"Good ya know, but ya didn't stop here just to see how I'm doin'. What's up?"

"I wanna introduce ya to a couple of my friends, Tony, and Angela."

"Hi, what can I do for you."

Nicky got right to the point as he did with each person to whom they had stopped to talk.

Without any emotion, he asked, "Whaddya think of the president?"

"I hate him."

So far that was the consensus although up 'til now the responses had been much more colorful. If she collated the answers in her head and then spit them out, the neighbors thought *Abbas was a jerk off, asshole, shithead, scumbag whom everyone hated and who was ruining the country.*

"Angela here voted for him."

Oh great, thanks, Nicky thought Angela.

"Are you shittin' me? How could you vote for that faggot?"

"Well in my defense," Angela started.

"You'd have to be a damn moron."

Angela's impression of Connie as a quiet, reserved woman was obviously off the mark.

"Well I"

"He's a rat bastard."

Ah, a new adjective to add to her collection of Abbas descriptions.

"Well back then…"

"I've gotta hear this one; I'll bet it's a beaut. Go on. Whatsa matter, the cat gotch yer tongue?"

"I was stunod ok. I'm sorry. Can't a person make a mistake?" Angela blurted out.

Angela braced herself for a barrage of more condescension.

"There, doesn't it feel good to finally get that off yer chest."

The two women stood looking at one another without moving and then they both broke out in laughter.

Nicky went on to tell Connie about the next meeting at Angela's house and what they were trying to accomplish.

"Well I'll think about comin' to the next meetin' but ya know I gotta be careful right Nick?"

"Yeah I know, but this is pretty important Con."

"Ok," she sighed." I guess I'm in."

As they walked away, Angela couldn't help but wonder what her story was. Why was she so hesitant?

"Well, she appeared less than enthused for someone who claimed to hate the President so much. And what was that about 'being back in the real world?"

"She's gotta be careful not to violate her parole and end up back in the joint," said Nicky

"She's an ex-con?"

"Yep. Served ten and a half of a fifteen year for assault with a deadly weapon. The original charge included with intent to kill, but they couldn't make it stick because there was an element of self-defense."

"What did she do?" asked the unusually quiet Tony.

"Some guy in Buddy's bar came on strong. At first, she was being nice because he bought her a few beers. And she liked the attention. But the more he drank, the more he, well let's just say he started taking liberties with her, trying to feel her up. Stuff like that. I guess he figured since he bought her a few brews he had a right. I don't know. In any event, Buddy testified that he was about to whip out the bat and whack the guy upside his head when Connie broke a beer bottle across the guy's face and used the shaft to slash open his arm. He had a concussion, black eye, and took five stitches in his face and another twenty down his arm. He damn near died. He lost so much blood. She said it was self-defense as the guy was trying to rape her but he said that she had come on to him and had welcomed his advances and that all she had to do was stop taking the beers he bought her and to tell him she wasn't interested. The jury seemed sympathetic to Connie, but the pictures of this guy all bruised and bloodied, really hit home. He looked like he'd been run over by a truck."

They walked silently for a while then resumed their recruiting. By the end of the day they had eight new members who promised to be more fun to be around and more committed to their goals, than the current crew. And each had agreed to bring a friend or two to the next meeting.

Chapter 27

As Secretary of Defense, Hakim was used to being called into national security briefings or into the situation room. That was his job. But to get a call from the president on a Sunday morning was troubling. He had no idea what the president would want with him, unless he was being fired.

It was 8am when he arrived at The White House. The president had told him to meet him in the oval office. There was no secretary standing guard, only secret service. Unlike himself, apparently Julia's job was safe and she got to enjoy her only day off. Hakim knocked.

"Come in."

"Mr. President." He was a little nervous as he approached the large oak desk. Seated in one of the chairs was Omar Khalid. "Good morning, Omar." Omar nodded.

"Sit Hakim! Sit! Can I have one of my staff get you something, some coffee or tea maybe?"

"A cup of coffee would be great, Mr. President. Thank you. "

The president buzzed a staff member and ordered a coffee and two cups of tea.

"I'm very concerned", said Abbas. "Very concerned. I wanted you both here because I was up all night. I have this nervous feeling in my stomach."

The president filled Hakim in on the snake incident, of a few nights before. So now you are up to date on what happened and we can move forward. "Omar, what did you find out during your investigation?"

With the exception of when they were alone, Omar never addressed his old friend by his first name. "Mr. President, I conducted the investigation as we had discussed. The staff all checked out but a review of the electronic sign in log revealed several suspicious people who had been at the White House that day. It seems all were accompanied by staff members throughout their visit with the exception of one."

The knock on the door interrupted their conversation, as their coffee and tea was handed to them.

The president sipped his tea while he waited for privacy. "Go on Omar."

"Mr. Marquis Williams who works for our exterminating company, Capital Critter Control, was permitted to do his job without anyone tagging along. That's standard procedure. He entered his badge number and we have his photo. I called over to the company and spoke to the owner. He said that The White House was not scheduled for a visit and that he didn't have anyone named Marquis Williams working for him. I transmitted his photo while we spoke and he didn't recognize the person in the photo."

"I knew it. I knew it. This is serious gentlemen. This is very serious. This is the second attempt on my life in just a few months. Is that a coincidence? I don't think so."

"Of course, I've shared Mr. Williams photograph with the Capital Police, FBI, and other appropriate agencies, continued Omar. " So far no one has been able to match the photo with anyone in their database. He doesn't even appear in any of the state DMV records."

"There is something going on gentlemen and we need to figure out what and we need to find out fast. Let me ask you this Hakim. Do you believe that the military is fully behind me? Do they have my back?"

"I'm sorry, Mr. President, but I don't understand. What do you mean do they have your back?"

"As Commander In Chief, can I count on our military to defend me?"

The president seemed nervous and his speech pattern was rushed. He was rubbing his left arm. It looked as though a rash had developed. Of course he was nervous. Who wouldn't be after what appeared to be a second assassination attempt.

"Mr. President. I can assure you that I will do everything in my power to make sure that you and the first lady are safe."

"Yes, yes. I understand that but how about the military? Are my soldiers willing to follow my orders?"

"Of course they are, Mr. President."

"Every single member with no questions asked and without hesitation?"

"Mr. President. I can't say with absolute certainty that everyone agrees with your policies but"

"I need to know that I can trust the people around me, especially those who are supposed to protect my country and my presidency."

"But Mr. President, the only way to do that would be to ask every single soldier."

"I see. I see. Maybe we could have them sign an oath of allegiance or something. You know stating that they would always be on my side, supporting my decisions, and defending my presidency. How about that?"

The president was scratching his neck now as he seemed uncharacteristically agitated.

It was obvious that Hakim was uncomfortable with the direction of the conversation but Omar understood the need to reassure the president. "Mr. President. I don't think you need to do that. The members of our armed forces took oaths when they enlisted."

"Of course you're right". He seemed to be calming a little. "I just get nervous because I hear stories about my ancestors and how life was in their country. Every year they had a new leader, it seemed. Leaders were threatened, killed, resigned and some just disappeared. People were never satisfied. I've done a lot for this country, Omar, but are the people satisfied?"

"I understand, Mr. President, and I know that you understand this but things are not done that way in the United States. We have not had hostilities in hundreds of years. Change here is made through the ballot box."

"Yes Omar. You're right of course. I just feel that I need to know for sure, for peace of mind. But I guess there are no guarantees in life."

"No Mr. President, there aren't. But soldiers are trained to follow orders."

The president nodded. They finished their beverages without anyone saying more about it. There was some idle talk but the mood had changed and the president seemed calmer although the rash on his arm looked pretty bad. He had scratched it so hard that it had bled.

"Is there anything else, Mr. President?" said Omar.

The president stared as if deep in thought.

"Mr. President. Is there anything else you need to discuss?"

"No Omar. Thanks for your help, gentlemen. Go on home and enjoy your day off and I'll see you here tomorrow."

"Yes, I will."

"Thank you, Mr. President."

As he and Hakim walked quietly down the corridor from the oval office, Omar couldn't shake this uneasy feeling that something wasn't quite right.

Chapter 28

Tony phoned Angela and told her that after their recruiting trip, he had walked around his old haunts and talked to about ten guys that he knew. Most said they would come, bring girlfriends, wives, and friends. Tony joked that he hoped that those who brought their wives would leave their sweethearts home.

At 1 pm, people started filing into Angela's small apartment. She had put out a few extra chairs, but it was obvious those would not be enough. Many of the clergy members present at the last meeting were no-shows. Tony and Angela watched as the count rose to over 70 people. Angela was astonished, not just that this many people would show but that they would even come close to fitting inside her tiny apartment.

She passed around a pen and paper to be used as a sign in sheet. Having everyone's name, nickname, address, phone number, and email address would make it easier for her to organize future meetings.

As the pad was circulated, Angela started the meeting by introducing herself and Tony and then filling everyone in on the purpose of the group and what had transpired to date. Oddly enough, there wasn't a lot of griping. She asked if anyone would like to take minutes.

Buddy Riley's sister, Ann, a short, thin, redhead volunteered to be the secretary moving forward.

The first comment came from a tall man named Bruno Valente. "I get it Angela, but what's in it for me."

She saw heads nodding and heard some under the breath comments. One of her fears had been that some of the minor criminals might be more interested in themselves, then helping the country so, appealing to their heritage she explained how the president's policies were hurting neighborhoods like theirs and the ethnic culture in which they grew up. She laid out plans for some already scheduled protests both in Philly and in DC and told the group that they needed a lot of manpower to make these events impactful. These events had helped sway public opinion, but there was more work to do.

While not really that into politics and still unsure about how he would benefit, Bruno, at least, gave in for now. As if speaking for everyone he said "Ok tell us what you need us to do. Ya need me to go tune these guys up." Angela wasn't sure if this was meant as a joke or not since Bruno didn't even crack a smile but it sure elicited a few snickers among Bruno's friends. "He'll do it too," yelled someone from the kitchen.

After the banter had died down, Angela thanked Bruno for his enthusiasm and his support and asked: "Does anyone else have anything they'd like to say?"

Anthony Carfagno, or Antny as everyone called him, stood and spoke. Antny was a former member of The Centurians Motorcycle Club. As opposed to gangs like The Hell's Angels, The Centurians were all cops who rode. Antny had retired from the force after being shot four times breaking up a bank robbery in West Philly a few years back. He was on full disability, but Angela thought he looked pretty good. He was one of the guys she'd "do" if she had the chance as it was obvious that he worked out. "What we need to do is organize. Give everybody a job whether it's to secure weapons, get some snitches who can provide us with some info, or even cook for meetings, although some of you fatties look like you could stand to lose a few if ya know what I mean." Everyone laughed at that last comment, but Antny said "Hey I'm serious man. I'm sick of this shit and so is my wife Sandi over there." Everyone's eyes turned to check out Antny's wife. Angela was disappointed to learn that Antny was married but even more disappointed to see that his wife was so attractive. While she knew she should stay focused on the important things, Angela couldn't help but eye Antny up and down. Oh well, thought Angela," seems like the best are always taken." Of course, she still had Tony and after the dry spell that she had had, that was pretty damn good.

Angela thanked Antny and told the group that he made a lot of sense.

Suddenly, another guy in the kitchen came bursting forward, bigger than life. Of course, that was the rather rotund Nicky Gervasi. Angela had spent an entire day with the guy and learned something new about him at every turn. Apparently, everyone else in the room already knew Nicky, and they knew him by his handle. "Nicky Killer at your service," he roared. "I say we get a bunch of guys, ride down to DC, and wait for those assholes in Congress to leave their cushy offices and then we whack em. If we kill all of them jerkoffs, maybe we can put some goombas in there that will do the job for us; you get what I'm talkin' about."

Angela expected some laughter, but there wasn't any. She whispered to Tony in his ear "Is he serious, Tone?"

"Serious? He's downright scary. That's why no one laughed. His nickname isn't Bobo the Clown, remember. I don't think anyone laughs at Nicky Killer unless he laughs first because you never know when he's serious or just joking."

Angela, trying to appear professional as the leader and control the meeting interrupted him in a very formal way. "Mr. Gervasi", she started. Nicky interrupted her "hey you can call me *Killer*, sweetheart." Angela just smiled, ignoring his last comment, which seemed like forced bravado. She was seeing a different Nicky than the guy she had met a few days ago. "That would be a great idea except that some of our other distinguished members, who couldn't be here today, are members of the clergy, and I think they might frown on flat out 'whackin' them."

Nicky spoke up. "Well if they ain't here, they ain't a part of this fight. Am I right or what? What bright ideas do they have?"

Tony spoke now. "Well, Nicky" and he was interrupted by Nicky, who said, "yo, who said you could call me Nicky." Angela saw that Tony had stopped talking. He had a look of sheer fright on his face. A few days earlier they had all been friends but apparently with Nicky you just never knew which guy would show up. Then she noticed that he was smiling "I'm just messin' witcha, Tone."

Tony let out a soft breath of relief, smiled, and continued. "These men are former ministers and deacons. They think that we can start replacing the members of Congress by getting the vote out against them and putting in our people. Once we take over Congress, they can repeal some of Abbas' laws and executive orders."

"No shit?" said another man who failed to identify himself. "Are these guys stupid or what? Do you know how long it would take to get these putzes outta office? I'm with Nick. Things are drastic, and they call for drastic measures. Who else is with Nicky?"

There was deafening applause. Angela was surprised to see so much passion from a group that had just formed. But Angela and Tony felt their control of the meeting slipping away. Angela had to smile at the thought that a bloodthirsty mob of mostly dagos had replaced the once milquetoast committee of 8 do nothings. It was good to see and yet she knew that this was not just a matter of going to Washington to get rid of one man. There was an entire culture that had developed in DC and changing one man would not accomplish what was needed. The situation required more than a few people. A much more coordinated effort designed to change the complete political landscape was needed.

Suddenly an older woman of about 65 rose to speak. "Hello everyone, I'm Joanne Shapiro. I just moved here from

New York with my husband, Asher. He would have been here today, but he had to work. We're from Flushing, Queens; born and raised. For the past few weeks, we've been having similar meetings with friends of ours back home who attended synagogue with us. The group is growing and includes some very influential Jewish leaders now, including a rabbi from my old synagogue. My understanding is that the New York group is working toward the same ends that we are, and I thought it might not be a bad idea if we could talk to them to learn what they plan to do. Maybe they even have a Jewish group here in Philly because I heard that there is a Christian group in New York. Anyway, I was just thinking."

Angela liked Joanne immediately. She was an obvious New Yorker as she pronounced the city like "New Yawk" and asked if she could have a glass of "Wahtah." Angela loved that Joanne's idea made perfect sense.

After some discussion, the group agreed to meet again in one week. In the meantime, Ann Riley would distribute the loosely framed minutes of the meeting and Joanne Shapiro would call her former rabbi in New York to check on his progress and discuss a possible joint meeting between him and the leaders of this group.

Angela and Tony agreed to drive up to New York together to represent the Philly group at the meeting. Nicky said that he would like to go. Angela said ok, although she had reservations. What crossed her mind was the thought of one of the Jews pissing Nicky off and getting whacked. Joanne said that she'd like to go as well to make the introductions and because she would like to spend some time visiting with her mom in Queens and maybe even have a Rueben at her favorite Jewish deli.

The meeting adjourned and for the first time, Angela and Tony felt that there was some hope – that they had some people with gumption or 'balls' as Tony preferred.

Chapter 29

Dr. Baltasar Jabili, a retired surgeon at Boston General, received a call from Josh Redmond, a longtime friend of his. Dr. Jabili met Josh during the liberation of Azmarin, where he worked as part of a humanitarian effort.

They stayed in touch over the years, but it had been a while since they had spoken so he was surprised to get a call from Josh.

Dr. Jabili was a known activist so Josh was fairly sure that if there were any truth to the rumors of political dissension among the Muslim community in Boston, Dr. Jabili would be the one in the know.

"Hello, Josh. What a pleasant surprise."

"Hello Baltasar, how are you and how is your family?"

"We're well, my friend, but you know what it's like getting old. I get up in the morning, and I am surprised to find muscles hurting that I didn't even know I had."

"I'm sorry to hear that. Here's my advice; start working out. I'm still running five miles a day and lifting at the gym every chance I get. I feel strong and full of energy."

"So, what is the reason for this out of the blue call?"

Josh didn't want to share too much detail, but he did want some help.

"Well Baltasar, I've met with some people in New York who are heartbroken over the current administration. I hesitate to call it a movement because it's more like a grassroots effort but they would like to see some changes made within the government. There are rumors of a group in Philadelphia with the same agenda, and I've verified that what I've heard is true. One of the members in New York also heard about similar concerns among the Muslim community in Boston, and I thought that if there was anyone who would know for sure and who might know the people I should contact, you would be that person. Can you help me?"

"Well, my good friend, I can tell you that there is some truth to those rumors. I am not directly involved, but the sons of my dear friend Ulfat are."

Dr. Jabili explained that he had been a close associate of Dr. Ulfat Khalid when he lived in Syria, as they both worked in a military hospital in Damascus. After a moment of silence, Baltasar asked the general if he knew Dr. Khalid.

"I know the name, Baltasar, because the president's chief of staff is Omar Khalid but other than that I don't think I knew Dr. Khalid".

"Perhaps he was killed before we met. In any event, Dr. Khalid was a close associate of mine and a patriot who was killed in one of the Syrian uprisings along with his wife and daughter, only his sons survived.

"He sounds like the kind of guy I'd have liked."

"That's for sure. You mentioned Omar Khalid. Ulfat was Omar's uncle, so his sons are cousins of the White House Chief of Staff. They lived with Omar for years and came to the US with his family. When I spoke to the two boys a couple of weeks ago, they told me about a group of dissenters."

"Are you suggesting that Muslims might go against another Muslim?"

"I don't know. And I'm not sure they'd be interested in speaking with you, but I think you need to talk to the boys, Josh. I'm not involved but I can make the introduction."

"I just can't imagine that they would help me."

"Well you have something in common. They hate Omar."

"That is a good start. Will you reach out to the boys in short order? Time is of the essence."

"I will, Josh, and please let's keep this conversation between us for now."

"You have my word. Thanks Baltazar."

Chapter 30

Josh received a call the following day from Qasim Khalid.

Qasim explained to Josh, who he was, some background about his family and how he knew Dr. Jabili. Josh was impatient but sometimes hearing someone speak, their phraseology or even their pauses, told a lot about their personalities.

"Tell me Qasim. I've heard rumors that much of the Muslim community in the Boston area is unhappy with the way the current administration is running the country. Is that a fact?"

While the introduction, and recommendation, by Dr. Jabili went a long way with Qasim, he was never the less a little guarded.

"I don't know too much. I just met a few people who seem to be as you describe."

"Is this a large group, Qasim and has there been any talk among the leaders there about trying to have the president impeached or maybe starting an opposition party to defeat him in the next election?"

"The group is small right now, and there is talk. But talk is cheap General Redmond. Usually, nothing comes of it."

Josh decided that this game of rope a dope wasn't going to get them anywhere. "Well, I can tell you that there are groups in New York and Philly, who want just that and that they are meeting and discussing those very issues. I was calling you to see what your mood was. There is a great deal of hesitancy among the members in those cities, especially the primarily Jewish group in New York, towards working with Muslims; even if they have common goals. Their fear, Qasim, is that no matter how much they hate President Abbas, Muslims will stick together and can't be trusted."

"General, I came to America as a teen. When my father was killed in Syria, I went to live with his brother's family. I spoke some English that my parents wanted me to learn. They said, 'Son, in the west there is freedom and civilization. You must go there if you are to succeed in this world'. I've learned a lot since I've been here about people and religions. I have strong faith but I hold no ill will toward any religion. I believe my father was right and I'm just sorry that he, my mother and my sister were not able to share what I have found here. You know General, I believe that Islam is the story and I have learned a lot from Christians, who have what they call 'The Word'. I have learned ways of better understanding the Quran and what it asks of me and I hope that I am a better person and that I might be an example."

Before the general could utter a sound, Qasim continued with a rhetorical question.

"How can that be, you might ask? What is it that Islam demands of me? It is the 'Great Jihad' of the soul--perhaps our 'Way of the Cross', the darkest night of one's inner self. In my old country, I lived in a world of ignorance and darkness. Many grew long beards, professing to be holy, only to teach the ignorant to hate and destroy. I had no freedom to struggle for my soul. Can this be done without freedom? Where else but here could someone become what Allah wanted? Can you not see the irony, General? My uncle, who stood for everything father hated, decided to bring my brother and me to the one place where this was possible. In America, and maybe only in America could I be a true Muslim able to practice what Allah asks of each man. My parents taught us that we are all children of Allah and in our own way must seek our destinies."

"So General, I see America as a true Muslim country as it is truly a Judeo-Christian country because God saw fit to bless it. And The Constitution affords the freedom for each of us to thrive and worship him in our own way."

"Of course, there is prosperity. Allah wants his children to enjoy the fruits of their honest labors. Wasn't that what the prophet promised the people freed from Byzantine corruption 1,400 years ago? And didn't Islam bring science and learning to the West at one time? And now the West has it, and it must be sought out and without pride used to advance the world."

Josh hadn't wanted to sit through a lengthy speech, but it would have been rude to interrupt, and it did give him some insight into Qasim's personality. Here was a man of conviction. He seemed sincere and spoke with passion.

"And what about President Abbas?" asked Josh.

"Ah, Ahmad al-Abbas.   I fear that he loses his grip. He imitates the emirs who seek to control the fanatics who can only recite the Quran but understand nothing. He suppresses the voices of the people as the imams did in my country and the mullahs did in Iran. He is turning America into what I fled."

Suddenly, Josh realized how important it was to understand that people are either good or not regardless of their religion. He didn't know if he could convince Saul, Aaron, and the other Jews in New York of this but he felt confident in his assessment of Qasim as a real American. He loved his passion and that was something that he wanted to tap to energize all of the groups.

Josh politely listened to Qasim speak about his brother and how much he hated Abbas. He then took over the conversation. After going into more detail about their plans, Josh asked him if he would be willing to join in their crusade, so to speak. He told him that he was having a meeting in a few days in New York and wanted the group to meet him and his brother, Makim, if not in person, at least via video chat.

Qasim agreed, and Josh felt, for the first time, that this was truly bipartisan and a just cause.

Chapter 31

The Burj Al Arab Hotel in downtown Boston looked just like its namesake in Dubai, only more modern. The hotel in Dubai built 50 years ago, was older but still one of the nicest hotels in the Middle East. This hotel, conveniently located next to the silver line, opened just three months ago, so everything was shiny and new. Situated on Boston Harbor on the site of the once famous, Seaport Boston Hotel, which had been thoroughly destroyed by fire on Christmas Eve 2043, The Burj, Arabic for Tower, with its unique sail shape, made you feel like you could sail it into the Atlantic.

While the original plan had been to meet for dinner at Qasim's house, Tarif had phoned late last night and suggested that it would be better if they met in a more public place for lunch instead. Although the logic of that escaped him, Qasim had agreed. He guessed that maybe a little paranoia was setting in. He expected that this meeting would tell him a lot.

Qasim arrived just before noon. He assumed that Tarif had selected this particular hotel because no one would pay much attention to two men of Arab decent having lunch in an Arab hotel.

As he sat at the table sipping an Arak, he thought about Tarif's motives and what role Tarif might play in his plans. While at first he wondered, now he worried about the reason they couldn't meet at his house. To him, that seemed like the more secure place to meet, if that was in fact what Tarif was thinking.

"Assalamu 'Alaikum," Tarif interrupted his thoughts.

Qasim replied,"Wa'alaikum Assalam" as they shook hands and exchanged a kiss on the cheek.

"Tarif, it's nice to see you again." Qasim motioned to the waiter to bring another Arak.

"How is Heela?" Qasim remembered Tarif's wife as an intelligent, dark skinned woman who came to the US as a little girl from her home in Saudi Arabia. She was a head turner but unlike many American-born women who have men drooling over them, Heela was down to earth and fun loving.

"She's doing very well," Tarif said while looking around the restaurant. "Wow, this place is something. I suggested this by reputation, but I've never eaten here before. What's good on the menu?"

Qasim studied the menu a minute and offered his opinion that the lamb roast along with kabsa was excellent. "Of course, it may not be as good as Heela's."

"Well," said Tarif, "Heela doesn't make kabsa too often as she finds it easier just to put Rice-A-Roni in a pot. Don't forget that she came to this country when she was three years of age. She's more American than Saudi. So, I think I'll try the roast."

They ordered another drink and then placed their food order.

While waiting, they continued their small talk. Everyone was well. Heela was a doctor at Boston General. Their two high school age children were doing well in private school in Cambridge where Tarif and Heela lived. Well, actually where they lived on the weekends. During the week, Tarif resided in an apartment off Dupont Circle in DC. As deputy chief of staff, Tarif had a lot of flexibility in his work schedule. He flew to Washington on Sunday night and worked through Thursday. He then returned to Boston on Thursday night and spent the weekend with his family, although more times than not he was on his cell with DC discussing some simple problem at a White House dinner party or special affair. Now and then something important came up, but he was usually pretty relaxed on weekends.   In any event, other than the commute, life was good.

The waiter served the food, and it was as good as Qasim had suggested. Tarif wished he could ask for seconds, but he was more interested in where this meeting was going.

"So Qasim, you didn't ask me to lunch to discuss family and food. What's on your mind?"

"Well actually, I invited you to dinner, but why quibble," Qasim joked.

Tarif said nothing, so he moved on.

"So how is the job working out and what kind of work are you doing?"

"It's a good job, but it's just a job, you know. I'm mostly helping your cousin Omar manage the White House staff. That's all there is to tell."

Good answer but not so fast.

Really, Tarif? That's all you do? I would think that the deputy chief of staff would be more involved in the running of the country.

Qasim was trying to be subtle, but that wasn't his style. Surely Tarif guessed by now that he was being vetted for some reason and, as he was about to speak, Qasim threw him off guard by asking "Why did you not want to meet at my house?"

After a slight hesitation, Tarif said that he may have been overly cautious. He explained that he had been able to get people in the Boston area to mention Qasim by name when he merely asked if they had witnessed or heard about any new Muslim civic groups forming or about any unusual meetings being held. He explained that he was afraid other members of the president's "A" team might have been able to do that same thing. Although the president had specifically asked Tarif to see what he could find through his contacts, the paranoia in the White House was spreading. If anyone even suspected Qasim of wrongdoing and learned that the two of them had spent a considerable amount of time at his house, it could mean big trouble for Tarif. Spending hours there, he explained, could be misconstrued as a lot more than a friendly hour-long lunch between old friends.

He let that one go but stayed on task.

"I understand. Let me ask you this. What do you think of President Abbas and his agenda and direction for this country?"

Tarif was thinking, and Qasim half expected him to dance around some of these questions by spouting the old party line.

Instead, Tarif's candidness was like a breath of fresh air.

"To be honest, Qasim, I don't like the president very much at all, and I hate your cousin, Omar. I don't believe that they care about anyone but themselves and the power that they can wield. The president has persuaded his friends to push new legislation that would allow him to rule forever. Oh sure it's starting out as doing away with term limits but I know his agenda and what he wants is a lifetime job as president."

"Does he confide in you?"

He's been speaking more freely with me of late even though I'm more of an underling, given that I report directly to your cousin Omar. Certainly Omar is Ahmad's main guy. However over the past week or so the president has asked me to join the meetings.

"I don't know the President that well, Tarif. Is he a suspicious man by nature?"

"He is. He's the kind of person who fears the unknown and hates surprises. If you present him with a serious problem, he's great at finding a solution. But if there are a lot of unanswered questions; if he doesn't have all of the facts, it drives him nuts."

"And what is his state of mind right now?"

"He believes that there is something afoot, and he doesn't like it or, at least, he doesn't like the idea of it. And, after the attempted assassination, he isn't taking any chances. Until he knows for sure, he'll be very uneasy. Anyway, he said in the last meeting that he wants all hands on deck regarding finding out what possible threats there are."

"Why did he suddenly call you into the meeting, Tarif?"

"For one thing, he believes that, like Omar, I am totally devoted to him. Also, he's heard the rumors of radical anti-Abbas groups forming in the big cities on the east coast. The president told me that he had great Intel in Philly and New York. I can only assume that he has no Intel here in Boston and, knowing that I'm from Boston and come home regularly; he's hoping that I'll uncover some plot. He will laugh and say 'I know I'm just paranoid.' But when I don't respond in any way, he gets an anxious look on his face."

"Do you think he's just paranoid, Tarif?"

"Ah but that's where this gets interesting my friend. What I think doesn't matter, does it? The real question is for you to answer. Is he just being paranoid or is there justification for his concerns?"

Qasim wasn't much for cat and mouse games. "Tarif, if there was something underfoot in Boston where would your loyalties lie; with trusted friends or with your bosses?"

"My grandfather was from Egypt you know. He had an old saying that applies here. He would answer you as I do now

'If you marry a monkey for his money, the money will go away, and the monkey will stay the same."

"Are you toying with me, Tarif, because I don't understand your answer? So let me rephrase my question. I know that you have a good, respectable job with a good salary. There is some risk. How important is keeping your job to you?"

"As I said, Qasim, I don't like the president, and I'm concerned about the future for this and later generations. He has an agenda, and he's pushing toward it no matter what."

"Then I can count on your discretion and loyalty."

"You can, Qasim."

Qasim smiled but still wasn't sure about Tarif. Was he someone who could be trusted to help them or was he a faithful member of Abbas' inner circle out to get information from him?

"Tell me then. What has the president up his sleeves?"

Tarif explained what he knew of the Abbas' thinking regarding changes to his foreign policies in the Middle East, about the handling of protests, and about the actions that he had planned to ensure that he and his cabinet would rule without much distraction.

After hearing Tarif divulge some obviously secret information, Qasim felt a little more comfortable sharing some of his thoughts. He was still cautious, but he felt that he had few options. He needed someone on the inside, and while he still could not totally trust him, he felt that he should engage him to a point and decide later whether to include him further. In other words, Tarif would be on a short leash until he proved his allegiance.

He explained what he and his brother had been talking about. He discussed the issues he had with the current administration and the group of Arab Americans who had been meeting in Boston twice a week to hatch a plan to unseat the president. Qasim felt it imperative, at this stage, to make Tarif believe that he was talking about using peaceful means to accomplish their goals. He then asked Tarif for his thoughts.

"Well my friend," said Tarif, "I'm not sure that anyone can accomplish what you want peacefully. I'm not privy to everything that is going on within the Administration, but I keep my eyes and ears open. I don't like what I know, and can only imagine that what I don't know is far worse."

Tarif explained that the president planned to issue more executive orders in the next week that would further restrict the freedoms that Americans had come to expect. Despite the first lady's objection, apparently among those under consideration were fairly strict travel restrictions on women.

"Do you know how that alone will change the face of American business where women have routinely run companies and flown worldwide?" said Tarif. "This on top of the newly instituted clothing rules for women and the banning of all abortion and any means of contraception. Women in most of the world have the right to vote, but Abbas is seeking ways to restrict that right. I hear that he wants to review the entire Constitution, especially as it relates to first and second amendment rights. He's already shown a disdain for the first amendment. He believes that too much freedom of speech only results in problems and further unrest. And, after the first lady's shooting, he would love to get handguns off the streets. Of course, the NRA will never stand for that."

Tarif spoke with passion.

"Look at what has happened in America regarding religious freedom. If you're a Muslim, you can attend *Jum'ah* every Friday. If you work, your employer must now give you paid time off to attend the lunchtime service. Did you know that there are over 30,000 mosques in the US? Catholics make up only 8% of the population. There are only 6,000 churches and only 1200 practicing priests. While there are no policies against other religions, and there is no outward hostility that I know of toward Jews and Christians, most Catholics feel the need to take shelter; praying at home. Protestants fare a little better, but Jews have a tough time because teenagers, for some reason, have targeted synagogues for acts of vandalism, including burning some of them to the ground. I'm sorry" said Tarif. "I've monopolized the conversation."

"No you have not, my friend," said Qasim. Keep talking, he thought. He was providing the type of insight that he was hoping to hear. "What is your opinion of American Jews?"

Tarif hesitated as he never expected a question like this and didn't know how to answer it. He hoped that Qasim was a friend who could be trusted and not someone trying to set him up.

"Why do you ask?" said Tarif. "Are you plotting against the Jews?"

Qasim laughed. "No Tarif, did I not tell you my purpose? I have not lied. I only ask because I've been contacted by a retired US Army general who is Jewish. He and a rabbi in New York want to talk to me about some of the things that they are doing. The general said that his group has the same goals as we." Still not entirely trusting Tarif, he withheld names.

"Well, I have some friends who are Jewish. We're not close, but I get along with them. But I know that you don't trust them, Qasim."

"You're right. Personally, I'm not a fan of Jews, but I outright hate Abbas. I can live with the Jews in this country if we are each allowed to mind our own business. But Abbas is screwing up the country. After my conversation with the general, and hearing what he had to say about the passive Christian plan to oust him, I'm convinced that the Jews and those of us who consider themselves American Muslims now are the only ones who have enough of what the Jews would call Chutzpah to dethrone him."

"Chutzpah?" said Tarif. They both laughed at the sound of a Muslim using a Jewish word.

"In any event, we don't have to like one another. We have a common enemy and a common goal. If we respect one another maybe we can work independently on the same mission even from different places. On top of that, it was mentioned that a former member of his synagogue, who happened upon a Christian resistance group, had contacted the Rabbi. So you see, Tarif, despite the diverse backgrounds and many differences that exist in the populace, the president has, in fact, unified the country. People of all faiths and nationalities seem to be of one mind with a common enemy."

"And you want me to join your group in Boston," said Tarif.

"Sort of but I need much more from you, my friend. I want you to be our man on the inside of the president's circle of influence. At the very least, we'd like you to be able to report on the president's state of mind. Ideally we'd like to know his plans and actions so that we can be prepared. Can you do that, Tarif?"

"We are of like mind, Qasim, but I'm not in Abbas' inner circle. I'm in the White House but only as the deputy chief of staff. I'd have to be in another position to be asked to attend all of the meetings and to be included in the behind the scenes planning. And, the people in place now are the president's closest friends and advisors. He would never appoint me to a post unless something happened to one of them that prevented them from carrying out their duties."

"I see," said Qasim. "Let me ask you this. If you could have your choice of any job that would put you in a better position to help us, which would you like?"

Tarif's hands were sweaty. This conversation went in an entirely different direction than he first expected and even when he realized where things were headed, he never imagined what he was now hearing.

"Well," replied Tarif. "I guess the easiest would be as chief of staff. As the deputy chief, that would be my next promotion and would be easier to justify than making me say, umm, Secretary of Defense. But the president wants Omar as his chief of staff, and I don't think he would replace him with me unless he learned that Omar was unfaithful to him. Omar is too trustworthy and would never do harm to the president."

"What do you think of Omar?" said Qasim.

He knew that he had already said that he didn't like him, but Qasim wanted no ambiguity. His mission was too important to leave things open ended or to chance.

Tarif hesitated to choose his words carefully.

"I've said that I don't like him. He's too much of a hard-liner having come from Syria and all" said Tarif. "He's my boss, so I'm obedient. I do what he wants, and I stay out of trouble."

"If the opportunity presented itself, would you take his job and then help us in our mission asked Qasim?

"Without hesitation," was his reply.

The quickness of his answer surprised Qasim, who still wondered about an ulterior motive.

"Good. Leave everything to me. Just lay low and under the radar. Keep doing your job. I will be in touch when the moment is right. Oh, and to refresh your memory, Tarif, my brother and I are also from Syria. But don't worry. We hate Omar almost as much as we hate Abbas."

Tarif sighed in relief.

"We will be in touch."

Tarif pulled out a billfold, but Qasim said "Thank you for joining me for lunch. Lunch was my treat. Give my best to Heela, will you?"

"Of course, Qasim, ma'a as-salaama."

"ma'a as-salaama," replied Qasim.

Qasim, still sipping his drink, watched Tarif leave. His head was spinning, and he wasn't sure if it was the arak or all that they had just discussed. And while he hoped he had a new ally, he would have to remain guarded in his handling of Tarif.

Chapter 32

It was early January before the joint meeting in New York could finally be held.

Angela found scheduling to be a real challenge given the time of year and previous commitments. In fact, almost a month had passed since the idea had been proposed and she was beginning to think that it would not be possible.

Rather than sit idly by, Angela had gone down to DC for Christmas to join in one of the ever increasing number of anti-Abbas protests being staged around the country. She needed to keep the adrenaline going. She had wanted Tony to join her, but he seemed more interested in family time during the holiday. In fact, he had wanted her to meet his family but Angela wanted to keep engaged in the cause. They had actually argued over this. She was in love with him and hated him at the same time. She wanted him to be as committed to their cause as she was and yet, at times, this didn't seem to be a priority for him.

"Relax, we're playing the long game" he had said.

"Screw you and your long game," she had yelled back.

"I don't understand why we're fighting. What's the problem here Ange?"

She loved him, but he was a wimp and a pain in the ass sometimes. She didn't have the patience for this *long game.*

"Nothing, I'm sorry. You enjoy the holidays. I just need to take care of some things."

But the truth was that she was frightened about the prospect of meeting his family. She wanted things to stay the way they were. So she went alone and managed to sneak into the White House with the press corps to hear the president's nationally televised Christmas address. During the Q&A, she had asked the president why he was trying to dismantle the First Amendment. Proving her right, the president ignored her question, asking for another. As the guards escorted her from the room, she yelled: "Why are you screwing over women?" This question, first echoed by Carol Carson, caused a stir and by his body language, she knew that the president remembered.

While Angela had been anxious to get this meeting scheduled, Josh Redmond, like Tony, had been happy to see the delay. He didn't sit around doing nothing. There was a lot of work to be done and the delay gave him a chance to travel up to Boston to meet face to face with the Khalid brothers. That had been important to Josh ever since he had spoken on the phone with Qasim. While he felt comfortable after their phone conversation, it wasn't until he was able to look him in the eye that he was sure that what Qasim had told him was the absolute truth. Now he was convinced that the brothers could be trusted.

Before the formal meeting began, the leaders from Philly and New York met privately in the back room of Rabbi Rudzinsky's Jewish center.

In attendance from Philly were Angela, Tony, Nicky Killer, and Joanne Shapiro. Joanne had been a real asset in growing the group. Since joining, she had brought in several Jewish members of her Chestnut Hill synagogue. These were all respected civic and business leaders in the area. The Philly group that just a few months earlier had been 10, now numbered in the hundreds. They came from all parts of the city. Each met separately, and each had its own leaders, but they were all in touch and coordinating with Angela, who, whether she wanted the job or not, was the de facto leader in Philly. That was exciting for her because just organizing things was like running a large company.

The New Yorkers at the meeting included the Rabbi, his son Aaron, Josh, and to prove that a common enemy can bring together strange bedfellows, Muhammad ibn Ali, a New York lawyer and scholar who once lived next door to the Khalid brothers. Despite what many believed, Muhammad was named after one of the earliest legal scholars and Imams, not the boxer. Saul did not like the idea of Muhammad attending the meeting but Josh said this was a one-time thing and insisted that having diverse opinions would be good for their planning.

"Welcome," started Rabbi Rudzinsky, after the initial introductions. "To get started, I hope that we can be on a first name basis and do away with formal titles and surnames when we meet. I think it would make for a closer working group." Everyone agreed, so Saul continued.

"I was dragged into the fray by my son Aaron who had been attending meetings in Queens. A small group turned into hundreds, and I realized that this thing was going somewhere. We now have over 500 members in our group in Queens, but not all attend meetings. Thank God for that or we'd need to rent Queens Field. Saul smiled; half expecting some laughter at what he thought was a humorous quip. No one so much as cracked a smile, so Saul continued.

We've created a hierarchy whereby we've broken New York into districts based on who was in the group that could lead and where they lived. Other Jewish leaders around the country have also called me. What we are doing here in Queens is being duplicated in Chicago, Cleveland, Phoenix, Los Angeles, San Diego, San Francisco, Dallas and St Louis. Those are the ones I know about for sure but in talking with other leaders in these cities, many have reached out beyond their sphere. For example, Rabbi Berkowitz in St Louis has already connected with the people in Kansas City. So it seems that we're moving in the right direction."

"I have a few comments and a question or two," said Angela. "We started small, and that was a blessing and a curse. On the one hand, it was easy to control the communications of the small group, but we didn't have any leaders. As we grow, how can we ensure that our plans are kept secret and not leaked? Won't it be difficult to keep people from talking to friends and relatives? Also, in Philly, we found that as we grew we didn't have enough leaders to control this, and we're at sort of a loss as to the next step." How did you get more leaders and how big can this become? Oh, and when does it get totally out of control?"

"Well Angela," interjected General Redmond, "I have the same concerns about security. But I've found in my life that we can only control so much. If people understand the significance of maintaining silence at all costs and provide information on a need to know basis only, that's about all we can do. We have to have faith in our people to do the right thing.

Also, we have to understand that we can't control what the president and his people learn or how they react to the information. We have to assume that they have spies and are learning some of what is happening, so we have to leak some bogus information and use some misdirection to keep them off their game. Those involved in other cities are doing the sort of things that we want the president to know about and to focus. Their roles are important, but they are diversionary, more like obstructions.

As for leadership, there are different types of leaders. My friend Saul here is an outstanding role model and a leader of faith. Priests and ministers can also make great leaders. But these men all have one thing in common, and that is that they are pacifists by nature of their roles. I've been in charge of literally hundreds of thousands of men. The hardest part is remembering all of their names," he joked. Everyone snickered. "Seriously," he continued, "Saul and I have been discussing this, and I've been working on some plans that I'll share. The one thing I can tell you is that since DC is on the east coast, the groups on the east coast are going to have to step up and do the lion's share of the work. We need to decide on the best approach to bringing lasting change to the government in the shortest amount of time. I don't want to put words in your mouth Angela, but I understand, from talking to Joanne, that you believe that the way to bring about change is through the ballot box. Being an officer in the military, I've traveled all over the world, and I've witnessed changes in government. I have my views of how that comes about, but I'd like to hear your thoughts on that."

"Well, General."

"Please call me Josh if you would," interrupted the general.

"Ok, Josh, our initial group, was made up entirely of clergy except Tony and me. Their view was that we could take back the country by non-violent means. I agreed initially, and I'd love to see that happen, but the group has grown, the clergymen have taken a back seat, and some very colorful people like Nicky have convinced me that I'd be dead before we'd get the change we need. So in short, Josh, I'm open to discussing anything that will bring about a quick and lasting change in leadership."

Nicky chimed in "I think we just let me and my boys go down there and tune em up for good."

While that repeatedly seemed to be his standard answer to everything, it still brought laughter from everyone but Josh.

"That's not bad thinking, Nicky," said the general. "I was thinking of a little more elaborate plan, but you've got the basics down." Now even he smiled.

Josh brought the Philly group up to date on several fronts. He talked about how a friend of his had put him in touch with people that he knew in Boston. Josh spoke of the Muslim brothers, Qasim and Makim Khalid, and mentioned that they were cousins of Omar Khalid, the White House Chief of Staff. "At the suggestion of my friend I decided to vett them and their group. In fact, I met with them in Boston a few days ago. I'm confident that they are on the up and up and can be invaluable to our cause.

Despite Muhammad's presence, Saul was quite candid about his feelings toward working with the brothers. "How can you expect me to sit with Muslims and work with Muslims? That goes against every Jewish bone in my body."

Aaron was equally surprised to hear that he might have to be involved with Muslims. "How do we know we can trust them? Maybe they're plants. Maybe this is a sting set up by Omar Khalid to trap us."

"I understand your hesitancy. All I can tell you is that I'm a pretty good judge of character. That's why I suggested meeting them. I wanted to look at their faces, look in their eyes, and decide for myself if they could be trusted. I'm confident they can be, or I never would have suggested this. Qasim and Makim hate the president and want a change as badly as we do."

Saul and Aaron didn't look convinced, but they nodded; an indication that they'd like the meeting to continue.

Josh then mentioned how, like New York, the Muslims in Boston had reached out to others in their community and how they expressed their views that it was much harder for them to identify who could be trusted. Apparently the race card, similar to the one that got the first African American President, Barack Obama elected in 2008, had come into play. Many Muslims who voted for Abbas hate him. But because he's a Muslim he got their vote out of a sense of duty. So identifying possible confidantes was difficult. Josh said that he was told that the Boston group numbered only 12. "But," Josh said, "one of the 12 is a White House insider, and that could prove invaluable to us."

"I feel that expansion is not only essential but inevitable. As we grow, other like-minded people will gravitate toward one another. We all believe in a divine creator. Sure we have our differences. Some say God or God the Father. Some may call him Yahweh; some prefer Jehovah, and others call him Allah. And we have our differences regarding scripture interpretation and whether Jesus was a prophet, the son of God, or neither. But we share a common purpose. No matter what our reference, we all believe in a supreme being who created us and whom we worship. And I hope I'm speaking for everyone when I say that we all believe in each other's right to worship as he or she deems appropriate. That, my friends, is called "religious tolerance", and it was one of the cornerstones of the founding of this country. Further, we share a common enemy in President Abbas and his administration. This president threatens this basic religious freedom and promises to take away many of our rights, thrusting the United States back to ancient times. Are we not agreed that this man must go?"

Everyone had nodded their heads in approval and then clapped for Josh.

"This common thread that binds us will result in a cohesive effort with a single mind and a single purpose, but I understand that each group would prefer to work independently on specific operations because of their distinct differences. I'm ok with that because I think it can work. Don't forget that geography and religious beliefs already separate the groups. We basically have three primary groups: Mostly Christians in Philly, Jews in NY and Muslims in Boston."

"We just need to recognize and accept our differences, organize, put together the final plan, and execute that plan. I expect various groups to start solidifying in the coming months so that we'll need a liaison in each city."

The Philly contingent remained silent. It was obvious to them that these folks were much more organized and further along in the process than they.

Aaron was the next to speak. "I know I'm a young guy, but I've been a foot soldier out on the streets, rallying support, and finding out what was happening. While my dad is an obvious pacifist, I've been helping General Redmond put together a plan that we believe has a high probability of success. But I have to get this out on the table. This plan is not without risk, and I have some very real reservations about having Muslims play a part in this operation. There is the risk that these Khalid brothers are a part of a sting. There is a danger that we could all be found out, imprisoned, tried for treason, and executed. There is the risk of total failure where the government repels our actions with the result being mass casualities and no change. There is a risk of this happening. But I guess I'm willing to go along with Josh's gut because I'm convinced that none of these is worse than the outcome of doing nothing."

The applause was deafening. Angela, speaking for her group, said that they were on board and that she would bring the Philly group up to speed and on board as well.

Hearing that, Josh brought up Teleview, MicroTech Corp's new 3D 9G video conferencing software on his computer. He dialed Qasim and Makim, who were waiting in Boston.

The brothers, expecting the call, answered on the first ring. Josh welcomed them and after a few introductions and pleasantries, they got down to business. Saul sat with his arms crossed, obviously not happy with these recent events but apparently willing to go along for now. Josh told the brothers that he'd like an update in a few minutes but that he wanted to fill them in first. The general finished telling the brothers about the Philly group agreeing to join forces and the New York group starting work on a final plan. Aaron then asked the group to vote for and elect General Josh Redmond as the supreme commander of the Nationalists, a term that from then on they alternately used with Patriots to describe those fighting for their freedom. The group approved Josh through acclimation. While seemingly a no-brainer, this was the most important decision these three groups would jointly make.

Josh thanked everyone and, after a very brief acceptance speech, told them that it was critical that no one discuss their goals, mission, or any sensitive information via text or email. He was confident that sooner or later, the president would order the NSA, CIA, and FBI to monitor those. He told everyone about his purchase of a *secured* phone from Intercontinental Cellular and would place an order for 15 more such phones so that from this moment forward, all communication, among the leaders of the groups, would be either by secured line or in person. He purposely held back telling them about his other secure phone and the Assembly of Nine. He was hell bent on people having only the information that they absolutely needed to do their jobs. All information, he told them, was to be on a "need to know" basis."

What went unsaid was that Josh wanted to keep the minute details away from the religious among them. They served the purpose of community organizers and could muster a group of people who trusted them. But the less they knew about the details of what was being planned, the better.

He then asked Qasim for an update on their end. Qasim spoke in detail about what Makim had found out about a few Muslims in Boston who were meeting in private discussing what they could do about the current administration. He then briefed everyone about his meeting with Tarif and how important it was to have an ally on the inside.

Everyone listened intently before Josh spoke. "That's an outstanding idea, Qasim, and it fits right in with our plans here. But are you sure that Tarif can be trusted?"

"No General. I'm not 100% sure but can we be 100% sure of anything? I just don't see any other options that will give us eyes and ears inside the White House. I believe that Tarif can be a valuable asset. But I also think that we have to make sure that we always keep one very skeptical eye on him."

"I understand," said Josh. "Ok then. I guess the most pressing need at this point is to remove Omar, the White House chief of staff, from the equation so that Tarif can be promoted." He asked if anyone had any ideas.

Saul was the first to speak. "From what I've seen in politics, everyone has some skeletons in the closet. I'd suggest finding out what Omar Khalid is hiding and then use that information to affect his departure either by forcing the president to replace him or by strongly suggesting that he resign."

Muhammad ibn Ali, who had been unnervingly silent, spoke up. "I don't know Omar personally but Qasim and I have spoken at length about him and, while he's a terrible human being, there is nothing in his background that could be proven and of use to us in this sense. Do you agree with that Qasim?"

"Yes, I do. I've known Omar all of my life and lived with his family for years. On the one hand, he's very sneaky and did things that I would not be proud of myself. But he's not an entirely dishonest man or a criminal and, while not a good husband regarding how he treats his wife, he is at least faithful to her. He doesn't drink, gamble, or frequent prostitutes. He works hard for his money and brings home a decent paycheck that he uses to take care of his wife. He even gives a lot of money to his mosque. We can look, but I don't think we'll find any skeletons in his closet. I don't see any way to discredit or blackmail him."

Nicky chimed in; "Are you suggesting that we whack him?"

"While I don't like him, I'd much prefer to do something to trap him into some wrong doing. Then we can use that to have him fired from his job."

Josh then told Qasim that he would like to talk to him the next day about some ideas on how to peacefully remove Abbas from office.

Chapter 33

Nicky hung around after the others had left because he wanted to speak to the general about his strategy. While the general spoke about entrapping Omar in a way that would force the president to remove him from his position, Nicky wasn't buying it for a minute. He had street smarts, and a keen sense of what was happening and that sense told him that the nuances suggested in the meeting were not the general's style.

"General, it doesn't make any God damn sense to me that you would want to play some political bullshit game just to can someone from his job. I think that a more direct way would be better, ya know....and faster."

"I was brought into this by Rabbi Saul. He's a good friend of mine, and while I'm sure he knows on some level that things are likely to get ugly, he's also a pacifist who doesn't want to be a part of any violence. So while I'm working on a better plan, it helps our cause to have the Rabbi believe that his group is interested in some peaceful way out of this mess. Does that make sense to you?"

"Yeah but what's the real plan?"

"We start by *whacking* Omar," said the general bluntly.

They both laughed at the General's use of a word that was more common to Nicky's vernacular. "Fuckin' A, I'm in. What can I do to help?"

"Nicky, I know several people who could do this but they are active duty Special Forces. We need someone good who is not in the military. Do you know anyone?"

Nicky nodded. "Does the Pope know any prayers, General?"

"Good. I thought you might. Don't do anything yet. Poke around a little; feel some people out, and wait for my call."

After Nicky left, Josh sat down to relax; relieved that he had someone to do some of the grunt work. He liked Nicky. To the general, he was like a good soldier who would follow him into battle no matter the danger involved. Oh sure he was rough around the edges at times. Yet Josh sensed that under his rough veneer was a smart, resourceful guy. Most important, though, he was confident that when Nicky said that he'd do something, he'd produce results. So far there had been few in the group ready to act, and that had to change.

Chapter 34

Most of his high school friends would describe Ronnie Tartaglione as a punk. He was slight of build and the kind of kid who instigated trouble and then ran away when things started to get out of hand. It wasn't unusual for Ronnie to get into the middle of the fracas, help it escalate, and then sneak away while the remaining combatants ended up brawling.

In school, he was a smart ass and a class clown. He had an IQ of about 120, but while smart enough to get good grades, he never applied himself. He'd much rather be out playing football or basketball or even just chasing girls.

While attending the local Catholic high school, he was constantly in trouble. He was dismissed because of his poor grades, first from the football team and then the basketball team. Trouble seemed to follow him during his sophomore year and by the middle of the term, he was expelled for smoking pot on school grounds and painting graffiti on the outside walls. His parents enrolled him in a public high school, but he dropped out during his first semester there. He had just turned 16.

At a loss for what to do with their son, his parents asked his uncle if he would take him under his wing for a while. Uncle Larry and Aunt Betsy lived in the middle of farm country in Southern New Jersey. Uncle Larry ran an auto repair business, was a member of the NRA, and an avid hunter. Aunt Betsy stayed at home and baked and ran the household. Childless herself, she was thrilled to have her nephew to dote on.

It was there that Ronnie started to realize that his talents could not be tied to a classroom because he was more of a 'hands on' kind of guy. Under his uncle's tutorage, he became quite the auto mechanic. More importantly to his future career, he became quite the hunter. His uncle taught him to shoot at a target range he had set up behind an old barn. Ronnie started by shooting cans with an old .22 long rifle and later progressed to shooting even smaller targets at even greater distances. Uncle Larry would brag to anyone who would listen that his nephew was the best marksman he'd ever seen.

Eventually, his uncle took him out hunting, first for small game like rabbits and then, during the season, deer that ran rampant across the area. For his 17th birthday, his aunt and uncle bought Ronnie the first really expensive present anyone had ever given him; a multi-load .308 Winchester with a scope and a box of Remington 125 grain reduced recoil loads. Once he got the hang of the rifle's recoil, he switched to the heavier 165-grain bullet that provided greater killing power. Within a few months, Ronnie was shooting deer from 350 yards as if he had been born with a rifle in his hands.

One requirement that Aunt Betsy placed on him was the he had to accept homeschooling to complete the requirements for his GED. While not thrilled, Ronnie agreed and was much more motivated working one on one with his aunt than he had ever been in the classroom. And, he loved his reward for doing a good job; hunting trips with his uncle.

Once he passed his GED though, Ronnie realized that living in rural New Jersey was not what he wanted out of life. In fact, he had no idea what he wanted to do. So, he enlisted in the Army.

It wasn't long before his TI's, and CO recognized that Ronnie had real talent and recommended him to "MAST-Military Academy for Sniper Training."

Ironically, the smart aleck goofball with a chip on his shoulder that Ronnie had been before he entered the service was replaced by a serious young man being groomed for a very serious job. Initially, Ronnie was assigned as one of the sharpshooters in an infantry squadron. The Army charged his squadron with taking out the most elusive but strategic enemy targets. The expert marksmen were tasked with killing the key military leaders in an attempt to disrupt the enemy chain of command and decision-making. He was never told "Ronnie you are now an assassin", but as he was singled out for assignments, and as his targets became high profile leaders, that is exactly what Ronnie Tartaglione had become. And he was good at it. In fact, he was one of the best. By the time he was discharged, he was credited with 229 kills, the most ever by a US Sniper. The "credited" count is the score the government admitted to. The reality was that Ronnie had likely killed over a hundred more.

In the Army Ronnie found his passion; killing people. But once retired, he didn't know what to do with himself. He had been trained as an auto mechanic and was a darn good one but between the changes in automotive technology and his lack of interest, that didn't seem like a good option. He was smart but he didn't want to use his GI Bill benefits for college. That just wasn't for him. His wife, Tina, kept on him about finding a job, and he'd halfheartedly look at the on-line job postings, but there was never anything that interested him.

After a while, though, he just got frustrated and pissed off at Tina's nagging, and he'd lash out at her. Eventually, she just accepted that he would never be a nine to five career guy like many she knew. So she stopped harping on him and let him do whatever he wanted to do while she went out to work. What Ronnie did mostly was wander the streets and chat up sports with anyone who would talk to him. A lot of people thought that he was a little odd so even finding someone to talk to was hard because let's face it, how many people could relate to someone like Ronnie? Very few could understand the inner workings of a guy who killed people for a living for 20 years. He picked up odd jobs every now and then, but there were few employment opportunities for a guy like him. That's why Ronnie was psyched when he got the call from his old war buddy about a possible job.

Chapter 35

Old man Giovanni liked to call his little establishment "Giovanni Ristorante" but looking around the room; Nicky Killer knew that it was just a friggin pizza joint with some table cloths on the tables. Putting a few pasta and parmesan entrees on the menu didn't make Giovanni's a swank restaurant. No, it was nothing fancy which is why he loved the place.

Today he thought he'd have a cheese steak with extra cheese and lots of fried onions. Nicky almost single-handedly contributed to Philly's rep as the fattest city in America. He loved pasta, pizza, cheese steaks, hoagies, and Philly Pretzels. Coke too and not that diet crap, only the high octane stuff. If it was fattening, it was on Nicky's diet.

As a young boy growing up on South Colorado Street, his mother used to try to get him to eat eggplant disguised as lasagna, but Nicky wasn't having any of it. He wanted the real thing. "If you wanna change it up ma, put some sausage and extra cheese in it."

All of which explained why he was a 46-year-old with a 46-inch waist to match. He had been a good-looking boy back in the day. After floundering around for a few years after high school, he enlisted in the Army at 23 and left South Philly to go overseas to fight the towel heads, his favorite nickname for the Taliban.

He was 5'11 and weighed about 160 pounds back then. His friends jokingly said he was in the infantry because he was too stupid to get out of the way of the enemy. In fact, it was during the third Iraq war while engaged in a firefight in neighboring Kuwait that Nicky, using a machine gun that was part of the Browning M1933 series, was credited with taking down over 50 enemy troops and two jeeps single-handedly. The talk started about *Nicky the Enemy Killer*, a nickname which was eventually shortened to *Nicky Killer*. That rep had served him well in life as most people were afraid of him because rumor had it that he was crazy. He didn't think he was crazy but, to foster the myth; he'd say stuff like "Who am I to say? I ain't no psychiatrist. Maybe I am a little nuts?"

While on a TDY at Camp Taji, near Bagdad, Nicky met a 20-year-old who was also from South Philly, Ronnie Tartaglione. Being stationed together made them both feel right at home and he and the kid, as he referred to Ronnie, hit it off right from the start. The big thing they had in common was that they both liked to kill the enemy. The only difference was that while Nicky loved killing hordes within minutes, Ronnie was a Special Forces sniper who enjoyed the hunt, even if his count was only one. "Quality is what it's all about, not quantity," Ronnie used to joke. His forte, and what made him perfect for the mission that Nicky had in mind for him, was killing high profile enemy military and heads of state.

When Nicky returned from the Army, he found that the old neighborhood had changed. Many of the Italians were long gone, replaced by Asians and blacks. His parents and many of their friends had moved to the Washington Township area in Southern NJ. Nicky bought a home and lived near his parents for a while, but after they died, he joined the resurgence in South Philly.

As their parents, who had moved to the burbs, got older and either died or had to be admitted to residential living facilities, their kids started to cash in on the appreciation of the houses that were selling for almost a half million dollars. They then began moving back into the city. Taxes were lower compared to the burbs with the average cost of a nice house being $200,000. So the old neighborhood, which had been run down and dilapidated, was a decent place to live. When Ronnie was discharged from the Army, he thought about selling the tiny row home to the developers and moving to the burbs, but Nicky convinced him to stay in South Philly near him. South Philly was once again becoming "a Little Italy."

"Yo Nicky," came the familiar voice as Ronnie entered Giovanni's.

He stood to greet his friend as they usually did, "Yo Ronnie," and they gave each other a brief bear hug.

"How ya been Nick?"

"Been doin' great ya know, I have my days but other than that I'm doin' ok. And what's the use a complainin'. Don't nobody listen anyway."

"How's Tina"

"Ah, ya know Teen. She never changes. She's the same girl I met 25 years ago. We've been married for 17, ya know. 'member, weren't you at the wedding?

Nicky could never forget Tina. After she and Ronnie had been married a couple of years, Ronnie was away on an assignment. Being away was common, and his assignments were always overseas. Nicky was home on leave and attended a party thrown by a mutual friend, Sissy something or other. He spotted Tina from across the room. She looked gorgeous. She was about 5'5" and weighed about 115 lbs. She had shoulder length black hair and the most engaging smile. Nicky mentally undressed her, secretly wishing she were single. *Don't be a pig*, he had thought to himself.

Tina saw Nicky and walked across the room to give him a hug. She had felt good, and he had to keep reminding himself "She's freakin' married." As the night wore on they both mingled and chatted with friends. Nicky overheard Tina telling friends that she and Ronnie had only been married two years, and she'd already been to Ft Rucker, AL, Ft Ord, CA and Ft Benning, GA all for short stints while Ronnie was stateside. They always lived in temporary housing because they weren't going to be there long before her husband would be getting orders to go overseas again. That's why they bought one of the older, more affordable, row homes in South

Philly. It was their home base, but Tina spent way too much alone time there.

At the end of the evening, Tina asked Nicky if he would walk her home. The great thing about South Philly was that everyone lived within walking distance of everyone else. Good thing too because there was never a place to park. Tony thought that his neighbor, Mr. DiLori from across the street, hadn't moved his car in 5 years because he didn't want to lose the parking space in front of his house.

So he walked the four blocks with Tina, and when they arrived, Tina had asked him if he wanted to come in for a drink. His response was "Do ya think that's a good idea?" To which she replied, "Well if I didn't I wouldn't have asked ya in."

She made herself and Nicky a drink, and as they sat on the couch relaxing, Tina started talking about her life.

"When I was younger, I was always drawn to the bad boys, ya know, the kinda guys who always seemed to flirt with danger. Ronnie was that kind of guy. He had a chip on his shoulder that said 'I'm someone, don't mess with me.' I remember one time we were walking down the street, and I was wearing something that I guess was sorta low cut. Anyway, these two dudes stared at me when we walked by, checkin' out my tits. Ronnie turned on them and beat the livin' shit out of both of them. I swear he would have killed them if I hadn't stopped him. That was scary, but ya know it made me feel good that I had a guy who loved me that much."

"But my mom didn't like Ronnie at all. She thought he was a thug. She was always trying to get me to date these smart, uninterestin' guys, but I fell for Ronnie, and I've loved him ever since. And I still do, Nick. I do. You know that. But this is messed up. He's rarely home and when he is, we're either fighting over his fits of anger or his mind is somewhere else. Then, out of the blue, we have to pack up and move to a new base. After a few months, he gets orders to go to some God foresaken place in the desert or something, and I'm back

168

here alone for the next six months." She touched Nicky's arm. "Everything's about him or the Army's needs. But what about my needs Nick? I have needs too. Ya know what I'm sayin'?"

For several minutes Tina talked about her private life. Nicky sat there; uncharacteristically quiet. Finally, she said "I'm gonna take a shower. I could use some help with my back." Again, Nicky sat silently. "Do I have to hit you over your head or what? What the hell is wrong with you, Nick? I know ya think I'm hot. I've seen the way you look me over."

Thinking that he might just sit there for hours, Tina took him by the hand and led him to the bathroom. She turned on the water to the shower, undressed, and slipped behind the curtain. Nicky undressed and entered the shower behind her. He rubbed against her so that she could feel his boner against her ass. Her wet body was even sexier and more beautiful than he could have imagined. With a soapy hand, she reached down and started playing with him. With her other hand, she touched herself. She was so wet between her legs, and not from the shower. Nicky stared wide eyed as she moved both hands in unison. They kissed, and he ran his hands all over her. She stopped short of climaxing, fearing that she would make Nicky come right there in the shower. No, she'd be patient, but she was ready to explode.

After washing one another, they stepped out of the shower and dried off before entering the bedroom. She took the towel from around his waist. He was excited and ready for her. She then let her towel fall to the floor. He let out a half-hearted protest "we shouldn't be doing this, Tina". "I know" but there was no way she was getting this far and not getting laid. As she lie back on the bed, she reached for a condom that she had placed on the night stand. As she put it on him she said "I want it big, and I want it all the way in." What followed was the best sex that Nicky had ever had. Tina was insatiable. She liked everything and every position, and there wasn't anything that she wasn't willing to try.

Nicky spent the night at Tina's, and they had sex several times. On his way out the door, he asked if she was free later on. She said "Nick, this was great, but I'm married, ya know. I love Ronnie, and I don't wanna hurt him. I needed this badly; I was all wrapped up in knots. You were great, and I'll never forget tonight. But I don't think we should make more of it. It was one great night, but all it can ever be is just one night."

That wasn't the last time he saw Tina. In fact, they had been in one another's company many times over the years. But that was the last time he saw her that way. They were just friends now.

That sobering thought brought Nicky back to the present as the waitress dropped the cheesesteak in front of him. *Sheesh, look at me now*, he thought to himself. *I couldn't screw more than once now, and that would only last about a friggin' minute.*

Yesterday, he'd received a call from Josh, who told him that neither he nor Qasim had been able to come up with a solution to the Omar dilemma. He told Nicky that it had been decided they needed what he called a 'final solution' and they both felt that Nicky was the guy who could get things done.

"Do you understand what I mean?" Josh had asked. Nicky may not have gone to college, but he wasn't stupid. He knew exactly what Josh wanted.

Nicky took a bite of his cheesesteak and leaned over the table close to Ronnie's face and whispered. "Ron, I've got a job for ya if ya want it, but this is one of those top secret missions like the ones ya used to go on when you was in the Army. Ya can't tell nobody, not even Tina."

"You're not sending me over to some rat infested third world country are ya?"

"Nah. It's here in the States, but it's the kind of job that you're perfect for."

170

"What's the pay?"

Holy crap thought Nicky. He hadn't thought about pay, and the question surprised him.

"Suppose I said nothin' but it would make you feel patriotic? How about that?"

"How about I say 'no way? Pay me and I do the job. Otherwise, tell your boss, whoever he is, to go screw himself."

Their pointed conversation was interrupted by Kathy, their waitress, who Nicky sensed had been eavesdropping. She looked like she'd been eating all of Giovanni's profits. When she had taken their order, Ronnie joked "Now there's a live one for ya, Nick."

"No way. I wouldn't do her with your dick," Nicky had replied.

"How's everything? Can I get yous anything else?" said Kathy.

Nicky said everything was good as she left him the check. "There's no rush but yous can pay me when you're ready"

He thought it best to shift the conversation away from money, hoping that if he could get Ronnie excited about the "hunt" that he'd be more willing to cooperate. So, he quietly explained the target and asked Ronnie if he was ok with that and if he thought he could pull it off. After a brief discussion of some options, Ronnie said "This is a tough one but yeah, I can pull it off. I just need to go down there a couple a times to scope things out, but I can do it."

"Good. Then you're with us?"

"Sure, if you pay me enough."

"Look Ron", Nicky whispered. "This guy running the country is a jerkoff, and so are those assholes he put in to help him. We gotta get rid of them, and this is important. You didn't seem to have any problems killing people before. You even seemed to like it. What's the problem with doing this for me?"

Ronnie smiled. "This isn't about what I like, Nick. I have no problem killing someone. That's what I do. That's what I've loved doin' for the past 20 years. Mess with Tina or cross me and you're a dead man. But I don't give a shit about Omar. I don't even know him. He hasn't done anything to me. I'll do it but only as a job; for pay."

"Ok I'll tell ya what, how 'bout I see if I can getcha a few grand," said Nicky.

"How 'bout ya see if ya can get me fifty grand?" was Ronnie's terse reply.

"Fifty large? Sheesh, that's a lot of dough. Ya just said it was a piece of cake."

"I didn't say it was a piece of cake. It's a freakin' nightmare. I said I could do it. How many people do you think there are who can pull off killing a high ranking government official? And how much do you think they would charge? Fifty grand and we got a deal. Otherwise, thanks for my cheesesteak. Oh, and this meeting never happened. Ya hear what I'm sayin'? "

"Ok, I'll get ya fifty," he said. Nicky finished eating his cheesesteak thinking *Shit, I shoulda been a sniper for that kinda money. And where the hell am I gonna get him fifty g's.*

Chapter 36

"Fifty thousand dollars?" said Josh into his secure phone. "Are you nuts, Nicky? What do you think I am a bank? I'm just retired military. I don't have that kind of money. Are you even sure this guy can do what he's promising?"

"Trust me," confirmed Nicky, "This guy could shoot a penny out of a squirrel's mouth from over a mile away. He's the best I've ever seen."

"What's this hot shot's name?" fired back Josh.

"Ronnie Tartaglione. You may have heard of him since he was an Army sniper for almost 20 years."

Josh had indeed heard of Ronnie. In fact, it was likely that everyone who had ever been in the Army had heard of him. Ronnie was a legend.

"Give me some time. I'll get back to you."

Josh hung up the phone, frustrated. On the one hand, he didn't have fifty grand. At the same time, he knew of Ronnie Tartaglione by reputation, and he knew that if anyone could pull this off, Ronnie could.

Josh dialed a local NY number.

"Hello Josh," said Saul. "What can I do for you?"

Josh explained a mainly false version of the situation to Saul about needing fifty grand to bribe a high-ranking government official to get him to step down so that someone who was loyal to their cause might be promoted. Though Saul had been at the meeting where they had spoken via Teleview with the brothers, Josh felt obliged to repeat everything about the Khalid brothers and their friend Tarif and how important it was to his mission to have eyes and ears on the inside. It was all true, except Josh never told Saul about how he was planning to spend the money.

"That's a lot of money. I can get you twenty-five grand but not the whole thing" was Saul's reply.

Josh thanked him for his help even though the money wasn't enough. He immediately dialed Nicky's number in Philly. "Ok, it's a go. I've got Ronnie's money. He gets half upfront and the rest when he's completed the job."

Josh was more than a little concerned about the money. He wasn't sure yet, but it was possible that he might also need an ordnance handler. He knew a guy from one of his Middle Eastern assignments but hiring him would cost him a pretty penny. He didn't know how or where yet, but somehow he'd figure out how to get the rest of the money he'd need.

Chapter 37

It was a beautiful spring morning with the bluest of skies over South Philly. Only a few birds were tweeting, mostly little sparrows, but Ronnie loved the sound of birds. Having spent so much time in the desert, he didn't get to hear birds chirp very often or for long periods. Besides having sex with his wife, that was his favorite part of being stateside.

He packed his luggage, kissed his wife, and left his home for DC.

Soon after being hired for the job, he had contacted an old high school classmate, Eddie Moretti. He loved Eddie's name because it kinda rolled off the tongue. Eddie made his living getting people whatever they needed. Ronnie had him rent a car for him under an alias with one of his many fake IDs. He and Eddie weren't friends. In fact, he thought Eddie was kinda stupid giving him a friend's discount. *What a dope* thought Ronnie. *I was gonna pay him 2 g's to rent the car, and all he wanted was the money for the rental plus a c-note for his trouble.*

He put the luggage in the trunk of the rental and hung a suit bag on the hook above the rear, driver's side window. Ronnie wore gloves so there would be no trace of his fingerprints on the car or the rifle. He also brought a portable vacuum cleaner that he would use to clean the inside of car and trunk. He had done this sort of thing hundreds of times, and since the car was rented to some fictional person, there would be no way to trace the car to Ronnie.

He stopped at the corner store for a cup of Joe and then headed south on I-95 on the short jaunt to DC.

Within three hours Ronnie was parked on the first level of a parking garage on H Street in the nation's Capital. This was his third trip to DC and each time he did the same thing;

packed lunch, parked on H Street, and went to a local park to relax for the day. Tina had wondered where he was going, and he explained that he was making a presentation about providing some security services at the Pentagon. She never asked for details. He loved that about her.

The park was relaxing for Ronnie. He enjoyed sitting on a bench or laying on the grass under a tree and reading his new Kindle Blaze. At the end of the day, he'd go back to the garage and then move from the garage roof to a roof at the corner of H and 15th. There he'd wait until 4:30 pm when the White House staff left for the evening. Everyone scattered to various parking garages, got in their cars, and sat in bumper to bumper traffic for what seemed like hours.

On his first two visits, Ronnie drove his own car and sat in traffic with everyone else. That hadn't been much fun, so his plan for this trip was to put all of his nondescript belongings back in the trunk, take a walk in the park again, and never return to the car.

The final part of his plan called for him to leave the park around 7 pm, walk a couple of blocks to get a cab to ride to Union Station. There he would change into his business suit and board an Amtrak train to Wilmington DE where his wife, Tina, would pick him up after what she thought was his long day of meetings at the Pentagon.

Chapter 38

It had been a very long day, and Omar was glad that it was over.

The day had started badly when Omar woke up with a splitting headache. He had taken a couple of pain relievers and sat over a cup of coffee reading the Washington Post. This routine had become a ritual that he loved as it started his day in a relaxed way. Well, the day usually started on a positive note but not today.

"Shit". He spilled coffee on his white shirt. "Now I have to change and I'm in a hurry."

After picking out a nice blue dress shirt and matching tie, Omar left for the short drive to the White House. The typical drive at 7 am from Silver Spring, MD was about 25 minutes or so but there was a lot of road repair going on and today's trip took him 45 minutes.

He felt cursed as nothing seemed to go right the rest of the day. It was just one of those days that made him grateful knowing that it would end and tomorrow would be a new day. He wasn't *a clock watcher* but today he couldn't wait to leave, play a little tennis, and then go home to relax for the evening.

Omar finished barking the last of his dinner party orders to the White House Staff at 4:15 pm and headed to a dressing room to change. Every Wednesday after work, Omar played tennis with some friends at the new "Fifth Set Tennis Courts" on NW 15th Street. It was one of the few things to which Omar looked forward.

He left the White House at 4:25 pm sharp, slightly ahead of the other daytime employees. President Abbas had wanted to hold a meeting to see if anyone had learned anything regarding a potential intifada but Omar had asked if the president could hold the meeting the following morning.

"After all," said Omar, "how much Intel do we have today that will not be just as valuable tomorrow morning?" The president seemed more tired than usual. He welcomed the chance to finish work, attend the planned dinner party, and relax with Maryam in the sitting room before retiring for a much needed good night's sleep.

Omar turned north on 15th toward H Street, and as he started his walk, he began to sing softly a tune from an old Walt Disney movie from 100 years prior.

"Just whistle while you.....

The word "work" never made it out of his mouth.

A little red dot had appeared on his forehead before a single bullet from a Barrett .50 Cal rifle ripped through the air putting a nice, clean, round hole in the center of his forehead.

Omar was knocked backward and laid dead on the sidewalk. The time was 4:30 pm on the dot.

Chapter 39

Police and news vans were all over 15th and H Streets; one group trying to find a killer, the others looking for a story.

News of Omar's shooting spread quickly, via VAPTs from the nation's Capital.

President Abbas called Omar's wife immediately so that she would hear the bad news directly from him. She was devastated. He wished that he could go to her to give her comfort but he had pressing business.

He told his secretary "Julia, I need you to do two things for me. First I need you to contact the remaining cabinet members. I want everyone in my office tomorrow morning at 7 sharp."

"Yes, Mr. President."

"Then I need you to go over to see Omar's wife. Someone should be there to comfort her and handle the press."

"Yes Sir. I'll get right on it."

The president picked up the phone and dialed Tarif Mansour's office. "Tarif," said the president, "Have you heard the news?"

"I just heard Mr. President. I'm so sorry. I know how close you both were. I'm in shock."

"As am I Tarif," said the president. "Are you up to the challenge of being the White House Chief of Staff?"

"Yes Sir, I am Mr. President. I just hate to get promoted this way."

"I understand, but I need a trusted friend to be my right-hand man, and you're the best person for the job. So, it's yours. I've called a meeting of my cabinet for tomorrow morning at 7 but I want to see you right away to discuss your duties and to get your ideas on how to best move forward.

"I'll be right there, Mr. President."

Chapter 40

Two blocks away from the site of the shooting, Ronnie sat in the park reading his Kindle waiting for some of the commotion to die down. It had been a good day for Ronnie. He had time to relax, do the job for which he got paid fifty g's, and in a couple of hours, he'd be home. Killing always made Ronnie a little horny, and he was looking forward to having sex with his wife. These feelings were hard to deal with when he was in the military as his kills were always overseas. He did have a few women he'd have sex with from time to time. The irony of his messin' around with some foreign babes while his wife was faithfully waiting for him in South Philly was lost on him. Somehow he justified his actions by telling himself that it was essential for him to wind down after a kill.

At 7 pm, Ronnie left the park and started walking to catch a cab to Union Station. A metro police officer stopped him briefly to ask if he needed help. Guessing that he looked a little confused, Ronnie asked: "What happened officer?" The officer told him that a senior White House staffer had been killed, so there was a massive manhunt on.

Looking shocked, Ronnie said "No shit. Wow. To think I was just a few blocks away in the park reading. Is there a cab stand nearby? I usually just grab a cab on the street here, but I guess with all that has been goin' on, the hacks had to get outta Dodge so as not to get in the way of you guys, right? "

"Yeah, it's right on the next corner. Just hang a left and you'll run into it. Got it?"

"Roger that" and with that Ronnie was on his way home.

Chapter 41

Tina got the call from Ronnie at around 6 pm telling her that he was taking the 8 pm train to Wilmington. He said his efforts in Washington had paid off and because of that he was going to make some more money. He asked her how her day was and then asked if she could pick him up at the train station around 9:45 pm

"What happened to your car Ronnie," she asked.

"That was a car that I was driving down to DC for a car dealership. They were supposed to give me another car here for me to drive back but there was a snafu, and there wasn't one. So I'm taking the 8 pm train back. It's not a big deal Teen. It's just that I need you to pick me up."

Tina hadn't heard him so upbeat in a long time, and she couldn't wait to see him to find out more about the money he was making.

She'd never been to this train station before. Usually, they used Philly's 30th Street Station but that station was under major repairs and parking and getting around was a nightmare. Plus, she wasn't a good driver, having learned to drive just a few short years ago. So Ronnie suggested using the Wilmington Station, which was much easier to navigate.

Ronnie gave her vague directions, telling her it was in the center of town on the waterfront at French Street. She put the address into her GPS but still managed to make a wrong turn. The GPS gave her new directions, and she finally arrived at the Amtrak Station at 10 pm.

She had prepared herself for Ronnie to have been waiting there for 15 minutes, angry as hell. But when she arrived at the station, there was no sign of Ronnie. She went up to the Information Desk in the center of the station and asked the clerk if the 8 pm train from Union Station had arrived and he told her that it had arrived on schedule.

She thought that he might have gotten pissed at her and went outside for a smoke, but he wasn't there either. She waited, figuring that he might be in the men's room. After a while, she started to get worried. She had an Amtrak security guard check the men's room, but he said that there wasn't anyone in there. She tried his cell, but it went directly to voice mail. "Hey, you've reached Ron. You know what to do."

Beep.

"Hey Ron, It's 10:15 and I'm here at the train station in Wilmington, and I don't see ya. Are ya outside? Did ya miss the train or go to 30th street or somethin'? Call me right back."

After another half hour with no word, Tina explained to the desk clerk that she was picking up her husband who should have been on the 8 pm train from DC but that he didn't appear to be on it.

"Could ya check the passenger list to see if you have him on another train? His name is Ronnie Tartaglione, and he would be on a train from Union Station in Washington.

The clerk punched in a few characters, asked her to repeat the spelling, typed it in again and then said that there was no record of any Ronnie Tartaglione on any train out of Washington, DC.

"Ok thanks," said, Tina. "Maybe he missed the train and decided to rent a car instead."

She left another message telling Ronnie that she was headed home and that she figured he had decided to rent a car instead and that she would see him at home. She assumed that if he took a train, he would call her when he arrived either at 30th Street or Wilmington. If she didn't hear from Ronnie by tomorrow morning, she would have to call the Philly PD.

Chapter 42

It all happened so fast. One minute Ronnie was hailing a cab and the next he was in handcuffs.

"You have the right to remain silent. Anything you say can and will be used against you in a court of law. You have the right to speak to an attorney. If you cannot afford an attorney, one will be appointed to you. Do you understand these rights as they have been read to you?"

Ronnie protested. "What's this all about? There must be a mistake, officer."

"Do you understand your rights, sir?"

"Yeah Yeah but I ain't done nothin' wrong."

With that, Ronnie was pushed head first into the rear of a police cruiser.

Shit, he thought. *If they were on a fishing expedition, they'd have said they knew I was in the area of the shooting, and they wanted to see if I saw anything. But, handcuffs and Miranda? They had something. How did I screw up?*

At the station, Ronnie was interrogated by a ranking detective who seemed to know a lot more than Ronnie would have thought. First he was asked some of the expected questions. "What is your business in DC? Can anyone verify that? Where were you at approximately 4:30 pm this afternoon? Did anyone see you?"

He told the detective that he was planning to move to DC and spent the day looking for work and sightseeing.

All were standard until the Detective asked: "Did you drive a rented 2048 Toyota Kira today?"

Ronnie's face went white, but he refused to answer.

"Have you ever fired a Barrett .50 Cal rifle?" More silence.

"Look," said the detective. "We know that you were a sniper in the Army. We have two witnesses who saw you get out of a 2048 Kira early this afternoon and walk over to the roof of a building on H Street and 15th Street. You can play coy with us, or you can come clean. Which will it be?"

Hearing all of these clichés would have been funny if it weren't for the fact that they seemed to have him dead to right. Further interrogation revealed that a witness saw Ronnie take a rifle out of the car in the afternoon, stroll over to the roof again, put it back into the car's trunk, and then head out to the park. A search of the car revealed the long range rifle that they were sure would match the ballistics of the bullet that killed Omar Khalid. It was just a matter of time.

Ronnie finally spoke, "I would like to exercise my right to have an attorney present."

Outside the interrogation room, the detective dialed White House Secret Service.

"Yeah Sadeem," said the detective, "We've got your shooter. We read him his rights at the scene, and he just lawyered up."

"Thanks," said Sadeem, "Don't let him see his lawyer. Under the 'Patriot Act of 2038' and the 'Treason Sentencing Law', people suspected of terrorist actions or of killing any high ranking government official do not have the right to speak to an attorney. Hold him for me and we'll be by to pick him up for questioning."

Chapter 43

Back home that night Angela and Tony relaxed in front of the TV for the first time in weeks. They talked about Monday's meeting, how well that had gone, and about what Nicky had told them a few days ago about hiring someone to kill Omar Khalid. That was supposed to be a secret so they now knew that Nicky could not be trusted with confidential information. Who would have thought just a few months earlier that a Sicilian-born Mafioso would be their compatriot?

She flipped channels as Tony mixed them a drink. She loved Vodka mixed with fruit juice, and she liked that Tony had a heavy hand with the vodka. This time, he brought her a combination of juices; passion fruit, pineapple, guava, and lots of vodka.

As was usually the case, there was very little on the tube, but she was able to find a rerun of an old TV show called "Papa's Family." It had been one of Angela's favorite shows, and she loved being able to share it with Tony. They laughed heartily at the humor. It was good to laugh. They hadn't done that in months.

Suddenly the show was interrupted by A SPECIAL REPORT.

The announcer told the audience about the shooting outside of the White House. "In Washington, Chief of Staff Omar Khalid was shot and killed by a sniper as he left The White House at the end of his workday. According to a report just in, a suspect has been arrested and taken to Metro Police Headquarters for questioning."

The report went on to describe Khalid as a hard working member of President Abbas' staff. Then the reporter provided some background information on Khalid and his family, lots of speculation about motive, what weapon was used and a few other details before it was announced that the president had appointed Deputy Chief of Staff Tarif Mansour as the new White House chief of staff.

So finally, things were moving ahead as planned.

"Tone," said Angela, "This is really happening, and suddenly I'm scared."

"Me too Ange, we're really in this thing. It's not a game. This is real."

"Hold me tighter," said Angela.

They embraced, kissed, and the passions and tension of the last few weeks were released as Angela took the initiative. She knelt on the floor and unzipped his pants, ready to show him how much she really loved him. She was patient letting her tongue tickle his most sensitive spot. Tony ran his fingers through her hair and pulled her head down so that she could fully pleasure him. Angela stopped long enough to pull her top over her head. She was not wearing a bra, and Tony couldn't get enough of her beautiful breasts. She stood and took off her pants and panties. With hands on hips, she was posed completely naked in front of him.

"You like?" she teased.

He nodded. "Do you want to go to the bedroom?"

Angela shook her head and, moving the coffee table out of the way, started pulling his pants down partially dragging him off of the couch. Tony took off his shirt leaving him naked as well. They kissed long and hard as their tongues moved playfully inside each other's mouths. While still embraced, they slid to the floor. He nibbled on her ear lobe and then kissed her on her neck as he ran his hands over her breasts and then slowly moved them downward. She spread her legs wide as both his fingers and his mouth moved lower. He suckled her breast, first the left, then the right as he let his finger probe her vagina thrusting in and out, alternating between deep thrusts and just barely placing his fingertip inside.

Focusing his attention on a more direct path to her pleasure, he let his moist middle finger tickle her little bud. She closed her eyes and reached down, slowly stroking his erection.

He did everything he could to not come in her hand but it was getting harder to hold out as he heard her moans getting louder and felt spasms starting to rise throughout her body. Suddenly she started shaking and screaming in ecstasy.

"I want your dick," she cried out as she rose to straddle him. "Fuck me." With one swift motion she engulfed his penis and had him deep inside. She moved slowly but rhythmically over him as he raised his hips thrusting to meet her up and down movements.

"Come with me Tone. I want to feel that."

He was running his hands all over her. As her pace quickened, she could feel that he was close.

"Don't stop! Don't stop!"

She felt him coming as his fluid filled her. His spasms continued until he was fully drained.

While their first love making session had been over in a matter of a few minutes, this time they were able to hold out a lot longer, giving each other immense pleasure. It was close to an hour before they were both spent

They snuggled for quite a while making "pillow talk" before deciding that it was time to clean up and go out to dinner. Facing the mirror Angela said "Today, Angela Marie Mastronardo you are officially a slut," she paused before adding "and a terrorist."

Chapter 44

After showering and dressing, Tony and Angela went to one of her favorite Italian restaurants, Dante & Luigi's on 10th Street. This was an old family run business that had been here for almost a hundred and fifty years.

As she ate a stuffed calamari appetizer, she noticed that Tony was just staring out the window. He was unusually quiet.

"What's the matter Tone," Angela said.

"Ange, I love you. Marry me."

She almost choked. She went through her 20s and 30s attending all of her friends' weddings and now at 44, she figured that marriage just wasn't in the cards for her.

"Are you serious?" was all she could think of to say.

"I've never been more serious in my life. I've loved you from the time we were teenagers. Don't you remember how I used to drive by and flirt with you," said Tony?

"Nah, I don't remember that," Angela remarked and could barely keep a straight face.

"Really?" said Tony. "You used to yell something like *you wish jackoff.*"

Angela laughed "And my guess is that I was right on two counts, you wished, and you probably jacked off a lot over the years."

"You can joke," said Tony "but I'm serious. I love you."

She loved him too but had never said those words to anyone before and even now she didn't say them out loud.

"I'm not trying to be funny Tony. It's just that with everything that is going on, I don't know if this is the perfect time to get married."

"When is the perfect time, Ange? There may never be a perfect time and this feels right. I love you Ange and I want to spend the rest of my life telling you that."

"How can a girl say 'no' to someone who professes his love with such passion? Yes, Tony, I'll marry you."

Tony stood and moved to her side of the table. He bent down and gently kissed her. She saw a tear in his eye. He really did love her. "Let's do it tomorrow Ange."

"That's too soon. I don't need a big wedding but I do want to have a small ceremony with family and friends there. And, I want Father Quinn to do the honors. Okay?"

Tony nodded, as he sat back down. He didn't give two craps where they got married. They could be married in the basement of his house for all he cared.

Chapter 45

The news in the morning paper was all about the president's chief of staff being shot by a sniper outside the White House. According to the story, an unnamed gunman shot Omar Khalid with a high powered sniper rifle from a half a block away. The manhunt led to the arrest of an Army Veteran, who was taken into police custody for questioning last evening. Because of the ongoing investigation, no further information was being released by the DC police department.

Ahmad sat in the oval office on this dark, gloomy day reading the reports of what had happened. He knew that this story was bad press for his administration. But he also knew that the media in the United States would move onto something else in a few days so long as there was a story that was more sensational. Cold cases are called that for a reason. It's not just the police who go cold on a story but also the press.

The phone rang. It was Sadeem Ali, the Director of the Secret Service. He told Ahmad that he now had the shooter and had been interrogating him all night and relayed to the president all that they had learned. Ahmad thanked Sadeem for his hard work and then told him to "handle" this Ronnie Tartaglione in the usual manner.

At 7 am the members of his cabinet filed in. He had the perfect idea for the next story. But first he needed to brief The Cabinet.

"Gentlemen," started Ahmad. "It should come as no surprise that with Omar's death, Tarif Mansour has assumed the responsibilities of White House Chief of Staff. I'd like to formally welcome Tarif to our inner circle." After everyone's congratulatory wishes, the president continued. "The Secret Service has the man who assassinated Omar Khalid in custody. They have been questioning him all night and have learned that the Mafia hired him to kill the chief of staff. He's claiming that business was conducted via email and phone with anonymous money drops, so he does not know who hired him to commit this despicable and treasonous act. The email was routed through servers in Russia and could not be traced. It's no longer working. The same holds for the phone which was a burner phone that has no doubt been discarded. But Sadeem intends to interrogate him until he gathers some additional information. "

Ahmad paused for effect to see if he'd receive any opinions from his cabinet. There were none as everyone sat stoically and listened. Ahmad continued. "I'm starting to believe that these reports of possible actions against my administration are more than rumors. I've had intelligence people from the NSA and CIA monitoring email, text, and chat room banter to see if they could find any threats. So far they've only uncovered some planned protests and the rantings of a few random malcontents who hate me but seem to be just letting off steam. Every president has had to be vigilant about these same types of threats and, as a general rule; they turn out to be *little people* pretending to be more than they are. I am concerned about why someone would target my chief of staff, though. Can anyone speculate as to why someone would target Omar, and not another key official?"

In an attempt to throw them off, Tarif was the first to speak.

"Mr. President, Omar has had some problems of late. After breaking his back in a car accident a few years ago, he was on a daily regimen of Neuvomorphine for pain. I've seen him taking these pills, and while I hate to talk about someone who cannot defend himself, we have to ask ourselves if this was not a drug-related shooting."

Nice try but it didn't work as the Secretary of Defense spoke up.

"Mr. President," started Hakim. "I can't believe that this was a drug-related shooting. Most of us have read or heard about drug deals gone bad. Has anyone ever heard of someone being shot with a high-powered rifle over a drug problem? This act was carried out by a well-trained marksman using an assault rifle from a distance. Does that sound like the work of a drug lord?"

Syed Rashad chimed in. "I tend to agree with Hakim, Mr. President. I would suspect that this was simply a matter of opportunity. Omar played tennis every Wednesday like clockwork. On most days, his behavior patterns, like most of ours, were somewhat random. But every Wednesday Omar left at the same time, 4:25 pm, like clockwork. The one thing I can't help but think is that either the gunman was sending you a message, Mr. President, or that Omar was only the first and that this is part of a bigger conspiracy to kill each of us as the opportunity presents itself."

"Thank you, Syed," said the president. "My thoughts have run along similar lines; which is why I've assigned each of you a Secret Service Agent for the next few weeks. In keeping with our current policies and procedures, Gentlemen, we do not intend to release this prisoner. He's admitted to the shooting so we'll keep interrogating him until we can find out if he was acting alone or in tandem with others, and if it was the Mafia behind this killing or something bigger still. The CIA and NSA will continue monitoring all electronic and phone conversations in our major cities for any clues to the possible subversive activity going on. Does anyone have any questions?"

After a moment of silence, the president moved on.

"Closely related to this is the need for a story bigger than this that will take the press and the American public off the trail of this one. As you all know, Saeed traveled to the Middle East recently to speak to several of our allies there. After consulting with him about his trip, I've decided that next month, the United States will be entering into a reciprocal intelligence gathering and protection agreement with both Syria and Iran. Initially, each country will deploy several military units to the other two countries with current military installations housing the foreign military. The first deployment will include both Syrian and Irani infantry units coming to the US to be stationed at Ft Belvoir in VA. Both countries will also deploy several fighter squadrons which we will house at Andrews AFB and several other bases. The Syrian agreement will be signed on May 5th in Damascus. On the following day, I will be in Tehran, to sign a similar agreement with Iran. I believe that my actions may result in strained relations with Israel, but I also believe that these agreements will strengthen our relationships in the Middle East and help us should there be any real domestic threats. My press secretary has called a 3 pm press conference during which I'll announce the new bi-lateral agreements."

"That's all I have," said the president. "If no one has anything else, we're adjourned. Please pick up your assignment envelopes on the back table as you leave. I'd like you to do your best to maintain your daily routines as if nothing has happened. Thank you for coming."

Chapter 46

After work, several members of the cabinet met for dinner at Zaytinya, one of the city's best Middle Eastern restaurants. The restaurant was noisy but the food was good and it gave them a chance to talk informally as no one seemed to know, or care, who they were. They managed to find an out of the way table along an outside wall where they'd be able to carry on a conversation.

While some declined, thinking it disrespectful to Omar's memory, a few wanted to speak in his honor and to celebrate Tarif's promotion. Tom Hilton and Larry Richter would have preferred a restaurant with a bar but since Tarif and Hakim joined them, they settled on an eatery that they would all enjoy.

Tom was the first to speak. "So, what do you make of this new plan, Hakim?"

"I think it makes sense. We have strong ties with both now, you know, and it's good to work together. It helps build strong relations and enables everyone to share information and strategies."

"So you aren't concerned at all?"

"Not really. You never know when you'll need a helping hand. I know our department has been helping others for many years."

"I don't know. Maybe it's a good idea but the boss seems a little on edge lately. What do you think Larry?"

"I haven't noticed anything out of the ordinary but you men are in his company a lot more than I am."

Hakim rejoined the conversation. "I think he feels that there are people who want him to fail and who are willing to act to make sure that he does. He's always been concerned because of his heritage so this is not new."

"I'm worried that he's focused on the wrong things. He's micromanaging and isn't seeing the big picture," said Tom. "What was discussed today is a very big deal and he doesn't seem the least bit concerned about the ramifications."

"I wouldn't worry. I know the boss better than most", said Tarif, "and now that I've been promoted, I'll be even closer and better able to help him. He's under a lot of pressure but he can handle it." He hoped that he had calmed his coworker's fears without letting on that he had the same concerns. Fortunately, they all had a strong allegiance to the president and Tarif hoped that their loyalty would be justified

He then changed the subject to more mundane issues as they talked over coffee. When the check arrived Tarif reached but Hakim picked it up. "Oh no, we invited you to dinner. This is our treat."

Tom and Larry kicked in their portion and bid their coworkers good night.

On their way out, Tom suggested a drink at a local bar. The place was nearly empty, which was good. That meant they wouldn't have to encrypt their speech as they did in the restaurant.

"I can no longer support this president," started Tom. I have never in my life heard of anything as ludicrous as this. What are people going to think about working so closely with two countries that until a year ago were our enemies?" he said. "I have no idea what he's doing. I'm not even sure he does. You aren't around him that much Larry but, trust me, he's losing it."

"You're right, I'm not but I've heard the rumors. People are starting to question his motives and state of mind. Is it true that he's carrying a pistol wherever he goes and that he's insisting that everyone who comes to the White House be interrogated by the Secret Service?"

"No," Tom laughed. "As bad as it is, it's not quite that bad. But he's definitely more paranoid. You know he was ok until the assassination attempts but now no one is beyond suspicion. I wish there was some way that we could restore the presidency to what it once was. I was always proud of our way of life and I, for one, would like to see a return to those ways. "

"I agree with you Tom and this has to stay between us," said Larry, "but I'm concerned enough that I've considered going back into the private sector. I've spoken to a few headhunters on the QT. I have to be careful though. If the president finds out, he may add me to the disloyal column."

"No doubt about that. You'd better be extra careful because lately he's had eyes and ears on everyone. I just hope that things calm down and maybe this whole joint exercise thing goes away. I don't see the point in it, to be honest, but you can't argue with the president."

"That's for sure. Let's keep each other in the loop on what is going on. I don't know where all of this is headed or even who we can trust, but I'd like to know that if things start to unravel, we could at least count on each other."

"Sure thing."

They finished their drinks and said their goodbyes as if they weren't going to see each other again. Of course the following day they'd be back at work for the president. Only, after the past two days, they'd be more vigilant and from now on they were confidants who had each other's back.

Chapter 47

Tommy Whitehead was a good soldier. He had been loyal to General Redmond since serving in his command at Ft. Bragg and again in several overseas assignments. The general was a man of integrity and someone Tommy admired.

His boss in the Secret Service, Sadeem Ali, considered him to be a good friend. In fact Tommy had been his best man. But Sadeem was a masochist of extreme proportions and not someone that Tommy looked up to. Respect was something that was earned and there was no doubt in Tommy's mind which of the two deserved his respect and loyalty.

His job right now was to keep an eye on the prisoner. He knew Ronnie Tartaglione by reputation and had been standing outside the interrogation room while agents grilled Ronnie. Tommy sat across from Ronnie. Neither said a word.

One of the other agents came in.

"Do you need a break? If you want to step out for a smoke or something, I can cover for you."

Tommy stepped outside and put on his cell phone projection bracelet, one of the Secret Service's new gadgets that turned your arm into a touch screen. It worked like the old smartphones, only it projected images onto the inside of his forearm, allowing him to send messages and make calls.

"General, this is Tommy. We have Ronnie in custody, and it doesn't look good."

"How's he holding up?"

"Not well, General." He's remained silent over the past day despite some very intense interrogation, but he looks bad.

He said he'd been hired by the Mafia. I'm not sure anyone believes that bullshit."

"What's the next step?"

"They've waterboarded him, Sir. The plan is to keep him in a room, shackled to the desk and not let him sleep. Then they're going to go at him several times overnight and possibly place rats in the room. If he doesn't break, they expect to do more waterboarding in the morning. I don't think he's going to be able to withstand that kind of torture, Sir."

"It sounds like we need to act. Is there any way to get him out?"

"No Sir. I'll be close by overnight, but other people are working here."

"Are you up for this Tommy? It's a lot to ask and I wouldn't if it wasn't important. It's damned important."

"Yes, Sir, I understand."

"Thanks, Tommy."

Tommy pushed the end image on his arm and went back upstairs.

Ronnie was alone in the room now, and there was a single agent outside his door.

"What's the plan?" Tommy asked the agent.

"I'm done my shift so I'm heading out. Nothing has changed except they probably don't bring in rats. Somebody mentioned maybe throwing some roaches, but no one thinks that will break this guy. Captain Leary just left. You'll be alone with him until around 3 when you'll be relieved. He's shackled and not going anywhere. Take a few shots at interrogating him but mostly make sure he doesn't fall asleep. They want him up all night. Agent Holloway is downstairs working if you need a break. And of course, the night shift supervisor, Captain Eberhart's here. Ok, that's it for me. I'm outta here."

"Got it. Thanks"

Tommy stood outside for a time until all of the day shift had left. Then he went inside to talk to Ronnie.

"Hey, Ronnie how are you doing?"

Exhausted, Ronnie said he was hanging in.

Tommy chatted for a while pretending to interrogate Ronnie. Then he hit him with some tough questions and tried to trick him up. He was so tired that it almost worked.   Tommy went at him several ways. Ronnie didn't give up anything, but Tommy had been through this many times. He knew that Ronnie was a good sniper, but he also knew that he had never been through an interrogation like this. He would not make it.

Tommy went in and out several times. He was supposed to keep the prisoner awake, but he figured what the hell. He'd give the guy some peace. He grappled with the idea of an escape but while there were only a few detectives in the building, the perimeter was heavily guarded.

Finally, around 2 am, Tommy reentered the room to find Ronnie with his head down on the desk trying to sleep. Tommy smacked him on the top of the head. Ronnie looked up and saw the silencer on the end of the 357sig. He closed his eyes.

Chapter 48

Two days after the killing of Omar Khalid, The Nationalists from Philadelphia arrived at Saul's Jewish center in Queens for their meeting with the general and Rabbi Rudzinsky. Instead of using Teleview on the computer to include Qasim and Makim, they joined this meeting in person and for the first time, all of the leaders from the three primary metro areas on the east coast were on hand.

Josh sat at one end of a long table with Saul and Aaron in the two seats to his right. At the other end sat Angela, Tony, and Nicky on one side of the table. Opposite them sat Qasim and Makim. Joanne Shapiro, who was in attendance to take minutes, sat alone in a chair in a corner behind Josh.

"Welcome," started Josh. "It's nice that everyone can meet Qasim and Makim in person. And I'd like to extend a special welcome to Tarif Mansour, the newly appointed White House chief of staff. Much has happened since our last meeting a few days ago, and I would like to bring you all up to speed."

Josh gave everyone an overview of what had been planned starting with the strategy to get Tarif into a key position and including the hiring of Ronnie Tartaglione and his background and skills before pausing for comments.

Saul sat upright, saying nothing. Josh could only imagine what was racing through his mind. He sensed the uneasiness in the room as he continued.

"We owe a great deal of gratitude to Saul for coming up with some money for our cause, but I owe him an apology for lying to him about this mission. Saul, I knew that if you knew that we were going to kill the White House Chief of Staff, you would have refused to help. I'm sorry, I hope you'll understand and forgive me."

"Wait a minute, General. You apologized to my dad but what about the rest of us?" said an outraged Aaron. "We've been talking about protests and how to get Abbas out of office. You never once mentioned killing someone. Don't you think you owed us all an explanation and a chance for us to express how we felt about it? We had to hear about this in the news."

No one else spoke, but some murmured and nodded in agreement.

"I'm sorry. I felt that we, I mean I, needed to act quickly and I made an executive decision. I value the views of each and every one of you in this room and in hindsight I could have confided in you. I'm used to the military way of doing things where command decisions have to be made and where inaction is the result of group discussion. I'd like to say that this will never happen again. But I can't. There will be times when I have to make a decision and don't have the luxury of time to call you individually or call a meeting to get your permission."

Tony didn't want to let on that Nicky had spilled the beans to him and Angela, so he feigned anger. "General, I understand what you are saying but I also know that in this instance, we had time to discuss it. This is inexcusable."

"I don't know what to say. I said I was sorry in this instance but, as I said, there are no guarantees. If any of you are uncomfortable with me making decisions, you're free to leave. I won't hold anything against you."

Saul excused himself and left the room. Josh waited patiently through the silence for several seconds.

"If no one has anything else, I'd like to continue my briefing. As you know, on Wednesday Ronnie carried out his mission, and killed Omar as he left the White House. The hit was clean, but the police took him into custody because of a nosy old man who watched him all day. He saw Ronnie go to the roof top next to the parking lot where he had parked his car. Coincidentally, he walked his dog in the same park where Ronnie went to bide his time while waiting for his opportunity. Being suspicious, this old man later watched as Ronnie pulled out the rifle from the car. Since his friend rented the car for him under an assumed name, there was no way to tie the car to Ronnie. However Ronnie was again seen walking back to the car and putting the rifle in the trunk before returning to the same park. The old man then called the police who dusted the car for prints. There were none. While there was nothing of use inside of the vehicle, the police search uncovered a high caliber rifle from the trunk. The worst part is that this witness gave the cops Ronnie's description. Ironically, were it not for this one person, Ronnie would have made it to Union Station and boarded his train home with no one the wiser."

Josh took a sip of water before continuing. "Ronnie didn't know everything about our plans as we purposely kept him in the dark but he knew about me and, of course, he knew Nicky. He also knew Angela and Tony, who live in the same neighborhood, but I don't think he made any connection between them and Nicky. My big concern is that while he didn't have the details, he may have guessed the nature of the overall mission and mentioned it to his wife."

This time, Angela interrupted to ask if they knew if Ronnie was still in DC Metro Police custody.

"You're ahead of me, I was just getting there," said Josh. "Many of you know most of this, but I want to bring you up to date. If this had been any other case, the DA might not have even pursued the case against Ronnie because all of the evidence was circumstantial. There were no prints or other hard evidence, and the only witness was an old man who could easily have been discredited in court. However this was no ordinary case, and no one bothered to call the DA. Instead, DC Metro transferred Ronnie to the offices of the secret service. Sadeem Ali, once the head of one of Iraq's most gruesome torture camps, took over the questioning using methods similar to those he had employed years earlier when he had interrogated prisoners in his native country."

"How do you know all of this General?" interrupted Tony.

Josh told them what had happened to Ronnie in pretty vivid detail, considering he wasn't there.

"I have an informant with the secret service, a good man who once served under me. He told me that Ronnie was going to break. He had no doubts. He understood the risks he faced, especially regarding consequences of his involvement. Not only did he risk his life, but he had a good career going with a nice pension. He risked everything because he strongly felt that our cause was just and his action necessary. I would have preferred extracting Ronnie but that wasn't possible. During the night, he mercifully shot and killed Ronnie and then escaped.

Now there were gasps in the room from almost everyone. Neither Qasim nor Makim showed any emotion.

Nicky, on the other hand, had tears in his eyes as he listened to Josh's explanation. He appreciated the sensitivity that Josh had shown by phoning him in advance of the killing, but he took it especially hard, given that he was the one who had dragged Ronnie into this. And how was he going to face Tina?

"I know what you're thinking," injected Josh, "but you have to understand what we were dealing with and what Ronnie was going through. Trust me when I tell you that Ronnie was not going to survive under any circumstances. Tommy said that once they got the information they wanted from Ronnie, they were going to kill him. Over his two-day incarceration that included no sleep at all, Ronnie was hung upside-down, deprived of air, kicked, whipped, and beaten. Tommy had no doubt that more beatings, electric shocks, and even the possibility of being sodomized were in Ronnie's future. Sadeem Ali treats his dog with more compassion and Sadeem has the reputation of getting prisoners to do anything he wants them to do including killing their best friends. This situation was not going to end well.

My informant is in hiding right now as the Secret Service is undoubtedly looking for him. I spoke to him this morning, and he's in a safe house that I had arranged in advance in DC, thinking that we might need it for Ronnie if the situation was such that he could not get out of DC and needed a place to hole up. The plan right now is for him to stay there unless he hears from me telling him that it's safe for him to leave. I won't do that until we're in complete control."

"One final item for discussion is Ronnie's wife. I don't know her or have any personal feelings about the situation. We don't know what she knows about Ronnie's mission or who hired him. My real concern is whether she'll keep quiet if she does know."

"Well," started Nicky, "I'd be surprised if she knew anything about his mission. I've known Ronnie for a long time, and he was a tight-lipped son of a bitch about his assignments. Tina was used to it and wouldn't have pressed him. However, I'm sure that she knows that me and Ronnie had a meeting in Philly. I guess if the feds pump her for information and she mentions my name, it won't be too great a leap to consider me as the guy who hired him. They won't be able to prove it. But I ain't takin' any chances. I need to lay low for a while 'til I see how this shakes out. But first I'll get hold of Tina to make sure that she's ok and see if we need to worry."

"Good idea. We don't need any problems."

Nicky interrupted. "What about the money, General? We promised Ronnie another twenty-five G's when he completed the job. I say we give Tina the money."

"Well, that would be a nice gesture, Nicky, except I don't have the other $25,000 to pay her. I only had the front half and assumed that we'd figure something out later."

Nicky was obviously pissed off. "Are you shittin' me? You told me you had the dough. We hired a guy and didn't have the money to pay him?" He stood to leave. "If she freakin' knows about the money, she's gonna want it, or she might try to get even."

"Technically, Ronnie is not around to collect, but I'll see if there is some way to get the money if I have to. Hopefully, I won't. It's not a high priority."

Nicky stormed out of the room.

With that discussion over, Josh ended the meeting with a final warning. "We can't afford to be lackadaisical or get sloppy. As always, stay off of your computers regarding our mission. Be careful about what you say to the others, especially outsiders, about our meetings and plans. We can't afford mistakes. There is a shredder outside the door. Shred your agendas before you leave."

He turned to Tarif.

"I need to know everything that Abbas knows, what he is thinking, and what his plans are."

Chapter 49

Sadeem Ali hated middle of the night calls. He arrived at work within a half hour along with about ten other agents on the on-call list. He screamed at everyone within earshot to go out and find that ass wipe, Tommy Whitehead. Tommy had just shot and killed, Ronnie Tartaglione, his best hope of finding out why he had assassinated Omar Khalid, who had ordered the hit, and what the "bigger" plan might be. He was sure that the killing of the White House chief of staff was about something much greater than this one outwardly meaningless act. After two days of interrogation, Sadeem had stepped over the line by waterboarding Ronnie Tartaglione. Although many considered it torture, to Sadeem, it was an old and very effective method of interrogation. After days of enduring extreme hot and cold, psychological games, solitary confinement, sexual humiliation, and some other techniques that failed to produce any results his prisoner was finally ready to crack.

Why would he do this thought Sadeem? Tommy was one of his best men. Hell, last month he participated in classes on sensory deprivation and bombardment as a means to break a person during interrogation. In fact, he was recently involved, with Sadeem, in using those methods to break prisoners.

"Dip the fingers in sulfuric acid and pull out all of the teeth." Sadeem then gave the orders for Ronnie's body to be cut up in small unidentifiable pieces and disposed of quickly. He then swore everyone to secrecy.

He could not let the White House know that someone killed Ronnie. He had to convince the president that he had somehow escaped and that the Secret Service was going to find him and bring him back for even more brutal questioning. The president would be angry, he knew, but he felt that he would accept an escape better than he could a murder because with an escape, came hope; hope that he could be recaptured, interrogated, and would provide answers that President Abbas wanted.

With butterflies in his stomach, Sadeem hesitated before picking up the phone to make his call. He looked at the clock. It was just after 3 am. "Crap, he's not going to like me waking him up at this hour with this shitty news."

After three rings the president answered the phone. Sadeem gave him a story he had concocted about the prisoner asking to use the restroom and then escaping through the bathroom window. It was a little far-fetched given the security that they had at the dungeon, but he felt confident that the president would buy it. Sadeem thought Abbas took the news about as well as one could expect. He hung up and, sinful as it was, decided that he needed a drink. It was early in the morning but in this job a small amount of alcohol to calm his nerves seemed defensible.

At the White House, the president was furious. "Damn it," shouted Ahmad as he slammed down the phone. Why was it that all of these bullshit phone calls happened during the night? Sadeem was a good man who did an outstanding job. Until now, Ahmad had complete trust in him. But he didn't believe a word of this crazy story about Ronnie Tartaglione escaping from the dungeon. That wasn't even remotely believable and if he couldn't trust Sadeem, who could he trust?

Chapter 50

It was 7 am and Ahmad was already seated behind his desk in the oval office. He was still fuming.

He clicked on the intercom for Julia and, without even the slightest pleasantry, said: "get me Victor Sanchez at the FBI. I need to see him here right away."

"Yes, Mr. President, right away."

Victor Sanchez was the 35-year-old lead agent for The Criminal, Cyber, Response, and Services Branch. While he didn't have a fancy title, Victor was an important man in the FBI. His responsibilities included leading the Criminal Investigative Division, Cyber Division, Critical Incident Response Group, International Operations Division, and the Office of Law Enforcement Coordination. Victor reported directly to the Deputy Director of the FBI and was the leading resource if you wanted to get something done about the real criminals in the country. He had a reputation for being the kind of guy who would leave no stone unturned to get to the bottom of any crime or mystery.

After a minute or so, the intercom beeped.

"Mr. President, Agent Sanchez will be here in 15 minutes."

Time passed quickly as Abbas went over the recent events and jotted down some notes for his meeting with Sanchez.

Agent Sanchez arrived in exactly 15 minutes as promised. The president told Victor about what had happened with the sniper and Sadeem's story about his escape.

When he had finished, he said "Victor, Sadeem didn't seem like himself. He had a slight hesitation in his voice, like someone who was lying. He was trying to cover his ass. Every bone in my body tells me that Tartaglione didn't escape at all. I think someone killed him to keep him quiet. The question is who, and who was that person working for?"

"What would you like me to do, Mr.President?"

"I'm concerned about Sadeem. He's a good man and has been loyal to me. But I think he's worried about something. I need you to see what you can find out about the sniper, Ronnie Tartaglione. Don't spend too much time worrying about whether he's alive or not. And, I don't care about his possible whereabouts. Like I said I believe he's dead. If he's not, those at the Secret Service who believe Sadeem's story will be looking for him. I could not care less about this one man. He is like a speck of sand in the desert. What was Ronnie Tartaglione doing? That's what is of most importance. Find some relatives or friends; people with whom he might have confided. Start with a wife or brother; anyone who can help. Sadeem gave me a brief bio on him, but there isn't much. He's a retired Army Master Sergeant, who was one of the best snipers the military had until he retired a couple of years ago. He was originally from Philadelphia so I would start there and I want you to keep this off the books for now."

"Yes Sir, I will."

"If you have to, arrange to go to Philly yourself to investigate. Maybe you can make up a story to explain being out of the office? I trust you, Victor, but I don't want another FBI office involved unless we have no choice."

"Thank you, Sir. I'm sure that won't be a problem. Is it alright if I take my partner along?"

"Can he be trusted?"

"Yes Sir, I'd trust him with my life."

"Very well but share information on a need to know basis. I'm not sure who we can and can't trust at this point. Is that understood?"

"Yes, Mr. President, I understand perfectly. I'm on it."

Abbas felt a little more relaxed after Sanchez left. He knew the kind of man Victor was. He was like a pit-bull when it came to these sorts of things. He wouldn't stop until he found out everything he possibly could about Ronnie Tartaglione and his end game. By the time Victor completed his investigation, he would know the type of underwear that Ronnie had worn, and he would be able to tell how many times he had gotten laid in the last week. More importantly, he felt confident that Victor would find out who had hired him. There was no doubt in his mind that Victor was the right man for this job.

Chapter 51

Inside a small chapel in South Philadelphia sat 10 of Angela and Tony's closest friends. They watched quietly as the couple, standing before Father Quinn and in the presence of God, stated their intentions.

Angela had always wanted a garden wedding. But neither she nor Tony wanted to wait until springtime and the frigid February temperatures that hung on through March made an outdoor wedding impossible.

There was a small reception in the church hall but there would be no honeymoon. Immediately following the reception, the newlyweds left for a meeting in Queens. They had dinner at Bruno's in Queens before heading over to the Jewish Center. They were the first to arrive.

Because of Shabbat, the meeting was called for 9 pm. Saul was there shortly after 9, and by 9:15 the leaders from both the Philly and New York contingents had arrived. Josh was glad to see Saul back in the group. The three men from Boston had declined to attend the meeting. Josh sensed a bit of an undercurrent at the last meeting, and it was obvious that Saul and Qasim preferred not to attend meetings together. Josh had suggested that there was nothing to be gained by Qasim and his brother driving down from Boston. He could brief them later on what had been discussed and get their feedback at that time. Saul seemed especially pleased with that solution.

While Josh usually opened the meeting, this night Saul began by greeting everyone. Today he made a slight deviation from the usual agenda by announcing the marriage of Angela and Tony and breaking out glasses and two bottles of champagne. He raised his glass to congratulate the newlyweds. Everyone clapped and Nicky jokingly told Tony that he didn't think he had the balls to go through with it.

While there hadn't been a lot of time for camaraderie, these little niceties helped bind them together, almost like a family.

Saul then introduced the general. It seemed a little silly to Saul since everyone knew him by now but it was a small sign of respect for their commander.

Josh began by telling everyone how the organization had grown. "I've been in constant contact over the last several months with leaders in every major city, and I can tell you that there are millions of Nationalists ready to take to the streets and that they are led by thousands of leaders just like the people in this room."

"Our biggest challenge has been keeping our meetings and plans covert as people have a tendency to talk when they shouldn't. The stakes are high and it seems as though everyone has done an excellent job of keeping our secrets. My friends at the NSA tell me that there has been no out of the ordinary chatter. I've spoken to each leader and stressed the importance of keeping our plans secret because it's time that we shifted into high gear on this. We have to act before Abbas can put up a defense."

"The first part of the strategy resulted in successfully removing Omar Khalid from office, and that has helped us with the rest. Tarif has been able to keep us informed of what the president is thinking, and it appears that, with Ronnie's death, Abbas has lost what he felt was an invaluable way to gather reliable Intel. Now he seems to be fishing around, hoping that something will surface. My fear is that is exactly what will happen. Tarif has warned me about the president. His behavior has been erratic. He's a very shrewd but paranoid man who believes that something is going on. While he hasn't been able to pinpoint particulars, Tarif believes it's just a matter of time before he goes totally bonkers trying to smoke out potential threats and squash any resistance movement. So it's time for us to act boldly and decisively. We want Abbas to believe that his only worry is some unrest among a few dissenters. In short, we want him so distracted by overt acts of civil disobedience that he doesn't see what's coming."

"The second part of the plan begins on Monday, July 4th at 0800 EDT. We've selected that date for obvious reasons. Besides the symbolism, it won't seem unusual if there is a lot of activity in and around our major cities on Independence Day. It also allows the Joint Chiefs, who are with us, to be able to take time off without any suspicion. They will work from the command and control center at my house on Long Island."

"The sympathizers will begin their pivotal roles with peaceful protests in the streets of our major cities. We're talking about what Abbas has defined as civil disobedience starting in Boston, New York, Philly, Baltimore, Washington, Atlanta, Nashville, Raleigh, Chicago, Houston, Dallas, San Antonio, Phoenix, San Diego, LA, San Francisco, San Jose, Portland, and Seattle. Thanks to contributions from some of my overseas friends and allies, many of our people will be armed. However, they are under strict orders to maintain peace throughout the protest even as it escalates when police and guardsmen arrive. Our goal here is to make these events seem spontaneous and coincidental, like the many anti-war protests that have occurred over the years. There will be some hurling of rocks and bottles to create havoc, but violence beyond that is to happen only in self-defense. While each of these groups will be operating independently from those in other cities, it will look like a coordinated effort to the authorities, and more importantly, to President Abbas. There will undoubtedly be some panic among city officials as they watch their police units spread thin and contemplate petitioning their state officials for National Guard support."

"The protests scattered around Washington will look the same as those in other cities but with a more highly concentrated effort around the capitol. We have identified several key people in the administration, Congress, and the military. Those friendly to our cause will play a big part in our plans. Others, while not directly involved, will nonetheless be protected. We've also identified those sympathetic to the president. They will be isolated and neutralized. Obviously, the president, his entire cabinet, and General Elway Bishop, Chairman of the Joint Chiefs will be targets for ouster. We've already identified their replacements who have agreed to fill these important roles. You will hear a lot of rumors and some will be true. We do have snipers and bombers with IEDs positioned throughout the city. Hopefully, we can have them stand down as the intent is to have a bloodless transition. However, I think it would be naïve of us to think that this mission will be carried out with no casualties. Like I said, as a precaution, we have people positioned in the Capitol Building, Pentagon, and The White House prepared to act combatively if necessary."

"As a result of the havoc in the streets of our cities, I would expect all of the governors in our ground zero states to go by the playbook and call out the National Guard. The president will undoubtedly follow protocol by calling an emergency meeting of his cabinet. He'll ask General Elway Bishop, the Chairman of the Joint Chiefs, and Sadeem Ali, Head of the Secret Service, to be a part of the meeting, most likely to start around 0930. Tarif feels that the meeting would be brief. But, since it's a holiday and people will have to drive from home through heavy traffic and crowds, in most instances, the meeting will likely start a little later, buying us some valuable time."

"Concurrently, the vice president will call the speaker of the house and senate majority and minority leaders to have them call for an emergency joint session of Congress. We caught a break when the government moved its fiscal year to July. A few congressmen may be away, but most will be in or near the city so that they can vote on the new budget on Tuesday."

"Our coordinated effort is to begin at ten hundred hours when Nationalists inside the White House will interrupt the meeting of the president's full cabinet and take all who are present as hostages. Unfortunately, any resistance from White House Security or the Secret Service will have to be met with immediate force. Even if there are Marines opposing us, we will have to act in kind. There will be no time for debate."

"The only member of the inner circle who will not be present at the cabinet meeting will be Tarif. He had asked to have the weekend off and, knowing that many of the White House staff would be on holiday; the president granted him the time off to attend a family reunion in Boston. He will not leave DC, however. I have plans for Makim Khalid that will require him to be in DC as well. Tarif, who will be at the Pentagon, will stay in touch with Makim in case he is in need of support."

"The plan also calls for the vice president and all members of The House and Senate to be taken hostage during their meeting at The Capitol."

"The Joint Chief's Vice Chair Admiral John Barrington and all of the Joint Chiefs will be at my house manning the C6I as it is known in military jargon."

"What does that acronym stand for General?" asked Aaron.

"C6I is the latest iteration of what was once C2, or Command and Control. It translates as Command, Control, Communications, Computer Security, Cyberwarfare, Collaboration and Intelligence."

By the blank stares he realized that only Aaron really cared about this level of detail. "This isn't something anyone really needs to understand. Let's just say that it's a high tech place from where we'll be able to see and control what's going on."

"Ladies and gentlemen, we have the right people in the right positions to pull this off with minimal bloodshed. We are very well prepared. But I still have concerns. Having citizens like yourselves involved is critical. But it also complicates

216

things, making this the most difficult and complex mission with which I've ever been associated."

"The field leader, loyal to our cause, is US Army Four-Star General Aloysius Barr, who will assume total command of our armed forces. There are hundreds of senior military personnel including Army, Air Force and Marine Corps Colonels and Generals, Senior Naval and Coast Guard officers who command over 2.5 million troops who have already pledged allegiance to our cause and promise the complete takeover of our military. Deputy Secretary of Defense Kotsopoulos will remain in Washington as he may be needed to take control of the military once we have taken hostages."

"We have identified about 25 who will continue to support President Abbas and would be willing to have their troops fight to their deaths. As I've stated, while we'd like to take them alive; that may not be possible. Things could go wrong. One way or another, for this mission to succeed, they will all have to be neutralized."

"My advice now is to be on guard. While it is my belief that this will be a successful operation, we should all be prepared for the worst. You have all spent a lot of time and done a phenomenal job mustering support in your districts. I'm grateful to each of you for the many sacrifices that you've made to restore our freedoms guaranteed under The Constitution."

After a few very minor logistical questions, the meeting was adjourned with Josh saying "Thank you for your loyalty to our country and your hard work. May God bless us and help us prevail and may he bless these United States of America."

Chapter 52

Victor Sanchez rang the bell on the front door of the brownstone row house on tiny Mole Street in South Philadelphia. His partner, Tyrell Ferguson, covered the back. Though the president seemed to believe that Ronnie Tartaglione was dead, Sanchez was not taking any chances.

Victor looked around as he waited to see if anyone was at home. It's a good thing he didn't expect any high-speed car chases, Victor said to himself. *These friggin' streets are even smaller than in DC, and there are little alleys everywhere. He couldn't even imagine trying to capture someone on foot here. "How can these city cops do their jobs?* Victor wondered.

The door opened a crack. The woman behind the door was a petite woman of about 35-40 years. She was very attractive with beautifully tanned skin, short black hair, and hazel eyes.

"Yes?" she asked.

"Mrs. Tartaglione?" asked Victor.

With some hesitation, she said "Yes?"

"Mrs. Tartaglione, I'm Agent Sanchez with the FBI."

"This is about Ronnie, right?"

"Yes Ma'am, it is," Said Victor.

"Did you find him? Where is he? Is he ok? He isn't in trouble is he? Oh my, God, he isn't dead is he?"

So many questions in rapid succession left Victor dazed but fortunately, all but the last question had the same answer.

"No ma'am," said Victor. We were called by Philly PD after you filed a missing person report. Because your husband left PA and traveled to DC on the day he went missing, this investigation is a federal matter that comes under our jurisdiction. So the FBI was brought in to investigate."

"I see," said Tina in almost a whisper. "I was hoping that you had some good news."

"I'm sorry that I don't," said Victor.

Tyrell came around from the back of the house realizing that no one else was in the house.

"This is my partner, Agent Ferguson."

Tyrell nodded "Ma'am."

The president had told him to keep this under wraps but Victor needed to interview her and he needed an office. "Mrs. Tartaglione, we have quite a few questions of our own. Would you be willing to come up to our center city field office?"

"Yeah sure, I guess," said Tina. "Just give me a minute to finish dressing and putting on my makeup."

While Tina was dressing, Victor called a friend in the Philly FBI office and asked if they had a room that he could use to speak with a potential witness.

Tina meanwhile was thinking about what Ronnie had told her before he left for Washington. He had just finished showering, and she thought it odd that he was standing naked looking in one of the closets. He never did that.

"Whaddya doing standin' there in your birthday suit, Ronnie."

"God, ya scared the shit outta me, Teen. Why'd ya sneak up on me like that?

Ronnie was holding a large manila envelope.

"What's in the envelope?"

"Teen, this is 25 G's. I'm hiding it under a floorboard in this closet so you'll know where it is."

Seeing the look of distrust on her face, he continued. "It's a partial payment on an ad hoc government project I'm working on. Keep it here or put it in a safe place and don't tell anyone about it, you got me."

She realized that she had been taking a long time to dress and didn't want Agent Sanchez getting suspicious, so she threw on a pair of jeans and an Eagles jersey and met Sanchez outside.

"Sorry it took so long, I had to use the little girl's room."

Once downtown Sanchez stopped to talk to someone in a fancy suit before ushering her into what she suspected was the hot shots' office. She half expected to be thrown into a room with a table, two chairs, and a two-way mirror. That's how they did it on TV.

Sanchez offered her some refreshments, and she accepted a soft drink.

"Thanks for coming down to talk to me, Mrs. Tartaglione."

"No problem. I just want you to find my husband."

"Mrs. Tartaglione, when did you last see your husband?"

"The night before last."

"So you didn't see him at all yesterday?"

"No, I didn't."

"Do you know where he was yesterday?"

"He said he was going on some kinda job interview or something."

"And you don't know who that was with or where that was?"

"No I don't."

"And you never bothered to ask him?"

"Nope."

"That seems very odd to me. A husband is going on some job interview and never discussed it with his wife?"

"Ronnie was sort of a private person, and he was used to being on his own."

"Would it surprise you if I told you that your husband went to Washington yesterday?"

"Not really. He mentioned a few weeks ago that he might have some business with the Pentagon, but he didn't tell me when or anything about it."

"And you weren't even a little curious about that?"

"Not really. He used to travel overseas all the time when he was in the Army, and he'd go off to all sorts of top secret briefings. I wasn't supposed to know nothin' so he never told me. Plus ya gotta know Ronnie. He does what he wants. He doesn't need to ask permission and he doesn't have to tell me everything."

"Well, the truth is that a high ranking government official was assassinated yesterday in Washington."

"I saw that on the news. What's that got to do with me and Ronnie?

"Mrs. Tartaglione, your husband was arrested as the prime suspect."

"You're nuts. Ronnie wouldn't do something like that. And you're just telling me now? What is this some sick game? I'm worried sick and you're playing twenty questions? Is he ok?"

"As far as we know but he's escaped from custody, and we're trying to find him."

Tina was shaking. She was relieved to hear that her husband was ok, but she couldn't hold back the tears. Agent Sanchez offered her a tissue and gave her some time to compose herself.

"So, as I was saying, he's no longer in custody. Where is he, Mrs. Tartaglione?"

"I told you that I don't know where he's at."

"Yes, of course you did. Did Ronnie happen to have any close friends, someone he might call if he was in trouble? Someone who you know would help him?"

"No. He was pretty much a loner."

"C'mon Mrs. Tartaglione. Do you mean to insult my intelligence by telling me that your husband had no friends at all, not even some old Army buddies?"

This questioning was tiring, and now that she knew that her husband was alive, all she wanted to do was go home and hope for a phone call. But it didn't seem like Agent Sanchez was going to let her leave anytime soon, at least, not until he learned something from her. He was going to find something out sooner or later so she might as well give him a little something so that he'd let her go. It was a rash decision and one that she'd regret.

Chapter 53

"Mr. President?" Julia spoke through the intercom.

"Yes, Julia." replied Ahmad.

"I have Agent Sanchez from the FBI on the phone for you."

"Thanks, Julia. I'll pick up."

"Agent Sanchez," Ahmad said as he picked up the receiver. "What do you have for me?"

Sanchez went into great detail about his time in Philly and his interview with Ronnie Tartaglione's wife.

"She was taken completely off guard, and I could see, Mr. President, that she knew nothing about this. I don't think she was involved at all Sir. "

Victor related to the president that Tina knew little about her husband's affairs except that he might be interviewing at the Pentagon at some point.

"The Pentagon had no record of her husband having any business with anyone there and that he had not signed a visitor log at any time in the past year. Mr. President."

"When we asked about his friends, she said he'd spoken to a couple of neighbors on the street from time to time but mostly to just say hello or to chat idly about the weather or the Eagles. She didn't even know any of their names as she didn't make friends easily and only knew them to wave to say hello."

"She finally told me that her husband had no family other than her and that his only real friend was an old buddy from the Army, a guy named Nicky. She said she didn't know this guy Nicky that well."

Excitedly Ahmad asked, "Have you located this Nicky yet, Agent Sanchez?"

"Not yet, Sir. I canvassed the neighborhood talking to some of their neighbors and asking about someone named Nicky. I finally found someone in the bar a few blocks away who guessed that it might be Nicky Gervasi."

"Have you been able to confirm that, Agent Sanchez?"

"Yes Sir, Philly PD knows him, and they know about some of his past ties to the area. He's known by *Nicky Killer* and has some ties to organized crime but isn't a major player. He's more of a wannabe. They gave me his address, and I spoke to some of his neighbors. Apparently he hasn't been home for several days."

"Did any of them know Tartaglione?" The president was anxious.

"No, but the name 'Angela' came up in a couple of the conversations. No one knew if she and Nicky were a couple or even what her last name was but they seem to be connected. I'm going to follow up to see if I can find out more. The Philly PD put out an APB to bring Nicky in for questioning in connection with Targalione's disappearance."

"Good work, Agent Sanchez," Said Ahmad. "Stay on it and let's see where this leads us. I'm confident that this Nicky Killer character is our link to Omar's assassination and more importantly to what I suspect is something even bigger."

"Yes sir," said Agent Sanchez. Sanchez wasn't as sure as the president seemed to be about Nicky Gervasi but then the president had been acting strangely paranoid since the attempt on his life. *It's his right,* thought Sanchez. He smiled, reminded of an old joke, *being paranoid just makes good sense when everyone is out to get you.*

After hanging up the phone, Ahmad skimmed over the notes for tomorrow's cabinet meeting. He was even more sure that something big was going down, and he was determined to smoke it out and stop it at all cost.

He punched the intercom. "Julia, would you get the Ambassadors to Syria and Iran on the phone. Ask them to meet me here for lunch?"

"Yes,Sir."

"And if one of them cannot make it, for whatever reason, patch that call through to me. It's important that I speak to them both."

"Yes, Mr. President," said Julia.

Chapter 54

Between all of the hours of interrogation yesterday and not knowing what happened to Ronnie, Tina was a mess. She sat there crying, looking at the manila envelope when the doorbell rang.

"Damn it, not again."

This time, it was Nicky. It had been awkward for the two of them after they had their one night stand a few years earlier because he kept after her, wanting to have sex again, and was always professing his undying love. She knew he was harmless; just a little horny. She was tempted once or twice but was sure that she didn't want to start that up again. She kept telling him. "Nick I tole ya that was just a one-time thing. Get over it will ya." They had finally settled into the friend zone.

Today seemed different, though. He was all business.

"I have to tell you somethin' he said. "I don't think Ronnie's comin' home."

She just stared at him with tears welling up in her eyes. After yesterday she was hopeful, but deep down she feared this might be coming.

"Why do you say that?"

"There's a lot more to this Teen. I don't know much, but I've heard that the cops took Ronnie into custody. That's all I know. Did Ronnie tell you anything?"

Tina was barely holding it together, but she explained what she knew which was just what Ronnie had told her but that she suspected that there was more because she knew that he had met with Nicky one afternoon and disappeared the next day. She also told him that she had twenty-five G's and that Ronnie had told her about the rest of the money.

Tina was a survivor and as distraught as she was she kept her head about her. "So what the hell happens with the rest of the money, Nick? When will I get it?"

"I don't know nothin' about what the money was for or what the job was."

He looked down at the floor as he spoke and with both hands in his pockets, he jiggled his change, an obvious nervous reaction.

"I was just the gopher, Teen."

He swore to her that he didn't know Ronnie's whereabouts but was concerned that something had happened to him. He prepped her for a visit by the FBI.

"They picked me up yesterday, and I spent 3 hours in center city at their offices. They kept asking me questions about what Ronnie was doing and who his friends were. Shit like that."

"What did you tell 'em, Tina?"

"Nothin' much."

"What do you mean nothin' much? Did you tell them about me?"

"Only that you guys were friends but nothin' else. I didn't even give 'em your last name. I told 'em that I didn't know nothin' else. Honest Nick."

"You have to play dumb, Tina. They got nothin' on me but now they may think I'm involved. I'm just a middleman here helping a friend with a good deal. That's all. If they ask you again, just tell 'em the truth that you've known me a long time and that Ronnie and I were in the Army together. But that we aren't close. Tell 'em you ain't seen me in ages. You know stuff like that. That's all, okay? And don't tell 'em about the dough. Are you ok with all of this, Teen?"

She didn't like that he kept calling her "Teen." Only Ronnie called her that. But she nodded in assent. Until Nick's visit she held out hope that Ronnie was alive but now she knew better.

"I'll tell ya what. I'll keep my mouth shut, Nick, but I want my money. I deserve it. So as long as I'm gonna get my money, I'll be the good soldier. Capisce?"

After he had left, Tina shook as she sobbed aloud for her husband. She didn't believe for one minute that Nicky didn't know what had happened to Ronnie. He knew. He was a big fat liar. She had prepared herself for years for this news, and yet she couldn't stop crying; knowing that she would never see her husband again.

Chapter 55

Nicky had knots in his stomach as he made his way back to his car. His hands were shaking. Why had he driven the lousy seven blocks to see Tina? Lazy lump. He could have walked and then he wouldn't have to worry about driving and finding a parking space.

He was worried about Tina. She seemed pretty upset after her visit with the FBI. She told them about him. And his showing up out of the blue didn't help. She was coming unglued.

He started the car, turned on the radio and just sat there for what seemed like an hour but was only about 10 minutes.

He had to go back to Tina's house. He couldn't leave things that way. He turned off the engine and took the keys.

He was only a half a block away, but it seemed like a mile. His bad knees were aching. The doc told him to lose weight. He should have listened to him. Maybe he would sit on her step for a while to rest, give himself time to think.

No. That wouldn't do any good. He had to see her. He had to face this. He climbed the five steps and gave a soft knock on her door. There was no answer. He looked around. He knocked harder, and that too went unanswered, so he tried the door knob. Damn it. It was locked. "I know your home Teen. I was just here" he whispered.

He rang the bell repeatedly and again looked around. He heard her coming to the door.

"Ok for Christ's sake. I'm coming."

Tina opened the door. "Oh no."

Chapter 56

The day following the final briefing in New York, Josh drove up to Boston to brief Qasim and Makim as he had promised to do.

He had previously explained a part of the plan in minute detail so that each would understand what was going to take place.

Qasim was going to remain in Boston on the 4th to oversee the protests in the Muslim communities. Like other major cities, there were several Christians and Jews in Boston who had agreed to do the same with their people. Those groups didn't like the idea of reporting to Qasim but Josh explained the logic of his being the point man. It wouldn't be an efficient use of his time, he told them, to have that many people calling him at home. This way each city would have one point person who could brief Josh. After some grumbling, they reluctantly agreed.

"What should I do on the 4th?" asked Makim.

"Makim, I understand that you are pretty good with firearms. Is that so?"

"It is," said Makim. "I've been using pistols since I was a young boy in Syria. I used to be really good with a rifle as well but having one arm limits me to some degree."

"I understand."

Josh laid out his plan for Makim.

"I need you to be in DC on the 4th. I hired a first-rate sniper but we haven't heard from him since the first part of his mission was completed a few weeks ago. I'm afraid he's either dead or been imprisoned. I don't know another reliable sharpshooter. Do either of you?"

Qasim and Makim both shook their heads no.

"I need someone who can wreak havoc on DC at the very beginning. It may be dangerous. We need you outside the Capitol in the early morning hours to keep watch on what is happening."

Seemed simple enough, thought Makim.

Makim had the feeling that there was more to this, but he just nodded to show his consent.

"Good. We may need to get you inside of the building at some point. I haven't figured out how but once inside we need you to prevent anyone from leaving. There will be a joint meeting of both houses so they'll be together. You have to be willing to threaten them. We'll send others who will help you totally seal off the building."

"I can do that," said Makim excitedly. He was sure that this was his chance to finally become a great man, like his father. "I know someone who works in the building. His name is Saadi El-Mofty. He will help me gain access. I am sure of that."

"Can he be trusted?" said Josh

"Yes. He is a good friend, and he owes me."

They discussed the plan in some detail, and Josh felt comfortable with Makim's part and that he knew exactly what to do.

"Do either of you have any concerns?"

When they shook their heads indicating that they didn't, Josh ended the conversation.

"Great it's settled then." If you have any problems or questions, use the secured phone lines, ok?"

They both nodded in agreement. "Good luck," said Josh. The meeting had been straightforward. There were no pleasantries and, when he had finished, he picked up his briefcase and left, without so much as a handshake. They were not friends. This relationship was all business.

On the drive back to New York, he got a call on his cell from Nicky telling him that Tina knew about Ronnie's deal. He said the Feds had been talking to her and that she was a nervous wreck.

He started to cry.

"She ratted me out, General. What else could I do? I had to kill her."

Josh realized that now he didn't have to come up with the rest of the money but all he said was "I'm sorry, Nick."

Chapter 57

Tarif was sitting quietly outside the oval office. For some reason, the president had more pressing business and had instructed Julia to put Tarif off for a short while. He would have gone back to his office to do some work but Julia told him that it wouldn't be but a moment, and the president specifically requested that he wait.

The two men approached the secretary and said something to her.

She pressed the button on the bottom of her phone.

"Mr. President," said Julia over the intercom, "I have the Ambassadors from Syria and Iran here to see you."

"Thanks, Julia, send them in."

They nodded as a courtesy as they passed Tarif. He nodded back.

He fidgeted in his seat wondering why they were here. Hell, he didn't even know why he was here. He knew the president had been increasingly disturbed about the dissension in the country. But he was always disturbed about something. Tarif feared that Abbas might question him and being a little paranoid and on edge himself, that the president might even think that he knew something about it, he had prepared answers. But now he wondered what was going on. Maybe he was totally off base. What could possibly necessitate an urgent meeting with these two men?

"Hey, Julia. What's the story? Why are Anas Al-Hamsi and Pooria Shahrestaani here?"

"You know that I couldn't tell you even if I knew. I'm sure the president will clue you in if it's something he feels you should know."

Stonewalled.

Tarif sat there for about 20 minutes after which the door to the oval office flew open.

"ma'a as-salaama," all three said in unison as the two men left the oval office. They walked passed Tarif without so much as a nod this time, and they didn't look happy.

"Tarif, come in." said the president.

Chapter 58

Josh watched the TV with growing concern.

NBC reporting: "The news out of the White House today confirmed the VAPT rumors that have been circulating across the country for the past week. In a prepared statement, President Abbas announced that he has entered into an agreement with Syria and Iran to conduct joint military exercises, first in the United States and later in the year in the Middle East."

"Here is the video of the president speaking from the Rose Garden."

"First off I want to dispel any rumors and alleviate your fears that foreign warplanes entered US airspace this afternoon unexpectedly. I want to ensure you that nothing could be farther from the truth. In fact, I'm excited to announce that The United States will be participating over the next month or so in joint military exercises with our friends from Syria and Iran. These exercises demonstrate a growing desire by our countries to embark on a new journey, one marked by a spirit of cooperation. While I was hoping for a large scale deployment for more long term exercises, we have jointly decided that this first step would not include any significant undertakings but merely joint firepower demonstrations by a few hundred troops from each country. The Irani troops and a light armored division have arrived and will be based out of Ft. Belvoir, VA. Our Syrian guests will be stationed here at Andrews AFB, at Ft. Bragg, in NC, Ft Dix in NJ, and Hanscom AFB near Boston. We asked our guests to arrive earlier than originally planned so that they might become acclimated to our customs here in the US and so that we can finalize the demonstration plans. At this time, we expect these exercises to begin on or about July 15th and end within a one-week timeframe; at which time all of the foreign troops will redeploy to their homelands.

Josh turned off the TV. He couldn't help but question the timing of these exercises. When had there ever been a joint firepower demonstration with foreign troops on US soil? The answer was never. Generally, the US only participated in CONUS operations. Joint military exercises with foreign forces were, until now, conducted overseas and typically involved a lot more than a few hundred troops.

Does this sly fox know more than we think he knows thought Josh? *And to what end would he invite Syrian and Irani troops?* Josh could not accept the reasons that were running through his mind right now. But he would have to stay vigilant and ensure that he was prepared even for the unthinkable.

Chapter 59

Victor Sanchez sped through the city realizing that he was late for his meeting with the president. There are just some people you should not keep waiting.

Naturally traffic in DC would be a mess. Whenever Victor had to be somewhere in a hurry, he hit horrendous traffic. It started on I-95 in Delaware where he found traffic backed up for miles as a result of a tractor trailer accident. Then he hit the typically heavy rush hour volume going through the Fort McHenry Tunnel near Baltimore and approaching I-495 around DC. He had left the Four Seasons Hotel in Center City Philly in time to make his 10 am meeting with thirty minutes to spare, but his cushion had degraded to about five minutes as he entered DC. As he turned off of New York Avenue onto 14th Street, he realized that the last mile and a half would take him another 15 minutes which precipitated his call.

"Call White House," he said to his car's dash.

"This is the White House, how may I help you?"

"This is Special Agent Sanchez. Would you connect me to the president?"

After a few seconds of music on hold: "This is the president's office."

"Hi Julia, this is Agent Sanchez. I have a meeting scheduled with the president, and I'm running a little late. I should be there in about 15 minutes."

"I'll let the president know."

As he pulled up in front of the White House, Victor hoped that the president would forgive his tardiness.

He checked in with Julia and had a seat in one of the chairs in the corridor outside of the oval office. Julia buzzed in on the president and he heard Abbas tell her to "show Agent Sanchez in."

"Good morning Mr. President. I'm sorry that I'm late, but I hit a lot of traffic driving down from Philly this morning."

"I don't care about that," said Ahmad. "I understand that you have some news."

"Yes sir, I do," said Victor.

"I've spent the last week in Philly trying to track down this Nicky Killer character. I believe that he has either fled the area or, knowing that we are looking for him, is in hiding. This is certainly a disappointment. But while we'd still like to find him, we've followed another thread that has provided some insight into what has been going on."

"As you suspected, Mr. President, there is a group of people in Philly who want to see you out of office. In speaking to some of Nicky Killer's neighbors, we learned that he had mentioned that at least on one occasion he had met with a group of local priests.

"Finding a priest isn't as hard as it once was. The Catholic Church, after years of hiding its priests, has streamlined its worldwide communications. We assumed, Mr. President, that the closest 2 or 3 parishes to Nicky's home would be most useful, so we were able to get a court order to monitor all emails and tap the phones of the rectories of these parishes in South Philly."

"Agent Sanchez, I don't have time nor do I care about all of this. I just need the important details of what you found out."

"Yes Sir, Mr. President. During one of the taps, we heard a conversation between a Father Richard Delaney from the Parish of the Holy Innocents and Father Edwardo Garcia

238

from the Parish of the Lord's Nativity in Northeast Philadelphia. During the conversation, we heard Father Delaney describe meetings he had attended up until about six months ago where several members of the clergy were trying to find a way to have you impeached. According to the conversation, though, things got too far out of hand as talk shifted to taking action that Father Delaney said were unsavory to the other clerics who were involved. He told Father Garcia that he stopped going to the meetings because of this."

Victor paused to catch his breath and to give the president a chance to ask any questions he might have, but quickly continued.

"One of the old women with whom we had previously spoken confirmed that Father Delaney was the name she had heard from Nicky, and this woman told us that he was once assigned to the Annunciation Church. For some unknown reason, Father Delaney has moved around more than one might expect, even for a Catholic priest. Even so, finding him proved a relatively easy exercise. He's a resident of The Parish of the Holy Family rectory."

"And I assume that was a good lead. Does this story have an ending, Agent Sanchez I have an important meeting coming up?"

"Of course, I'll try to be brief. We brought this Delaney in for questioning. To be honest, he doesn't look much like a terrorist. He's a short 5'5" and skinny as a rail with short red hair. He looks like a strong wind could blow him over."

"We told him that he was a suspect in terrorist behavior and had witnesses putting him at secret meetings. The priest, at first, denied it but after some individual persuasion, he admitted that he had attended a couple of meetings but stated that he had not done so in several months. He said that some thugs had replaced the small group of clergy that had been meeting in South Philly and that they all had joined with others from New York. Father Delaney insists that he bailed early on, but he told us that he heard about the group planning some activities for Independence Day."

Now the president interrupted. "Did he say what types of activities or does he know the names of any of the leaders here or maybe in New York?"

"He says he left the group before the meetings in New York started because he is not a violent person and was afraid that it might involve protests in the streets. He claims that when he was a pastor in North Philly, he saw firsthand how protests like these, could get out of control. He admitted to not liking you, Mr. President, but he didn't want any part of bloodshed. He did give up the name of the woman who was hosting the meeting in Philadelphia. She's a former businesswoman who is apparently bitter about the turn her life has taken under your leadership, Mr. President. Others have mentioned her before, Sir, but now we have her full name; Angela Marie Mastronardo. We've learned that she recently married a man named, Tony DiPietro. We're looking for them both, Sir."

"Excellent. Keep me posted on your progress. And, good work, Agent Sanchez."

"Thank you, Sir. Goodbye, Mr. President."

After Victor had left, the president decided it was time to plan his course, now that he was reasonably sure that it had not been just paranoia setting in. He didn't know everything, but he knew that something was up in at least a couple of the major cities and that July 4th was the date that he should expect some "Anti-Abbas" activities. What he had learned so far was enough information to enable him to put the machinery in motion to defend his presidency.

Chapter 60

Angela was taken by surprise when the two FBI agents, Sanchez and Ferguson, visited her and asked if she would be willing to come up to the office because they believed that she could help with an investigation being conducted. She wasn't sure what was going on but she agreed to go with them.

The Philly FBI office was in center city on Arch Street across from the old National Constitution Center. It was only about 15 minutes from Angela's house as Victor used four-lane Broad Street and managed to either miss or ignore most of the traffic signals.

After parking in the underground parking garage, they traveled up the elevator to the eighth floor. Ferguson asked Angela if she would like something to drink, before showing her into an interview room. She sat uncomfortably in an old wooden chair at an old wooden table.

Just like in the old movies, she thought. *Can't the FBI afford some decent furniture?* Sanchez had begun the questioning along with an Agent Tyrell Ferguson, but he had a previous engagement and left her in what he said were the capable hands of Agent Ferguson.

Agent Ferguson was a 6'4" well-built black man whom she guessed to be about 35 years old. He was extremely handsome, well-mannered and very professional. Angela was nervous at first but felt a little better as she sensed that, because he wasn't a hardened veteran, she might be able to manipulate him.

The part that made Angela nervous was that she didn't know what they had on her. Obviously, there was no evidence of foul play on her part, or they'd have already arrested her. No, this was not about them having anything on her. The Feds were simply on a fishing expedition. She figured someone gave them her name as a PI, but she couldn't figure out who would have ratted her out. So Angela Marie DiPietro, you are officially a person of interest. On TV, that meant that they did think the person was guilty of something. She wondered what it meant in real life.

"Mrs. DiPietro," said Agent Ferguson. "Do know a Father Delaney?"

That fag, she thought.

"Yes, I know Father Delaney. He's one of the priests living in a nearby parish. Why do you ask?"

"Well, his name was brought to our attention by a parishioner who mentioned that Father Delaney was involved in some meetings at your house."

"There were no 'meetings' at my house, agent. I do have some friends who come over from time to time to pray the rosary. As far as I know, while not popular, it's not against the law yet."

"Well Mrs. DiPietro, Father Delaney claims that when he was at your house, some of the other men were discussing problems that they had with the current administration and the president. Can you confirm that?"

Angela was deep in thought.

"Well, Mrs. DiPietro?"

He always started his questioning with well. It must be a requirement here at the FBI. Ok, she'll play along.

"Well what?" replied Angela.

"Well, did you ever hear anyone discussing problems that they had with the current administration and the president?"

"Well, I can't rightly say that I have." Angela was trying to act coy.

"Well, can you explain why Father Delaney would think that?"

"Well," Angela was getting the hang of this, "First off, Father Delaney hates my guts. Secondly, I think Father Delaney is more than a little nuts."

"Well, why would you say that?"

"Well, why would I say what? That he hates me or that he's nuts?"

"Well both," said Agent Ferguson

"Well when he was in here did you see him checking out the size of your dick through your pants?" so much for sophistication. "No, maybe not, you're a little too old for Father Delaney's taste. I'd guess you're about 25 or 30 years older than he likes them."

Agent Ferguson sat there with his mouth open.

"Surely you can't be too surprised, Agent." oh-oh, Angela was breaking the 'well' tradition. "Father Delaney was accused of being a pedophile some months ago by a former altar boy who claimed that he buried photos that would prove it. Ben Campbell was his name. I knew Ben and his family personally, and I believe without any doubt that the claims are true. The family has even filed a civil suit, that's pending, against Father Delaney and the Archdiocese. Philly PD took his initial statement and believed him as well. They thought they had the goods on the *good Father*, and I'm being sarcastic when I say that agent."

"I checked in the system, and Father Delaney did not have a record. What happened with the case?"

"Philly PD believed that they had plenty of time to investigate. So, they didn't immediately put the case together for the D.A. Sadly, in their typical vulture style, the press learned the young man's identity and started following him and taking pictures. Before the case could even get off the ground, the young man hung himself."

"What happened to the photos and what about the other boy who was willing to testify?"

"So far, no one has found the photos and the one other boy who came forward against Father Delaney decided that he didn't want to testify. So Delaney was released."

"Well, you sound like you have some ill feelings toward Father Delaney."

"You think?" said Angela.

"Look Agent Ferguson. Let me make this as simple as I can for you. I do not like Father Dickie Delaney. He knows that I don't like him, and he knows why I don't like him. He knows that I'm friendly with the Campbells, and I've told him in no uncertain terms what I think of him. I know that he's a child molester, and I will never let him forget it."

"Well if you hate this priest so much, why did you have him over to your house for these prayer meetings?"

"Was he at my house once or twice? Yes, but not by invitation. One of the other participants in the prayer meeting brought him along. I didn't want to make a scene because he's a priest and because everyone else liked him. He's a pervert and a predator, but maybe some people don't realize that. In any event, he came to two meetings. I was going to say something to him after the second meeting, but he left early. I didn't want him in my house, and he knew that so maybe that bothered him a little. Don't know for sure but he stopped coming, so that saved me the trouble of having to deal with a very sensitive situation."

"Well, I see that there is no love lost between you two."

"I'm glad that you understand. It's like a mutual aversion society. I hate him, and he hates me. I'm not surprised that if you called him in for questioning, he'd make up some story to get back at me."

"If I may, I'd like to recap your story," said Agent Ferguson as he was writing on a notepad. "You've had a few prayer meetings at your home, nothing more. Father Delaney attended a couple and then stopped coming. Father Delaney is a suspected pedophile and because of that, you do not like him. He hates you as well, probably because you won't let him get away with what he did. In your opinion, Father Delaney is lying because he hates you and wants to get even with you for calling him out repeatedly about your suspicions regarding his past sexual behavior. Is that fairly accurate?"

"Close enough," said Angela, "but for me he's not a 'suspected pedophile' but a real one and his 'past' sexual behavior is not necessarily in the past."

"I understand. That's all I had for you today, Mrs.DiPietro. You're free to go, but I'd hope that if I had further questions, you'd be willing to help me out."

"Of course, Agent Ferguson. I'm glad I could be of help. Is there a way that someone could give me a ride home? I don't have money on me for public transportation and it's a little far to walk in the rain."

"Well, I'd be happy to drop you off."

Angela was relieved. *Dodged a bullet this time and got to throw Dickwad under the bus at the same time. Well screw the good Father,* thought Angela. *That prick deserves everything he gets.*

Agent Ferguson called Victor Sanchez and related Angela's story.

"Good work, Tyrell. I think it might be a good idea for me to pay a personal visit to Father Delaney in the morning".

Chapter 61

As a young girl growing up in Birmingham, Karen often helped her mother prepare for what oftentimes became the social events of the year. The *Belle of Birmingham*, as many referred to her, took southern hospitality to a whole new level; sparing little expense and going to extremes to accommodate her guests.

One of the things that Karen disliked about being married to an Army officer was the constant moving. No sooner had she made friends at one base when they were off to another. Consequently get-togethers were usually limited to small dinners with one or two couples.

So to Karen, this cocktail party was not only an excuse to get her hair done, buy a new dress, and get a mani-pedi, but a chance to be a real southern hostess. To Josh, it seemed like the perfect way to get all of the Joint Chiefs together for a final walk through and to show them their place of business for July 4th.

As she left the house on the morning of Saturday, July 2nd for her favorite salon, Karen told Josh that she much preferred her party plans to his stuffy briefing.

The Redmond House, in Head of the Harbor, was unique in the area in that Josh, being a techie kind of guy, had brought their home into the 22nd century, 50 years before its time. The entire house was one big operating system and Wi-Fi hotspot. You could use cell and other wireless technology from anywhere. Retinal scanners armed and disarmed the security system and controlled access to in-wall safes. Every wall was a touchscreen. Tiny sensors were used in things like light bulbs, light switches, bio-locks on doors, windows, thermostats, and fitness devices. By using these M&C (Monitor and Control) sensors, homeowners could easily monitor and control things like the temperature, doors, security systems, TVs, and kitchen appliances from anywhere in the house or even remotely using a cell phone.

In the basement; Josh had established a Command Post which was technically bleeding edge. Retinal scanners and Nymi™ heartbeat biometrics sensors were used to restrict access and secure all electronic equipment. C6I centers were run by the government so it was odd that an ordinary citizen would have a secured facility at his home. But then again, Retired Two Star Josh Redmond was no ordinary citizen. While much smaller in scale, in some ways Josh's basement resembled the NORAD command center at Cheyenne Mountain.

Karen, annoyed that he had converted their home theater and entertainment room into this whatever you call it, asked him why he needed all of this equipment. Josh explained that the network was already in place but by commandeering the DOD and intelligence community's networks, his Joint Chiefs would be able to manage the entire operation and improve interoperability in real time with the touch of a screen. For a coordinated operation like this, timely information and optimum reliability and security were essential.

This technical stuff was beyond Karen's interest, and her eyes were practically glazed over as she mockingly humored Josh "hmmm, very impressive".

"Josh, would you play some nice mood music before the guests arrived."

"Sure honey", said Josh as he put on a mixed bag of 1960s and 70's rock that included Aerosmith, Pink Floyd, The Beatles, and his favorites The Stones.

"Oh my God, Josh, that is not mood music." She knew that Josh loved the old classic rock sounds of his grandfather's time but he could listen to those any time. She changed services to one with a mellow light classical feel and started humming.

"Really, Karen?"

Josh's protest was interrupted by the doorbell as their guests had begun arriving.

Along with their spouses, the guest list included Demetri Kotsopoulos, Deputy Secretary of Defense, Admiral John Barrington, Vice Chairman of the Joint Chiefs, General Raymond Rivera Secretary of the Army, Admiral Terrance Combers, Secretary of the Navy, General Bradley Gallant, Secretary of the Marine Corps, General Richard O'Meara Secretary of the Air Force, and Admiral Jesse Happ, Commandant of the Coast Guard. Kyle Simpson, Director of Homeland Security, was also in attendance but being gay presented unique social challenges for Kyle and his partner, Ty Landis, so Ty stayed away from these types of affairs.

These were the brave men who now ran the military. Josh could remember the days when the secretaries of the branches were civilians who didn't know shit from Shinola as they say. Of course back then they didn't play an operational leadership role the way these men do. Those pansies were mostly pencil pushers who worried about their branch's budget and fighting with Congress to get money for new weapons. They were more like lobbyists, kissing asses at every turn.

But the challenges of war became more complex as the face of the enemy became shapeless. President Ryan realized that only seasoned war veterans could understand the nature of radical warfare and make the kinds of decisions needed to protect US troops and the country. So, in 2024 it became mandatory for the secretaries of the branches to be high ranking military officers. This turned out to be one of the more brilliant decisions any president had ever made. Over the last 20 years having military minds making crucial decisions for their branches proved invaluable in defending the country from terrorists.

Karen warmly welcomed her guests in true Southern style. "Y'all just make yourselves comfortable." As they settled in chairs, she circulated among the crowd with a tray of hors d'oeuvres as Josh poured drinks for everyone.

After a short while, Josh gave a toast. While the wives all had a sense of what was happening, Josh thought it more appropriate to give a vanilla toast to friends and family. He did tell the men that they were only allowed one drink before he showed them his newly remodeled basement. "Afterward, you can all get shit faced for all I care, provided you don't try to drive home and take out one of my neighbors' mailboxes." Josh wasn't the funniest man around but being a retired general had its perks; everyone laughed.

Around twenty hundred hours the men left the women and adjourned to the basement to see a truly impressive command center within a Secure Compartmented Information Facility or SCIF. Like the rest of the house, the doors to the SCIF were secured with bio-locks and retinal scanners, requiring Josh's thumbprints and eyes to be scanned before allowing access. Not only were the walls of the SCIF serving as touch screens but the tables in the room were as well.

"Gentleman, starting on the 4th and until we have things under control, this room will be your home."

While each person in this room had undoubtedly memorized the operational plan before shredding it, Josh briefly laid out the primary plan one more time to ensure that there were no misconceptions and so that he could address any questions or issues. He hoped that things went according to plan. If they did, he and the military would have control of the country by the end of the day on July 4th. And, they will have neutralized the president, vice president, cabinet, Secretary of Defense, Chairman of the Joint Chiefs, and most of the Congress. They would all be captured or dead. That seemed like an ambitious schedule for a takeover, but the combination of Josh being a strategic genius and all of the key military and security leaders in the fold made it doable.

He initially had some concerns about the heads of the CIA, NSA, and FBI but Kyle explained to him that these men were running ops because it was their passion, it was what they enjoyed doing, and that their changing hats to the other team would not present a problem. "They are not combatants," said Kyle, "and because they know and trust the people in this room, they'll roll over for us. We just need to ensure that the teams at the various organizational headquarters at Ft. Meade, Langley, and Washington are in place to receive their orders and open the communication lines for a message from you at the appropriate time."

"Does everyone understand this plan and your respective roles?"

They all nodded so Josh moved onto Plan B by explaining what everyone already understood.

"I believe we've put together a sound plan and have the right people to implement that plan. But, as you all know from first-hand experience, sometimes that's not enough. Sometimes things don't go according to plan. There are many reasons for this. Unsuccessful missions sometimes occur because one or more groups fail to carry their respective assignments. This can be caused by a breach in security, or because of some uncontrollable events. We've all seen this happen. But chief among them is underestimating the enemy's intelligence gathering capacity and his ability to withstand an assault. That's why we need a contingency plan and why I'm presenting Plan B."

Josh went on to discuss his backup plan without providing all of the specifics. Ultimately, only he would know every detail of the plan; only he knew the end game. Like in battle, not everyone was going to be privy to every detail of either plan but rather, like actors, each would know their particular role in the plot and be in a position to execute that part flawlessly. Secrecy was critical. "Need to know basis" was always his way when he formulated a strategy because the fewer people involved the better and the less people knew;

the less they could divulge under interrogation or torture. Thinking back through history, Josh wondered how many individuals working on the Manhattan Project, or even in the military, knew the details of the plan to drop an atomic bomb on Hiroshima during World War II.

There were a few questions about his backup plan that Josh had to clarify, and there were some aspects that he chose to keep to himself for the time being. Josh would reveal more as the need arose, but everyone in the room accepted that this alternate plan was necessary.

"Gentlemen, remember what I said about security breaches impacting our success. Discuss these plans on a need to know basis only. Confide in no one except the few people who will be critically important to the completion of our mission. Is that understood?"

Everyone nodded in agreement.

"Good, let's go up and join our wives for what I hope will be a relaxing remainder of the evening."

As they filed out of the basement, Josh worried about the ability of patriotic Americans to essentially wage war against their own country. He hoped that Plan A would work as expected because he feared the consequences if they had to move to Plan B.

Chapter 62

After getting up early to visit Father Delaney before his 7am mass, Agent Sanchez decided to pay another visit to Mrs. Angela DiPietro

The knock on her door awakened Angela from a sound sleep. Through squinted eyes she made out the time to be 7:30 am. She ignored the knock but heard the bell ringing over and over. "Crap," she said.

She crawled out of bed, threw on a pair of pants, blouse, and sandals and peeked through the door's peephole.

"Are you friggin' kidding me," was all she could muster as she saw the face of Victor Sanchez displaying his FBI badge in front of her eyeballs.

"Yes, can I help you?"

"Mrs. DiPietro. This is Agent Sanchez with the FBI.

Opening the door; "Yes, Agent Sanchez. To what do I owe this honor?" She had a pleasant way about her, even when being sarcastic.

Looking around, she saw a line of blue and whites with their lights flashing as if they were leading a parade or something.

"Mrs. DiPietro, You're under arrest for murder and your involvement in un-American activities."

"Are you nuts? I didn't kill anyone", she protested

There was no need to Miranda her but if they couldn't get her on any conspiracy charges, he would read her rights to her before booking her for murder. Sanchez cuffed her and placed her in the back seat of the car with Agent Ferguson. Angela was worried, but she knew she hadn't killed anyone. Hell, they hadn't even told her who had been murdered. No, this wasn't about murder. The FBI was interested in something so much bigger. She wished that she had a chance to call or text Tony, in New York, to warn him but there was no way to do that now. No, he'd be okay and she felt confident that she'd be able to convey her innocence. She'd basically go uptown with Agent Sanchez, answer a few questions and she'd be home by dinner time. It was only Thursday, and Tony wasn't due home until late Sunday night. He's busy and won't even have time to think about her or what she was doing. He wouldn't even know that she was gone.

At the FBI building she was escorted into a large interview room. While nicer than the room she was in yesterday, it still had the look and smell of a stuffy 70-year-old building. There were no pleasantries today as Agent Sanchez began the interrogation.

"Is it okay if I record your interviews, Mrs. DiPietro? It will save a lot of writing and cramped fingers."

"I would like to request my one phone call so that I can call my attorney."

"I'm sorry Mrs. DiPietro. Perhaps I wasn't clear. You've been arrested for a series of crimes, one of which is plotting against the Government of the United States. Your rights under the Constitution do not apply because you are being charged with crimes counter to the Constitution."

"Are you kidding me? This is a joke right?"

"No ma'am it's not. You may not realize this, but if there is any truth to what Father Delaney has told us, you could be charged under the Patriot Act of 2038. Cooperate and I'll do everything in my power to help you. Now may I record this interview?" He avoided using the term interrogation.

"Sure why not. I've got nothing to hide." So we're back to Father Delaney, she thought. There was no murder. They're just chasing this bull crap story that the fag priest gave them. She was feeling particularly cocky now and was sure that they had nothing on her and would have to let her go.

"Mrs. DiPietro, I understand that you told Agent Ferguson that you do not like Father Delaney. Is that correct?"

"Actually, what I said was that I hate him."

"Right. According to my notes, that's because you believe that Father Delaney is a pedophile?"

"That's correct. He is."

"And it says here that you knew a young man who was abused by Father Delaney."

"Yes, but I already answered all of these questions yesterday."

"I understand, and I hope that you will indulge me a little as I may backtrack just to make sure that I have a clear understanding of what you're telling us. Is that ok?"

"Do I have a choice?"

"Mrs. DiPietro, when was the last time that you were in Father Delaney's company?"

"I don't know the exact date, but it was probably 2 or 3 weeks ago. Why do you ask?"

"To the best of your knowledge is Father Delaney involved in any illegal activity?"

"You mean besides being a pedophile?"

"Well, yes. Has he been involved in any other illegal activity, to the best of your knowledge?"

"Not that I know of."

"Do you happen to know if Father Delaney was a politically involved or motivated person?"

"I wouldn't know." She played dumb. "Why are you asking all of these questions about Father Delaney?"

"Mrs. DiPietro, Father Delaney was found stabbed to death this morning."

"Well, that's good news, right?"

"I don't know. You tell me. Someone used a large kitchen knife. The wound was straight to his heart, and the knife blade was pushed in with such force that the very tip came off in his chest. I think someone who can be that violent is likely someone who not only knew him but hated him with a passion."

The reason they brought her into the office was becoming clearer with each new revelation. "I think that getting a pedophile off of the streets is a good thing but, of course, I don't condone violence of any kind so I certainly don't think murdering someone is the right way to do that."

"Did you go to the rectory last evening?"

Voila here it comes, she thought. "No, Agent Sanchez, I did not."

"So what would you say if I told you that someone saw you near the rectory at about 7 pm last night?"

"I went to the bakery just down the street around 6:30 pm and the rectory is on the way back, so it's possible that I was 'near' the rectory around that time."

"Did you stop by the rectory last night to see Father Delaney?"

"No."

"So you didn't ring the bell to the rectory and go in to speak with Father Delaney?"

"No I didn't, and if someone says I did, they're lying."

"Do you know anyone who would want Father Delaney dead?"

"You mean besides me?"

"You? Did you kill Father Delaney, Mrs. DiPietro?"

Angela laughs out loud. "Saying you wished someone was dead is just an expression. That doesn't mean I killed him. I told you that I don't condone violence. But I would imagine that there are a lot of people who really would like to see him dead."

"Like who?" said Sanchez.

"Well, let me see," Angela mused. "There was another child who had planned to come forward about Father Delaney's, shall we be nice and say, 'indiscretions'? I would think that my friends, the Campbells, whose son, Ben, committed suicide over what Delaney did to him, might be holding a grudge. Wouldn't you think that agent? Then, of course, there are thousands of 'good people' in South Philly who questioned the reasons for Delaney's many diocesan transfers over the years or knew or read about the young man who had filed charges and then killed himself. I would think any one of those people might want him dead as well."

After covering more of the same ground with Angela for over an hour, Agent Sanchez brought in Sadeem Ali.

"Mrs. DiPietro, I'm Agent Ali with the Secret Service, and I have a few questions for you. Are you comfortable?"

"Comfortable wouldn't be a term I'd use. No, I'm not comfortable. I'm tired, and I'm hungry. I want to stop this waste of time and go home. I've spent hours here talking about some dead fag priest that no one except you people even cares about."

"I understand, but we're investigating the murder of a person of interest in a possible subversion plot. You, Mrs. DiPietro, have been named by several people as someone who, along with Father Delaney, attended meetings at your house."

Angela sat quietly, then said "I want a lawyer".

Agent Ali, ignoring her request, continued his questioning about her husband Tony, Nicky, Father Quinn, and several others who had attended meetings.

Angela's answers were consistent. Of course, she was at meetings at her house. It was after all 'her' house. Yes, Tony was her husband. He knew Nicky as a friend, but she didn't know him. Father Quinn was a pastor at a nearby parish. Everyone in South Philly knew Father Quinn. To the best of her knowledge, no one was doing anything illegal. They were merely assembling; a right guaranteed by the Constitution, for the purpose of praying the rosary.

"Excuse me," Agent Ali stepped out into the hall to speak with Agent Sanchez.

"She's hesitated on a few answers, especially when asked about Nicky. It seems odd to me that her husband would be friends with this guy and that she doesn't know him. I'm sure that she knows more than she's letting on and the president wants answers. I didn't drive all the way up from DC to leave without any answers."

"What do you have I mind?" said Sanchez.

"I know how to get the information that I need. Mrs. DiPietro is not a spy or trained military or paramilitary. No one has schooled her in resisting interrogations. I'd like to keep her here, instill some fear in her. I think she'll talk."

"How can I help?"

"I know she expects to be released, but I'd like to keep her. I don't think we can book her on any murder charges, and we certainly don't have anything to tie her to any subversive activity, but I think that as we get more information we can charge her with serious charges that will preclude her right to an attorney."

"Well usually we could hold her on suspicion for 48 hours without even booking her but under the new federal laws, we can keep her for 72 hours. Will that be long enough?"

"I think 48 will be plenty. I don't think extreme interrogation techniques are needed here. I think some badgering, some trickery, and some nutritional and sleep deprivation will work wonders. And, I'd like you to play good cop by stopping in once in a while to give me a break and befriend her. Are you okay with this?"

"Roger that."

"Good. Let's get to work."

During the ensuing 48 hours, Angela was held in the same room, leaving only to use the lavatory and even then only when she came close to peeing herself.

Eventually, she cried incessantly out of sheer frustration and exhaustion. *I'm not giving them shit* was her first instinct as she stuck to her bland recitations for the first 37 hours. The interrogation was circular in nature in that it eventually came back to the same topics, only with the questions asked with slight variations. Did she know that someone was going to kill Father Delaney? Was he part of some plot? Did she or her group have anything to do with Father Delaney death? Did she or her friends kill him to keep him quiet? Did she know of events planned for the 4th of July? Did she know who was leading any protests or conspiracies?

I can't take this any longer, Angela thought.

After a short break, Agent Ali continued. "So, there are protests planned for July 4th then."

"Who told you that?" asked Angela.

"Why, you did Mrs. DiPietro. I'm just trying to put things in perspective to determine where and when the protests are taking place.

Angela didn't remember saying anything about protests, but she was so tired that maybe she did. She was confused at this point. What had she told them? Had she asked for a lawyer and, if so, where was her attorney?

The two agents agreed that it was unlikely that she would be giving up any names, so they focused on the details of the protests. That information would, at least, be helpful moving forward.

"Look," said Agent Sanchez, after Ali had left the room to use the men's room. "I want to help you. Just tell us a little more about the plans and we'll arrange for you to go home. So, Mrs. DiPietro, on July 4th, there is going to be a series of protests. And you're one of the leaders?"

"I'm not a leader" cried Angela. "I'm just along for the ride."

"I understand. I'm just trying to determine your role in these potential events and ascertain some time line and where these protests are likely to occur. I'm sure you can understand, Mrs. DiPietro."

"All over the country; they're going to happen in every city in America. Now can I go?"

"Thanks so much for your help. Do you know who the leaders of the protests are then?"

Silence from Angela.

"I know you're tired so let's wrap things up, and maybe you can be home in your bed later tonight, ok? At what time are these protests to occur?"

Angela exhausted: "I don't know, early in the morning."

"Excellent. And who is your boss in this?"

Silence again from Angela.

"What is the purpose of these protests, Angela?"

"I don't know what you mean."

"Well you seem like a rational person, and I'm sure you wouldn't be involved in something that wasn't a worthwhile cause Mrs. DiPietro. What are you protesting?"

"What?"

Softly: "What is the reason for these protests, Mrs. DiPietro?"

An angry Angela DiPietro lashed out. "With all of the bullshit that is going on in Washington with this raghead president, you need to ask me the reason? Why not? Why isn't everyone protesting? They should be."

"If you say so, Mrs. DiPietro."

"I say so," said Angela. "And I have the right to legal representation. I'm not saying another word without an attorney present."

Outside the room, Agent Ali had been watching through a one-way mirror. As Agent Sanchez left the room, he said "hold her on charges of sedition for now and then have her transferred to Leavenworth."

"And then what?"

"You know what? Maybe nothing. But, if something extraordinary occurs on July 4th, we'll make sure she gets a speedy trial for the crime of treason and all charges related to it."

Chapter 63

Agent Sanchez, on his way back to DC after his trip up to Philly, made the 6 am call to President Abbas' private secured line. The president was dressing and it could have waited but he insisted on being called as soon as there was news to report. The president said that he didn't care what time of day it was.

"Mr. President, this is Agent Sanchez."

"Yes, Agent Sanchez, what have you for me?"

"Mr. President, based on the murder of a Philadelphia priest, who we suspected of being involved in some protest movement, and a few other tips, Agent Ali and I brought Angela Marie DiPietro back in for questioning. She was stubborn and wouldn't give us any names, sir, but after interrogating her for almost 48 hours, we were able to break her. I've texted some critical information to you and the vice president."

Sanchez went on to tell the president about the arrest, transport to Leavenworth, and the interrogation by agents from Kansas City.

He also advised the president of their planned stakeout of the DiPietro house, in the event Tony DiPietro returned.

Ahmad disconnected the call. Sanchez had merely confirmed what he had already guessed. Everything was in place, and there was no need for any action on his part. He'd be returning to his apartment for a few hours of shut eye before heading into the office. One way or another, the events that were to follow would prove to be monumental regarding their impact on US history.

Chapter 64

Tony arrived home late Sunday night from his trip to New York. He and Aaron had gone over their plans together like they were still in college prepping for an exam. Both were nervous, and neither wanted to make a mistake.

Angela had given up her apartment after the wedding, and they now lived in one of the newer three story row homes that his parents had purchased during the revival of the city. Major money had bought up some of the inner city shambles, leveled them, and replaced them with gorgeous 3 and four bedroom, multi-bath, townhomes with garages for off street parking. Parking in the city had always been a problem and one of the major reasons people like Tony's parents had moved to the suburbs. But with the new construction, the "old" style of South Philly neighborhood saw revitalization around 2025 as the children and the children's children moved "downtown." While there were still a few of the old style row homes standing, most had been replaced with the new three story townhomes with garages. It was a nicer place to live, although it still suffered from many of the same problems other cities faced; overcrowding, too much traffic, and smog.

As he approached their street, Tony felt a very eerie vibe. It was after midnight, but Tony half expected Angela to be sitting outside on the step waiting for him. He sensed that something was wrong. People were creatures of habit. The same individuals parked on the street day after day. Tonight, when he looked down his street, he saw cars that he didn't recognize parked there

The door to one of the cars opened, and someone in a dark suit stepped out and looked around.

Tony ducked into an alley to avoid being seen. He heard footsteps at first and then what seemed like someone running.

Tony ran down one alley and then cut up another that led to a larger street. He peeked out and not seeing anyone; he darted across the street, into another alley and then onto yet another street.

Again he paused to see if someone was chasing him. When it looked like the coast was clear, he turned and rushed to the intersection of Broad St. and Oregon Avenue, several blocks away.

At first, he thought he was just being silly but why would someone in a suit be sitting in a car near his house. It sure looked like a stakeout. And why would someone chase him? Well, he did act suspiciously he guessed. Not many people run down alleys in the middle of the night.

He was certain something was wrong though. He couldn't just walk the streets of South Philly. People didn't do that anymore, at least not during the night, without drawing unwanted attention.

They hoped it wouldn't come to this, but he and Angela had planned for the worst. They had thought originally about hiding out at a friend's or relative's house. It couldn't be someone involved in what they were doing. That wouldn't be safe. But they didn't want to get anyone else in trouble. He was only a block away from one of his frat brothers who had an old piece of junk 2030 Subaru that he always left unlocked. You can use it he had told them. Sure it will be unlocked. Who would steal it, he rationalized? Tony found the car where he always parked it, and sure enough, the car had been left unlocked. He sat in the back seat and called Ange's cell number. There was no answer so he disconnected after two rings.

Maybe she's over one of her friend's houses. "Damn, I knew I should have gotten a list of all of her friends with their addresses and phone numbers." He remembered a Janice something or other. Tony was so bad with names. If he was introduced to you one minute and you saw him two minutes later, he was likely to have already forgotten your name.

He thought of one call he should make so he picked up his phone. After five rings someone picked up.

"Hello?" He heard the voice of Joanne Shapiro on the other end.

"Hi Joanne, it's Tony DiPietro."

"Why are you calling me in the middle of the night? What's wrong?"

Expressing concern, Tony asked, "Is Angela with you?"

"No Tony. I haven't seen her. The last time I spoke to her was last Wednesday."

"Do you happen to know any of her friends, Joanne? She's not at home, and I'm at a loss."

"Sorry, Tony. Outside of when we chat from time to time at meetings, we don't socialize."

"I see. Well if she happens to call you...."

"I'll have her call you right away," Joanne interrupted.

He hung up the phone.

Tony realized that Angela would have called him if she was staying with a friend. The only way she wouldn't have called was if she was not able to call.

He hopelessly wished that she'd pop out in the morning all rested and ready to revolt. Suddenly his phone rang. Thank God. It was Angela's phone. "Hey Ange, where are you?"

"This isn't your wife", replied a male voice.

Shaken, he immediately hit the end button. He tossed the phone out of the car, jumped out, and stomped on it, breaking it into a hundred pieces. Luckily, he had his secure phone with him.

"Crap they have her." There was nothing he could do. With all of the pent up anger he felt, he would have liked to have been able to go for a run. But that was too risky. Realizing that it was 2 am he decided to get back in the car and try to grab a few hours of sleep.

Chapter 65

The pall of heat never broke in the city during the summer months but Tony tried to grab a few winks. It was a sweltering night and sitting in a car with no AC was torturous. Even so, he needed some rest. He dozed off and on and wished that he had been able to sleep more soundly and a little longer but the sunlight awakened him. He hoped that by the end of the day, he'd have Angela back and they'd be able to sleep like babies.

It was still early, but he felt that it was time to get moving. He wished he had his overnight bag with at least a toothbrush in it. He did have some mints, though, and that would have to do.

He got out of the car to breathe some fresh air, but there wasn't any. He cautiously walked the few blocks back to the park at Broad St. and Oregon Avenue. There weren't many places nearby where one could escape the city stench and feel a slight breeze, but this park was one of them. Even if there had been a breeze, the city dwellers who were daring enough to venture outdoors would have been treated to an olfactory aperitif of carbon monoxide, raw sewage, and steaming garbage; thanks to the city trash strike, now in its eighth day.

He ducked into a McDonald's to use their restroom to freshen up and grabbed a quick breakfast of Egg McMuffin and a cup of coffee.

As he was leaving, his burner phone rang. He knew it was Joanne as she was the only person besides Angela and Josh who had his secure number equipped with the latest cell phone projection technology. He touched the connect image on his arm.

Joanne said she purposely went to visit a friend who lived across the street from where he and Angela lived and was calling to let him know that her friend said that the police had been to his house several times over the past couple of days and that Angela had gone somewhere with them. She didn't know if Angela came home or not but the neighbor said that there had been agents watching his house all night and that a few minutes earlier two unmarked cars with 4 FBI agents inside pulled up to the front of his house. They knocked on the door, but no one answered. Finding it open, they walked in. She said she heard someone calling his name. They finally left, but there was still one car parked just down the street.

Tony was upset and worried about Angela, but there was nothing he could do now. He didn't even mention the call he had received from Ange's phone. He simply thanked Joanne for the info that confirmed what he already knew. He had hoped to see her at the start of the protest but now it was unlikely. He have to deal with this right afterward.

Tony started walking toward 13th street. He figured when the time came; he would be less conspicuous walking north up 13th rather than the larger Broad Street.

His palms were sweaty, and his heart was racing.

Chapter 66

Once he reached Snyder Avenue, Tony turned left and walked the one block west to Broad Street. It was almost 8 am. He was to lead a group of protesters who were meeting at the intersection of Broad Street and Snyder Avenue. The plan called for the roughly 200 people to walk north on Broad Street. He expected to encounter members of the Philly PD within a half hour of the start of their march, and he suspected that things might get a little out of hand. The Philly PD, while showing its softer side to tourists, was not exactly known for being hospitable to protesters; as evidenced by their abysmal record during the many civil rights demonstrations that had occurred over the years in North Philly.

As he approached Snyder Avenue, Tony was overtaken with emotion. There were easily 1000 people in the intersection waiting for him. A small loudspeaker was set up, and a couple of the guys had voice amplification apps on their phones, which Tony was able to tap into.

"Wow. I can't believe this turnout. I'm psyched man. I have a few announcements but before that, I have to find my wife. Angela Marie, are you out there? Come on up here with me." Of course, there was silence as no one stepped forward. Secretly he knew that she was being held and would not be there. And yet, calling out her name somehow made him feel close to her, like she was with him on this street.

"Ok listen up. The plan is that we are going to walk up Broad Street toward City Hall. There are groups from the Northeast and North Philly walking South and two others walking east from Southwest and West Philly. The plan is to converge on City Hall to protest against our pro-Abbas Mayor and the president's administration. Try to stay close together. We may engage some of Philly's finest. Do not, I repeat, do not do anything to antagonize the local authorities. We're merely exercising our first amendment rights in protesting. Is that clear?"

Everyone was quiet and in the military fashion, he yelled "I said is that clear." to which everyone yelled "yes."

"Similar marches are occurring today throughout the US, in every major city. We are not alone. Repeat after me "our voices will not be stilled.""

The crowd screamed their approval and headed north chanting "our voices will not be stilled."

With the exception of their voices, which seemed to grow louder by the minute, this city of millions was eerily quiet. It was downright bizarre.

Suddenly Tony realized that something was terribly wrong. It wasn't just that the streets, except for his marchers, were eerily quiet. They should have encountered members of the Philly PD in riot gear by now. The police always patrolled near Broad and Snyder as it was a major intersection in South Philly but after 15 minutes he had not seen one cop.

Tony tapped the general's number on his arm.

"Yes, Tony. How are things going in Philly?"

"Something strange is happening, General."

The General was afraid that he'd be getting calls like this today.

"What is it that you find strange Tony?"

"Well Sir, first off when I came home last night, Angela was nowhere to be found. It was very late general, and she should have been home in bed. I tried to find her but I couldn't. A neighbor said the police took her, but I hoped to see her this morning. She didn't show up at 8 am as we had arranged. Then as we started marching up Broad Street, I realized that there were no Philly police officers out here at all. Not a one, sir. It's very unusual."

Suddenly the noise of the crowd became overshadowed by loud engine roars. Tony looked around and then behind him.

His jaw dropped when he saw that foreign attack helicopters, outfitted with 50 millimeter M250 chain guns, two 7.62 millimeter M134 mini-guns, FIM-132 Stinger missiles, and AGM-124 Hellfire anti-tank guided missiles, were strafing a wide area of the street. The images that Tony saw looked like they were straight out of a modern day war movie.

"Oh shit. General, we've encountered tanks and military helicopters" was all that Tony could get out before the sounds of rapid gunfire and missile explosions deafened his ears.

He started screaming at the top of his lungs for everyone to take cover but there was no way to escape this type of firepower. People were dying all around him as Tony ran up Broad Street. He pushed people out of the way and banged on doors to see if he could find refuge for his charges. Unlike the suburban malls that bristled with activity on holidays, most city businesses were closed for the holiday so Tony yelled to the protesters to start smashing windows so that they could seek refuge indoors.

Unfortunately, the tanks were firing on those buildings as well, and mortar rounds were leveling buildings all around him.

While barking more orders for people to disburse, Tony felt the fury of a 50 mm chain gun, not unlike the stings of hundreds of fire ants. He fell hard to the ground and lay motionless. He could see the clouds casting a shadow over the Broad and Reed street sign, and he felt a few drops of rain begin to fall. Ironically he felt only a little pain but could feel his life seeping out of the tiny holes in his midsection. Tony's mind shifted to his new bride. He hoped that she'd be proud of him today. He said a short prayer for God to help her through what promised to be a difficult time ahead. With tears in his eyes, he whispered "I love you, Angela," as the rain slowly washed away his blood toward a nearby sewer grate.

Chapter 67

"Makim, this is Saadi El-Mofty, are you in position?"

"Yes my friend, what words do you have for me?"

"The Capitol building has been on lockdown as was ordered by the president. An emergency joint session was called, but many of the members are not here as they were not planning on attending any meetings until tomorrow. Some house members are meeting privately in one of the conference rooms. Some of the Senators have been waiting patiently, but they've decided to have breakfast in the Senate Dining Room before meeting with Vice President Rashad, who is on his way and will be joining them. He won't be arriving through the usual entrance though so you'll have to come to the Independence Street entrance on the south side. Hurry, Makim."

Saadi El-Mofty was the Sergeant at Arms who, while required to be at the full joint session meetings, oftentimes attended the House and Senate sessions as well.

He was to be off but, at Makim's request, he stayed in the city to ensure that he would be in the Capitol at 9 am in case he was needed.

He did not know what was planned, and that is how Makim wanted it. In fact, his brother didn't know the entire plan. Makim was thinking outside the box on this one and expanded the plan after receiving a call from Saadi telling him about the members of Congress who were already inside for the planned briefing by the vice president.

Saadi was Makim's best friend back in Syria. Like the Khalid brothers, he lost his parents during one of the Assad civil wars. Saadi was five years older than Makim though so he was able to live on his own. He was present when Makim suffered his tragedy. In fact, Saadi owned the blame, believing it was his fault that his friend lost his arm. Wanting to be a part of the uprising, Saadi had decided to plant a small IED beneath the car of Nizar Zaman, leader of Assad's Royal Guard. Makim was not supposed to be with his friend, but he was curious about what was going on and hoped that he might be of help. The original plan was for Saadi to blow up Zaman's car while it was parked in front of the presidential palace in the west of the city on Mount Mezzeh. However, since the palace encompassed the entire plateau of Mount Mezzeh and was surrounded by a wall with watch towers, the plan was not practical. Instead, Saadi decided that he would wait for a time when Zaman was asked to travel to the Tishreen Palace, located in the Al Rabwah neighborhood of Damascus. A problem with that location was that it was now more of a tourist attraction, so the potential for loss of innocent life was great. Saadi realized that if he waited until the vehicle left to travel back to Mount Mezzeh via Beirut Rd, he could minimize the loss of life of innocent civilians.

Makim watched through binoculars as Saadi dialed the phone number to detonate the bomb. The phone rang silent, as Saadi had planned, with the bomb not immediately exploding. The delay was by design, but Makim didn't know that. The car turned right onto Tishreen Rd. Makim, positioned on Tishreen Rd, thought that there was a problem when the device failed to explode at the time he expected.

Running at an angle to cut the distance between himself and their prey, he approached the car with his gun drawn; prepared to kill Nizar. When he was within several hundred yards of the car he tripped and fell to the ground. The bomb detonated totally destroying the car and several others nearby. The blast incinerated everyone in the car. Doctors said that it was a miracle that Makim had survived. His fall had saved his life but the explosion had ripped his left arm to shreds and caused burns over 30% of his body. Attempts by surgeons to save his arm were fruitless.

Makim never blamed his friend, but they both knew that Saadi was at least partially to blame. He had placed a 5-minute delay on the detonator so that the car would be moving away from Damascus when the bomb went off. Sadly, he forgot to tell Makim about the delay and though he screamed for him to stop, Makim never heard his warning.

When Makim called a few days ago to ask for help, how could Saadi say no?

Chapter 68

Makim, wearing khaki pants, loafers, and a golf shirt, looked like every other tourist. He arrived early at the Rayburn building just southwest of the Capitol to ensure that there would be no problems. Sitting in his car, he loaded his Heckler and Koch Tactical .45 Pistol and attached an AAC Ti-Rant .45 silencer. He stuffed the pistol in the rear waistband of his pants and left the car.

This promised to be much easier than he first expected. During normal working hours, this building was a hub of activity as it was home to over 160 members of the House of Representatives. But members of the House rarely used their offices on holidays. Even if they had to be in DC for a session, they worked in teams within the Capitol building.

Armed with a map of DC in his hands, and a map of the building in his pocket, Makim entered through the main entrance, the only one opened today. Generally, on weekends and holidays, all of the other doors to this building were locked, and there were just two guards posted at a desk near the front door. But with DC on high alert, there were five guards scheduled to work today. Besides the two at the main entrance, there was a guard stationed at pedestrian entrances on South Capitol Street, C Street, and First Street SW.

"Can I help you?" asked one of the guards. Makim handed him a map of the area and, pretending to speak little English, asked the guard if he could mark the nearest Metro stop. As the guard started to write, Makim aimed his pistol and shot the guard in the forehead.

The second guard, who at first paid little attention to what was happening, started to draw his weapon. He probably never heard the almost inaudible whip cracking noise. Yeah right, thought Makim. Two down. Makim loved his toys. He was not using the newest model of its type, but this piece was his favorite as it was truly stealthy. He joked to himself that, it was so quiet; he could barely hear the shot himself.

After locking the front door, he proceeded to walk through the building and with 'military like' precision took out the three remaining security guards.

With the front door locked it was unlikely that even one of the inhabitants with a key would enter the building today but to play it safe he made sure that he moved all of the bodies to out of the way locations. He hoped that any visitors peering through the front door windows would see no guards stationed, and merely leave, thinking that the building was off limits for the holiday. The worst case would be if one of the house members stopped in to use his office. Hopefully, he would simply think that the guard had needed a bathroom break. Makim was confident. He had time.

Makim entered Representative Cox's office on the fourth floor. He opened the window and positioned his rifle on a tripod. As he had explained to General Redmond, he had been a marksman as a young boy and was even better as an adult, but he usually used a handgun, as rifles were harder to operate with one arm. But for today's purpose, the tripod was almost as good as having his arm back. Today's plan was for him to cause a commotion. He would surely do that.

At 9:45 AM, Vice President Rashad, with three secret service agents in tow, walked up New Jersey Avenue from the Capitol South Metro Station. He crossed Independence Avenue and headed toward the House entrance of the Capitol on its south side.

Makim, seeing the back of Rashad's head as he started to turn toward the door, squeezed the trigger. The bullet ripped into the back of the vice president's head. He fell lifeless to the ground.

One agent knelt beside the body with his weapon drawn. The others drew their weapons and looked around for the probable location of the shooter. Three more rapid shots found three more lying dead on the sidewalk.

Capitol police, who were directing traffic at each corner, ran to where the bodies hugged the ground. Passersby flocked to see what had happened. Makim, not worrying about leaving any clues, left his rifle on the floor by the window and walked calmly across Independence Avenue almost parallel to the vice president's body. He looked around like everyone else seemingly bewildered and trying to grasp what had happened. He blended in nicely.

A police officer rushed up and asked Makim what had happened. He simply replied, "I don't know, but it looks like someone has been shot." The officer continued toward the bodies as Makim continued up the walk.

Waiting at the House entrance was his friend with the staffer nametag and credentials that he had prepared on Friday. Makim thanked Saadi and told him to leave from the opposite side of the building to avoid even the slightest hint of wrongdoing. He put the nametag and credentials in his pocket. He admitted his eight accomplices but told them to wait for him at the door. "I'm pretty sure I have this under control but I'll call if I need you." He headed for the Senate Dining Room where they were to begin the takeover of the building, holding those inside hostage.

Just outside the room, he met a young man bringing a cart with a mix of breakfast sandwiches and fruit on it. He pulled his handgun and, pointing it at the young staffer, told him to leave his white jacket and to run out of the building as fast as possible.

He affixed the nametag to the jacket, put it on over his vest, and rolled the cart inside; positioning it in the center of the dining room. He stopped to look around. There were at least 20 senators in the room.

Qasim will be so proud; he thought as he pulled out and depressed the small button detonating the explosives that he had hidden beneath the white jacket. The vest held enough nails, screws, bolts, and C4 to destroy the entire room and *everyone* in it.

Chapter 69

The command post was abuzz with activity. Karen had gone out to get two dozen donuts for everyone at the local Dunkers Best. Josh didn't think his men needed any more sugar to keep them revved up. Each had a donut and appreciated the gesture.

The early reports coming in gave Josh some concern. In Boston, New York, Philly, and Atlanta, the news was that the marchers were moving through the streets unencumbered. The same held true in the Central, Mountain, and Pacific zones. The leaders in various western cities didn't seem as concerned because the time difference meant that it was very early and police patrols at that hour were not as common. But even those locales reported that it was eerily quiet as there was little to no police presence.

"Gentleman," Josh began. "I was just on the phone with Tony DiPietro in Philadelphia. Tony was telling me that his wife, Angela, had neither been seen nor heard from since Thursday afternoon when he left for New York. During his report about the unexpected quiet, Tony said something that was inaudible. I heard him say 'Oh shit. General' but then there was so much static that I couldn't hear what he was saying. Suddenly there was nothing. I phoned his deputy as well as two others from Philly on our secured network, and no one answered."

"We know that the rallies all began at 0800 EDT. Please reach out to your field commanders and let's get some video feed so that we can see what is happening in each city. Even if they haven't started marching, call them and let them know that we would like them to report back to us after the first 15 minutes.

"Josh, you have to see this," said General Rivera. "I have a video feed from Col. Harrington in Atlanta." On the screen was live footage of the Nationalist's running and being gunned down on Peachtree Street. Their opposition was using rapid fire automatic weapons, LAV's with Bushmasters, and strafing fire from attack helicopters.

A call came in from Washington, DC. The general in charge there, oddly enough General Washington, reported that he was in touch with his key personnel in the Secret Service, who were stationed at the White House. These men were prepared to switch sides to help secure the White House with some of the general's Special Forces. They reported that there were Syrian and Irani tanks surrounding the White House; not in an offensive but a defensive posture. They also reported that there were 5 Syrian Attack Helicopters on the heliport. There was no way that this was going to be an easy takeover.

"What do you think we should do General?" asked Washington.

Josh didn't hesitate. "General have your men stand down for now."

"What do make of this Raymond?" asked Josh.

"I don't know. Washington's report confirmed my fear, Josh. I thought the LAVs and helicopters might be either Chinese or Russian made. Now I'm convinced that they are. However, the forces using them seem to be part of the Syrian and Irani military."

Another image came across the screen from one of the field soldiers in Chicago and, like those in Atlanta, these scenes were horrifying as Americans were shown being gunned down in the streets, offering little resistance. "General, I can see the decal on one of the planes," interjected US Air Force General O'Meara. "Give me a minute and I'll make it out." After about 30 seconds, O'Meara reported: "Sir, there is no doubt that the symbol on those helicopter gunships is the Syrian Eagle."

They stood there, stunned, as they watched image after image of the Syrian helicopters attacking the citizens of Atlanta. These weren't like normal military maneuvers, though. It was more like the Syrians had gone crazy firing on everyone that moved. At first, it looked like just protestors, but then it became apparent that the choppers were firing heavy machine guns indiscriminately into crowds of people and that American men, women, and children were being killed in mass. Tanks rolled over people blocking their paths like bowling balls mowing down pins. From the looks of things, it appeared that thousands had been killed in just a few minutes since they had started watching.

"Gentleman," said Josh. We had hoped to distract the White House and Congress with peaceful protest marches with maybe a scattering of violence. It now appears that our country is under attack by foreign forces. You will eventually need to go back to your posts in Washington to command your units but for now, you must get all of your units deployed against this apparent invasion by the forces from Syria and Iran. I'm going to make a statement via webcam that will be picked up by the major news sources.

Calls started to come in rapid succession followed by images. The images revealed a horror that no one anticipated.

"General, this is Qasim, and I have very bad news. We have major problems here in Boston as our foot soldiers are being gunned down by LAV's with both Irani flags and Syrian Eagles on the side, a few fighter jets also from Iran, and the worst damage has been caused by Syrian Helicopters with both machine gun and small missile capabilities. I've spoken to Tarif, and that seems to be the case in DC too, but I haven't had much time for TV. Is this what we're facing in other cities?"

"I'm afraid that is the story on the east coast and in some of the Midwest cities."

"Well, it's the worst scenario, General. The foreign troops seem to be firing with a vengeance on everyone whether they were protesting or not. I believe that they have gone rogue and had planned all along to take revenge on the United States for the years of fighting in their countries; fighting that saw thousands of innocent civilians slaughtered by coalition forces. I'll keep you posted, but it's very bleak here as it looks like thousands are dead. I have well placed friends in Syria and Iran, General, and as far as anyone knows there has been no declaration of war by either country. I expected some intervention by the US military, but I've seen no evidence that our national guard has even been deployed to defend the city."

"I'm not totally surprised. Abbas must have had even better intelligence than I thought and he must be crazier than I thought."

"If he can sneak away, Tarif is going to call you on the White House phone with some new developments on his end, General."

A very dejected Josh hung up the phone. He could only imagine what went wrong.

"Gentlemen I'm awaiting a call from Tarif at the White House to brief me on what is going on with the troops and our government. Please keep talking to those in the field. We are at war."

As he waited, he saw images of other cities on the monitors around the room. As was happening in Boston and Atlanta; protesters in Dallas, Houston, Phoenix, San Diego, Denver and one could only assume LA and San Francisco were dealing with devastating firepower from heavily armed military aircraft, vehicles, and then ground troops. The resistance is minimal as the Nationalists have nothing but handguns and a few rifles. They were planning to have to engage some local police and maybe some national guardsmen, most of whom would be ordered by their commanders to lay down their arms and side with them. No one was prepared for this.

"General," said Raymond Rivera, "we are not able to reach any of the leaders in the field. All of our communication lines are down. The video feeds have also gone out, so we're in the dark, General. All we have are the few phones with secured lines but those aren't enough to assist our ground troops. We can't even reach the National Guard commanders to see if there is some way that we could deploy them. We've been totally blacked out, Sir."

An ashen-faced Josh stood for several minutes in the center of the room just staring into space. Finally, his private phone rang.

"Yes."

"General, this is Tarif. I can't talk long. I'm afraid I'll be discovered. The president learned that I was not in Boston and he summoned me to White House first thing this morning. I can't say how but the president and his staff were able to smoke out your plan. Knowing that our armed services were likely compromised, the president asked Syria and Iran for help in defending the country from an insurrection. What was first promised, a few hundred troops, were expanded later to tens of thousands of troops and hundreds of tanks, LAVs, helicopters, and about several hundred fighter jets. The president promised that actions by these *allied* troops were needed to restore order and would not be viewed as an attack on the United States. These troops along with air and ground attack vehicles were redeployed from major bases to all of the major cities in the US. As the protest marches unfolded, the attack began. There was no provocation, General."

Josh was sick to his stomach about what was happening and upset by the indifferent tone of Tarif's report. While he appreciated the update from Tarif, it was troubling to learn hours later that the president had called Tarif to the White House. Equally disturbing was his use of the words "your plan", and hearing his unemotional account of the massive onslaught by enemy troops that caught them all by surprise.

Tarif continued. "At 0830 EDT the Secretary of Defense ordered all US troops to be placed on standby but that they were to 'stand down,' meaning that under no circumstances should they deploy without his direct orders. As you may have guessed, the entire secure DOD network including all audio and video feeds have been shut down. The only working communications is a new channel that was secretly set up last week for the president and Secretary of Defense to communicate with the Syrian and Irani generals who are controlling their troops. As of 10 minutes ago, it was reported that the attacks have claimed the lives of thousands of Americans."

"General, there doesn't seem to be any way to defend against this. I've spoken to President Abbas, and I told him about how our innocent civilians are being slaughtered in the streets. His view is that he has allies putting down a revolt. I suggested military action, or, at least, halting the Syrian and Irani forces so that we can assess the damage, but he said that he won't do that until there is complete order."

"I'm sorry General, but it looks like your mission has failed. The president will be going on TV to declare martial law in a short while. He will continue using foreign military until his advisors assure him that the US Military is again under his control. Of course, I'll stay on as White House Chief of Staff as I think that is where I can best serve my country."

"I see. Does Abbas suspect that any of the Joint Chiefs were involved in today's actions or does he merely think that he's stopped some independent rioting?"

"General, he suspects that there was much more to this plot but I don't believe that he has any real proof. He was able to gather intel about the street rioting and thought that if he could disrupt that, any other plans would be total failures."

"Thanks again, Tarif."

Josh hit the end button and looked around the room at the sad faces. "I was afraid that our first plan might fail but I never dreamed that a sitting president would call for foreign attacks on his citizenry. Gentleman, Plan B is our only recourse. I need you to follow the directions in your plans to a T. Your first job is to get on your secured private phones since the regular military network is compromised."

"First connect with your direct reports in the field. Tell them to stand down and inform them that you are on your way to Washington. They know what that means. Then call your bosses in Washington on the standard lines to see if they are working. If they are not, use your private lines for the 2nd call as well. Your message should be simple and short. Tell them that you just heard what is going on, and you're on your way back to Washington. Sound appalled. You need to sell this. Remember, you're coming off of a three-day holiday, nothing more. You are returning to take command of your troops, follow up on today's events, and make preparations to ensure that your regimens will be battle ready. Do this in the order upon which we had agreed. Every 5 minutes the next person will make his calls until you've all been able to speak to your leaders and either the Secretary of Defense or Chairman of the Joint Chiefs. Is that understood?"

They all nodded. "Good. God bless you all for your service and let's move on."

As they were about to leave, Josh's phone rang.

Chapter 70

Even though it was a holiday and a planned day off, the president had requested that his key people be on hand at the White House. That included his military advisors who, on a normal work day, manned their offices in the Pentagon.

Inside the White House, Defense Secretary Hakim Bahar had arranged for a conference room because he wanted to hold a special security briefing to discuss their next move in dealing with the uprising and securing government buildings and the streets of major cities with US troops.

In the meeting with the secretary were General Elway Bishop Chairman of the Joint Chiefs, Sadeem Ali, the Director of the Secret Service, and Demetri Kotsopouos, Deputy Defense Secretary.

Bahar began. "Everyone knows where we stand but briefly, the protesters are not giving up, even in the face of large numbers of citizens who have been gunned down by Syrian and Irani forces. In fact, in spite of that, the number of people who have taken to the streets of our cities has grown, and the number of cities in which protests are occurring has increased, now including many of the smaller cities like St. Louis, Memphis, Raleigh, and Richmond."

I was hoping that we could have the foreign forces stand down, but it looks like we will need them to continue the crackdown."

"Hakim," said Demetri, "I'm guessing that the news reports of foreign troops killing US citizens are pissing people off, and that has spurred more of them to action. We have to end this carnage. I've heard reports that there have been tens of thousands of citizens killed. I don't think we have much choice but to decide right here and now that our number one priority must be to protect our citizens. We have to decide how to deploy our troops to end this mess."

"If I may," interrupted General Bishop. "Demetri, I'm afraid that we have to keep our troops on stand by and not deploy them. We can't risk having the governments of Syria and Iran angry with the president if some of our troops decided to defend the protesters. After all he did ask for their help and technically these people are criminals; evidenced by their unlawful behavior."

Hakim asked Sadeem his thoughts. "Well Hakim, I tend to agree with General Bishop. The president will look bad. He's gone out of his way to bind with countries in the Middle East and to do anything to harm that hard work would be devastating to our efforts there. Personally, I see our jobs as ensuring we protect our leaders and that our federal buildings are secured. It's easier for me to do that if the rioters are kept at bay as they have been over the past couple of hours."

"I agree," said Hakim. "The only way that we'll be able to restore order is to secure our buildings and protect our leaders and allow the foreign forces to perform as we have asked."

Demetri spoke up again. "But what if this fighting continues for days, Hakim? How will any of us be able to look in a mirror knowing that we could have stopped this today and avoided more bloodshed?"

"In our jobs we're asked to make tough decisions, and this is probably one of the most difficult decisions we'll ever have to make. But I think we need to let this play out, and if there is more loss of life, I will be saddened, but I will also know that the protesters started this by taking to the streets and that our friends from Syria and Iran are simply helping us defend our Republic."

Demetri wondered how anyone could say, let alone believe, this last statement given that the Syrian and Irani troops were in position well before one protester took to the streets.

"If there is nothing else, gentlemen, I have to brief the president on our decision."

As the Secretary of Defense, sitting to Demetri's right stood to leave he was killed by a single bullet to his forehead. Stunned, General Bishop and Sadeem Ali turned to see Demetri aiming an HK 45C. The general opened his mouth as if he was going to protest but he was dead before uttering a word. Sadeem started to attack but, given that he was over 3 feet away and on the opposite side of the conference table, he had no prayer. Like the others, Sadeem was dead in seconds.

Demetri put the gun back in his jacket pocket and left the conference room to return to his office to make a call to The Pentagon.

He spoke to David Bushway, Executive Secretary of the DOD.

"David, this is Demetri over at the White House. I have some bad news. Secretary Bahar suffered a massive stroke during a meeting here. He died a short while ago."

"Oh my God. I just spoke to the Secretary an hour or so ago."

"Yes, he mentioned that which is why I'm calling. It's very upsetting, but I've been put in charge and will be carrying out a mission that he had proposed. This mission was discussed at great length, and agreed upon at our meeting."

Demetri updated David on a new plan that he had proposed during the meeting. David was a good guy and someone who never questioned orders. And for David, national security was priority number one.

Chapter 71

Josh answered his phone as everyone in the Command Post froze.

"General, this is Tarif again. Do you have the news on the TV?"

"No," said Josh. "We've seen enough on TV. Fill me in. What's happening?"

"Well General, I was called out of a meeting with the president. I don't know if you heard or not, but the vice president and at least 20 members of Congress were assassinated this morning."

Makim succeeded, thought Josh. "Fill me in."

"After shooting the VP, who was walking toward the Capitol, Makim made his way inside but instead of securing the facility, as you had planned, he armed himself with C4 and blew himself and everyone in the Senate lunchroom to bits. The president called us in to discuss the Capitol situation when all hell broke loose here."

"What do you mean, Tarif?"

"There had been a strategy meeting called by Secretary of Defense Bahar. Demetri Kotsopoulos, General Bishop, and Sadeem Ali were in attendance."

Tarif filled the general in on what Demetri had told him had transpired at the meeting.

"The President doesn't even know all of this yet, General, but as they adjourned, Demetri pulled a pistol that he had hidden inside his jacket and killed all three in a matter of seconds."

"Oh my God, where is Demetri now?" asked Josh.

"He's here with me now, and he wants to talk to you, but he's on another line so I'll finish up. Demetri called the Pentagon and told DOD Executive Secretary Bushway that Hakim had died of a stroke and that, as Deputy Defense Secretary, he was now in charge. His first order to Bushway was the re-installation of all military communications."

Josh turned to the members of the Joint Chiefs. "Try your main communication lines to see if they're open for communication with your field personnel."

A cacophony filled the room. "General, the lines are open," they all said, almost in unison as if it had been rehearsed.

"Holy crap" was all that Josh could manage.

"Josh," Demetri had joined the conversation from the White House. "Put me on speakerphone if you would. I guess that Tarif has filled you in by now. I may be tried for treason, but I couldn't stand by and watch thousands of Americans being slaughtered in the streets. I tried to talk sense into them, but they wouldn't listen. I had no choice but to take control. I've ensured that all of our military communications are open again. What we need to do is to use our forces to protect our citizens. I've just spoken with Deputy Chairman of the Joint Chiefs, Admiral John Barrington, and he and I are in complete agreement on this."

"Gentlemen, contact your field generals immediately. Order them to take whatever action is necessary to defend our country and its citizens. That includes deploying several brigades to our cities. I realize that the president asked for the foreigner's help, but I believe that taking this action is not only just but critical."

"I could not agree more, Demetri, and for what it's worth I think you're a hero, not a traitor."

"Thanks, Josh, I have one last thing. I've spoken to the president about this."

"You spoke to the president? Why didn't you kill him?"

"If I could have, I would have General, but he's now holed up in the White House bunker. He's really on high alert."

"He damned well should be."

"General, I'm sorry that you're disappointed, but I hadn't planned any of this. I was flying by the seat of my pants. I would have loved nothing more, but I had to check my weapon before seeing him. I thought for sure that someone would have realized that my gun had been recently fired, but they allowed me to put it in a basket outside the room."

"I understand, Demetri, and I'm not disappointed in you. It's just that it was a missed opportunity."

"No doubt but there was no way that I was going to be able to pull it off. There were four armed guards outside the room and another four inside. Plus the president was carrying. In any event, he was not happy, but he recognized that there was nothing that he could do about it. I don't think our original plan is going to work though unless we create a mess here at the White House so I'd suggest that we table that for now and start protecting our cities and people. We'll worry about the president later."

"I already scrapped our plans, Demetri, and we're moving on to Plan B."

"Good. That's all I have for now. Get to work, people. Good luck and keep me posted."

"Thanks, Demetri. We will."

Josh looked around the room, and the Joint Chiefs were already on the phones talking to their field personnel about what was needed and the best strategy to employ.

Chapter 72

With the Joint Chiefs headed back to DC, a dejected Josh Redmond finished packing their suitcases by putting their near perfectly forged passports into the zipper compartment. With Karen by his side, he set out from their home on Long Island on his predetermined escape route, ironically in a Ford Escape that he had rented under an alias.

Luckily for them, Josh's old wartime buddy, BGen Martin Tremblay, who had served with him in Iraq, was retired from the Canadian Army and living in Toronto now.

Josh suspected that Abbas would make sure that the military and Staties had all of the preferred major highways on high alert. Having ensured that no one knew what car they were driving would help, but Josh decided to take the safest available route. Instead of the more direct 8-hour drive north through upstate NY and PA, he and Karen were taking back roads through Pennsylvania to Cleveland, avoiding the Pennsylvania Turnpike at all costs. They would then drive to Detroit and from there into Canada.

They had gotten a later start than planned, leaving at 1 pm. First Josh had to secure his command center which meant gathering up and packing all of the small devices, like phones and flash drives and then wiping out everything on the larger electronic hard drives, screens, computer history, and even burning all of the previously shredded notes. He wasn't taking any chances. In fact, Josh had thought of completely destroying the entire basement but, always the optimist, he thought that it might come in handy when they returned home. Plus it was designed to withstand almost any attack, and he didn't have the time or know how to pull that off.

After he was sure that all was secure at home they drove both the rental and their Toyota sedan to the Smith Haven Train Station. Leaving their personal car at the station would throw everyone off track, giving them a much-needed head start.

Karen, being a soldier's wife, was used to moving around a lot. But Josh knew what she had wanted in retirement, namely tranquility and stability. In one of her more fanciful moments, before the chaos began, she actually spoke about loving their retirement home because it meant that they were truly retired. But here they were on the run. He knew that she didn't want to leave their home and yet she hadn't said a word. She understood why they had to leave and what was at stake.

The drive was going to take them over 17 hours, so it was important that they have some good music, as defined by Josh. So for 17 hours, Karen, who much preferred either jazz or classical music, would be treated to some of the best the 1960s had to offer including music by legends like Jimi Hendrix, Janis Joplin, The Doors, and The Beatles.

> "Pleased to meet you
> Hope you guess my name
> But what's puzzling you
> Is the nature of my game."

The Rolling Stones "Sympathy for the Devil," playing now, only served to remind Josh of the devil he was leaving behind.

"How long do you think we'll have to stay in Canada?" Karen always interrupted his favorite tunes.

"I don't know sweetie. A lot will depend on what happens over the next few weeks. If all goes according to plan, I'm hoping that we'll be able to return stateside by Christmas."

Josh was grateful that she didn't have a follow-up question. He could get back to Mick Jagger. Josh loved how this song conjured up his image of Ahmad Abbas

> *"Just as every cop is a criminal*
> *And all the sinners saints*
> *As heads is tails*
> *Just call me Lucifer*
> *Cause I'm in need of some restraint."*

Josh's mind raced. He hated to leave; to run away. He was a fighter and had hoped for a better outcome, one that would have him receiving a hero's welcome as he rode into the nation's capital as the champion of the people. He had dreamt so much about that in recent weeks that he had convinced himself that there would be no need for Plan B.

But, he had been wise to have this backup plan. It was the right plan, one he had concocted when he had been calm and thinking clearly, not dreaming. Once emotions get involved, bad decisions are made. And the last 12 hours had been one emotional roller coaster. Many of his friends had died or been arrested. He thought that there was hope following Dimitri's bold action. But now he and Karen were fleeing, and it made no sense to change plans. It was the time to follow the plan.

Josh recalled another time when he was forced to retreat. He was commandeering the takeover of Nad-e Ali District of Helmand province in Afghanistan. Expecting little resistance, Josh had ordered just one armored division into the city to back up a couple of infantry units. To their surprise, the city had become a Taliban fortress. Josh would have liked to have stayed to fight but remembering an old idiom that his father often used *discretion is the better part of valor*, led Josh to the conclusion that it was better to retreat and *live to fight another day.*

"Yes that is exacly what I'm doing", whispered Josh to himself. All of the Joint Chiefs were assuming their positions back in Washington. They had been well schooled in playing the part of disbelieving loyalists who supported the president. Josh had already seen an interview with Admiral Barrington in which he denounced the cowards who would discard the Constitution for their personal gains or because of a personal gripe with the administration. The admiral might just win an Oscar for his performance.

So here they were Mr. and Mrs. Benedict Arnold, as they were no doubt being characterized, on a nice leisurely ride through the country on a beautifully bright and sunny summer afternoon. In another 15 hours, they'd be in Toronto having breakfast with his friend, Martin, ready to work on the final details of Plan B.

As he headed toward Detroit, Josh made a spur of the moment decision to avoid the downtown Detroit area and the heavy security of the Detroit-Windsor Tunnel. He would take one of the bridges instead. Most people traveling from the east would logically take the tunnel.

If Abbas was onto him, as he suspected, it was more likely that he had beefed up security at those border crossings more so than at one of the bridges, especially The Ambassador Bridge, which was southwest of the city. No one would suspect that he'd arrive from the west.

The Ambassador offered a better chance for him and Karen to cross without much suspicion. It was usually more congested on holidays. But, considering the time of day and everything that was going on in the country, he figured that traffic would move quickly.

Josh swung his car south and then west ensuring that he would be approaching the city from the western side. He would encounter border patrol at the entrance to the one and half mile long bridge.

The shorter route would have been to take I-75 North from Toledo but Josh branched off onto I-275N that cut north between Ann Arbor and Dearborn. Karen was asleep. He wasn't afraid, but he was anxious. He'd been to Windsor many times but had always taken either the tunnel or the Gordie Howe Bridge.

His thoughts shifted to what was happening back east. He thought about calling their children but knew that wasn't the best idea. He was reasonably sure that they were safe. Instead, he turned on a radio news station but what was being reported as breaking news wasn't much different than what he had already heard before he left home. As usual, reporters were trampling over each other for every morsel of news.

Josh put in a couple of Moody Blues CDs. "Nights in White Satin" was infinitely more relaxing and he started to feel better, a little more at ease. Plus Karen could easily sleep through the softer music. He was going to take I-96 near Plymouth and head east but then decided to take I-94 instead.

He drove on I-94 through Wayne County for about 30 miles but then fear struck him again, so he opted to take the smaller Rt 39 toward Lincoln Park and drive up north from there on a parallel back road.

About 2 miles from the I-75 interchange, he saw a flashing light behind him. "Shit," he said aloud, waking Karen.

"My goodness, why the cussin'?"

"We're getting pulled over."

He pulled over to the side of the road and waited for the Wayne County squad car that pulled up behind him.

He reached under his seat for his old M-11 pistol. He held it in his left hand, between the seat and the car door.

298

"Yes officer is there a problem?" said Josh.

"License and registration."

Great, thought Josh.

He handed the paperwork to the patrolman.

"Did I do something wrong officer?"

The officer looked at the license. "I clocked you at 70 mph, Mr. Gladstone. The speed limit here is 50."

"I'm sorry officer. I'd appreciate it if you could cut us a break. I'll be more careful."

"Where are you headed, Mr. Gladstone?"

"We're headed to Windsor for a family reunion."

The cop looked over his fake license and then at the rental information.

"This isn't your car, sir?"

Josh wanted to say something smart like *no shit Sherlock* but decided to bite his tongue.

"No officer. Our car broke down, so we had to rent a car."

"I see. I'll be right back. Just stay in your car."

"I'm scared Josh."

"It'll be ok.

The officer returned.

"Can I ask you to step out of the car, Mr. Gladstone?"

"Is there a problem, officer?"

"Just step out of the car."

Seeing Josh's left hand moving up from his side, Karen screamed "No Josh!"

A single shot exploded when it hit the center of the officer's chest. *Collateral damage*, thought Josh.

With military like precision he went into *mop up* mode. He put on a pair of gloves, exited the car, and bent over to touch the cop's carotid artery. There was no pulse. He took back his license and other paperwork from the cop's right hand. He read his name tag; Sgt. Hanratty. "Sorry Hanratty," he said. *The poor son of a bitch was just doing his job,* he thought.

He was going to ask Karen to help, but she looked as lifeless sitting in the car as the slain cop did on the ground. He dragged the sergeant's body back to the squad car and flung him onto the passenger's seat before driving the car into an even more secluded area to the right of the road.

Back in the car, he asked Karen if she was ok. She was shaking and crying now. He wanted to help her, but there was nothing he could say or do for her right now. He sped away.

Once again he improvised deciding to pick up I-75 and take that to The Gordie Howe Bridge. He estimated that he was only about 10 miles away. One saving grace was that he was very familiar with the Canadian side of the bridge. Once across he'd take the Rt. Hon. Herb Gray Parkway onto Ontario Highway 401. That would give him a pretty fast traffic route until he could jump onto some back roads.

His mind was racing again. He still had to deal with the border patrol. And Karen's crying wasn't helping.

"I need you to calm down. And for God's sake don't scream if you see me lift this revolver. We were lucky. That was just one unsuspecting cop on a dark back road. There will be more people at the bridge. I don't want to kill anyone, but if I have to, I need to know that I can count on you to keep quiet. Otherwise, we're in prison or dead by morning. Do you understand?"

Karen sniffled but nodded her agreement. She was scared more about what she had just witnessed than what might happen to them. *So this is how men at war behave*, she thought.

Josh hoped that they would be ok since it was unlikely anyone would have found the Sergeant's body that quickly. But a part of him was still nervous. He was sure Sgt. Hanratty had run the car rental information through some system. Did anyone know that Simon Gladstone was Josh Redmond?

He approached the checkpoint with his hand on his gun. The border guard checked their phony passports, asked them about their plans in Canada and, accepting that they were law abiding US citizens visiting some Canadian friends, returned their paperwork and waved them through.

Josh let out a sigh of relief, turned the CD player back on, and drove across the bridge and onto Herb Gray Parkway.

Chapter 73

President Abbas was seated in the Oval Office, prepared to deliver the speech of his life. It was to be broadcast worldwide.

While TV crews were busy readying the oval office, the president reflected on all that had happened over the past several hours. It was disheartening to learn that fellow Muslims had sided with the infidels who wanted to remove him from office and do harm to his most trusted friends and advisors. The identity of the Capitol Hill Bomber, Makim Khalid, was learned through a letter that he had left in Representative Cox's office in the Rayburn Building across from the Capitol.

Makim Khalid, thought President Abbas, *was a swine who assuredly caused the despicable murder of his cousin, Omar. I curse you for your transgressions.*

Feeling certain that Makim's brother, Qasim was also involved, the president had ordered Agent Sanchez to have the Boston field office of the FBI seek him out and arrest him on suspicion of treason.

"Agent Sanchez, if you can arrest him, that will be fine, but I want him completely neutralized. Do you understand me?"

"Yes, Mr. President. We will take Qasim Khalid dead or alive."

Well, thought Ahmad, *Makim is undoubtedly suffering in his grave, and hopefully, his brother will soon be either in custody or joining him. And he, Ahmad Abbas, was very much alive and still President of the United States.* Loud enough to be heard by all he said: "Burn in hell, Makim."

"We're ready for you, Mr. President," announced the emotionless voice of the television director.

His heart and mind were racing. His palms were sweaty. The green light came on, and the president began.

"Good afternoon my fellow citizens: A lot has happened today, and I'm joining you in your living rooms to bring you a personal update on what has transpired and what I expect to occur in the days ahead."

"First let me assure you that I am committed to protecting the lives of every American and I will do everything in my power to protect our country and its citizens."

"Earlier today an attempt was made to take over our government. Vice President Rashad was shot and killed outside of the Capitol prior to a scheduled meeting with some key members of Congress. At about the same time, someone was able to infiltrate the White House and kill Secretary of Defense Hakim Bahar, General Elway Bishop, Chairman of the Joint Chiefs, and Sadeem Ali, the Director of the Secret Service. These are heinous and despicable acts, and when we learn the identities of the persons who masterminded these attacks, they will be dealt with in a most severe manner."

"Additionally, twenty members of the Senate were killed along with a suicide bomber who invaded their hallowed chambers. Ten members of the House are in critical condition at area hospitals."

"This was obviously a well-planned and coordinated attack and based on information that is still coming in, what has happened is only a small part of the master plan to take control of our government."

"Knowing that something was amiss, but unsure how deeply the infiltration into our government and Armed Forces was, I asked for some help from our allies; Syria and Iran, who, in accordance with our recent cooperation treaties, agreed to send a peacekeeping force to the United States. These troops came here under the pretense of participating in joint military exercises but were fully aware of the dangers they faced."

"Many citizens in our largest cities jammed the streets seemingly to protest this deployment, but I have irrefutable evidence that these citizens were nothing more than a diversion, a shell game so to speak, that was planned by the traitors who wanted to take control of our government."

"Sadly, the Syrian and Irani forces were forced to do a lot more than keeping the peace. They deployed many more troops than were needed; the result was the death of thousands of Americans."

"Your government could not allow this brutal and senseless killing of innocent American citizens to continue. We spoke to the leaders of these allied forces, and when the fighting not only continued but escalated, I had no choice but to consider their actions to be acts of war and to order our armed forces into action to protect our cities, our citizens, and our Republic."

"Over 500 F-37 Stealth Fighters, Osprey and Sioux Helicopters, and ten divisions of LAVs, with 50 teams each were deployed and were successful in their missions but not without significant loss of life and property. While there are still protests going on, I'm confident that our police and National Guard units will be able to restore order in a matter of a few days."

"Reacting to the news of our defensive actions, this afternoon at 2:45 pm EDT, the governments of Syria and Iran, declared that a state of war existed between their respective countries and the United States."

"Secretary of State al-Bashir called the presidents of both countries in an attempt to work out an appropriate end to hostilities, but they rebuffed his proposals. On my authority, he then expelled Anas Al-Hamsi, the Ambassador from Syria and Pooria Shahrestaani the Ambassador from Iran. They are on their way back to their homelands as I speak to you. The secretary then called for the immediate withdraw of all of our diplomatic personnel in both countries. Unfortunately, all had already been taken hostage by the governments of Syria and Iran. Also, Syrian and Irani fighter aircraft have attacked US bases in Kuwait, Bahrain, and Iraq."

"I have demanded the release of all American political prisoners. To counter this aggression, conventional and nuclear forces have been moved to DEFCON 2. I have also ordered the dispatch of additional troops to our bases in Turkey, Saudi Arabia, Iraq, and Afghanistan. Furthermore, the US Navy's Fifth and Sixth Fleets have been deployed to the Persian Gulf. "

"One hour ago, I declared martial law with a curfew of 8 pm across the United States. The only exemptions to this being mission critical personnel such as police, fire, and essential hospital employees. I'm hopeful that this curfew will be lifted in a few days when peace is restored to our cities."

"Lastly, my fellow Americans, I have asked the Selective Service System to institute the lottery system draft as a precaution. Our troops are spread thin and our preparedness may be compromised without additional troops."

"I know that these are troubling times, but I want to assure each and every American that I will protect and defend our country at all costs. I have no doubt that I will prevail."

"Thank you. May Allah bless you, may He bless our troops, and may He bless the United States of America."

Chapter 74

Karen missed her home but was enjoying her stay in Canada. Since they weren't going to be there for more than a week or so, it was more like being on vacation at a bed and breakfast than being in hiding. The only negative for her was that, while no one knew them in Canada, they still had to be careful to stay inside. When this whole thing is over, she thought, she'd like to come back for a visit and see the area.

The Tremblay's made them feel right at home. She got along fabulously with Lee as the two women had green thumbs and a passion for cooking in common. Josh and Martin likewise shared many interests, not the least of which was how to defeat the enemy. In fact Josh had commented earlier about how Martin's military acumen had helped him refine his plans. He seemed really happy to be there was well, but the tension was beginning to show on him. He spent a lot of time on the phone and on Martin's computer, making plans no doubt. She sensed that he was feeling a degree of urgency about getting back to the states.

Both couples watched anxiously as The President of the United States addressed a worldwide television audience.

"Can you believe that bastard is taking credit for saving American lives when he's the one who brought the foreigners and their death machines to the US in the first place? I'm the one who ordered our troops to defend our country. It was me who saved lives, not Abbas. Damn it that pisses me off."

The Tremblay's nodded their heads.

Karen, noting the irony of her husband's outrage, just smiled.

Chapter 75

Saul anxiously watched the TV reports of what was happening around the country.

July 11th was the 7th day of fighting. The VAPTs and news reports were coming in from around the country where anti-Abbas citizens had again taken to the streets demanding his impeachment.

"This is Rakeem Rasul of CNN reporting the latest on the uprising that is taking place around the country. We take you first to CNN Reporter, John Anderson, in New York."

"Thanks, Rakeem. Earlier today there was a great deal of gunfire and explosions could be heard scattered throughout the city. It was an ugly scene. I'm on the streets now and it's much quieter. The fighting started in the wee hours of the morning of July 4th as hundreds of thousands of people marched peacefully in all five boroughs, protesting the administration of President Ahmad Abbas. While there was a lot of confusion, it now appears that a peaceful protest turned ugly when, seeing armed military in their way, rebel protesters began to attack some small but heavily armed combatants. The ground troops began what would be days of carnage by firing into the crowds and things took a drastic turn when attack helicopters and light armored vehicles fired at will on anyone who was in their path. It has since been learned that these armed forces were divisions of the Syrian and Irani military."

The next several minutes of TV video displayed the death and destruction on the streets as the newsman continued with his report. "As scores of Americans fell dead on the streets of the city, US Special Forces and US Air Force Apache helicopters were ordered to protect the protesters from further assault. As you can hear, they are still flying overhead. The counter attacks successfully destroyed many of the foreign assault vehicles but not without much loss of life. The damage to buildings in New York City alone is estimated to be billions of dollars. After their great success in repelling the foreign troops, most of our military forces were called back to base, planes were grounded, and fighting stopped."

"The protesters returned to the streets the following day and for the seventh straight day, rioting has been the story on the streets of New York City and around the country. There are National Guard troops trying to maintain order as what remained of the Syrian and Irani forces have returned home. Thus far in New York, almost 50,000 people, mostly patriots, or Nationalists as we've heard them called, have been killed in seven days of rioting, but the streets seem eerily quiet as we head into nightfall." This is John Anderson reporting for CNN in New York City."

"We now take you to Philadelphia where Diondre Brooks is on the scene. Diondre, are you there?"

"Yes Rakeem, I can hear you."

"Tell us about what has happened there and what is the mood of the city," said Rakeem.

"For the first time in 7 days, it's quiet here in Philadelphia where the loss of life has exceeded 20,000 people. But the loss of infrastructure and buildings has been significant as well. What started as peaceful protests early in the morning of July 4th turned violent when foreign military helicopters began circling above the city. Seeing the protesters running through the streets, the pilots turned their helicopters to intercept the Patriots and opened fire on them using a combination of high capacity machine guns and sidewinder missiles. Hours later, planes and helicopters from Maguire and Dover Air Force Bases were deployed to protect the protesters and repel the foreign forces. The entire Philadelphia transit system was virtually shut down by the military at the onset of this uprising. Delays were reported soon after the fighting started, as Nationalists claimed responsibility for the mid-air explosion that completely obliterated a plane carrying some key government personnel flying back to Washington to brief the president. Since then, there have been few flights out of Philadelphia International Airport and the airport remains shut down for all intents and purposes. Much of downtown Philadelphia including its most cherished landmarks was destroyed."

Again, the video feed showed the impact of missile firings on Independence Hall, Carpenter's Hall, and The Constitution Center. All had been totally destroyed. The streets were littered with pieces of downed foreign planes and helicopters.

"Fire and rescue units have been working diligently to free people who have been trapped in subway cars and stations. Concerned friends and family members are holding vigils near city hall and at various subway station stops. People are waiting patiently for word about the fate of loved ones believed to have been riding the subway when the attacks occurred. We have only unconfirmed reports on the number of dead. There has been no official word on the extent of casualties and officials here are reluctant to even speculate on the number of missing. I'll have an update within the next couple of hours. This is Diondre Brooks reporting for CNN in Philadelphia."

"Thanks Diondre. We go now to our correspondent in Boston. Tom, what's the situation there?"

"This is Tom Reilly in Boston. It was announced earlier today that Deputy Mayor Brian McGonigle is now in charge. The mayor spoke to reporters at 9 am informing them that Mayor Gill had been killed in an automobile accident on his way to work. Because of the unknown circumstances surrounding the accident, the governor has ordered additional protection for the new mayor. City Hall is surrounded by armored vehicles, and some urban warfare tilt-rotor helicopters are flying overhead."

"No one here is certain what started the bloodshed on the 4th. Reminiscent of the first shot fired at Concord that began the Revolutionary War, both sides are blaming the other. But does it matter at this point? Whatever led us here, Boston Boston is in chaos. There has been an increase in violence as protesters clash with local police. Several people on both sides have been killed. Traffic in and around Boston is almost non-existent. Logan Airport is entirely shut down to commercial transport, with only workhorse military C130z's and a few Air Force fighter jets being allowed to land."

"The odd thing here, Rakeem, is that after the initial day of fighting, all was quiet in Boston. People were willing to stay in their homes and abide by the curfew until they realized that the president had partnered with the foreign military. As news of the president's role in the deaths of US citizens spread, Bostonians have again taken to the streets, demanding his ouster. Fearing retribution, some government officials who supported the president fled the city or went into hiding."

"Yesterday was a particularly bloody day that saw neighbor pitted against neighbor. The smoldering tensions between Abbas supporters and those sympathetic to the Nationalists boiled over. The anger in this city reached epic proportions as first responders dealt with acts of violence, vandalism, looting, and arson by angry mobs. President Abbas was burned in effigy with fire spreading to nearby homes."

"A short while ago Mayor McGonigle issued a plea for calm and temperance as the city struggles to respond to what has becoming an uncontrollable situation".

"This is Tom Reilly reporting for CNN in Boston."

"Thanks Tom. If you're just tuning in, this is Rakeem Rasul in the CNN Studios in Atlanta bringing you the latest news on the fighting that is taking place throughout the country."

Rakeem went on to offer a brief recap of the events of July 4th: the assassinations, the slaughter of US citizens by foreigners, American retaliation, and the newly imposed curfew, noting that the resulting bloodshed and loss of property in the US had been catastrophic.

"At the government's request, I'm going to show a VAPT that was intercepted by the FCC on July 4th. President Abbas believes that showing this treasonous communication will shed light on the events that occurred and offer proof of who was behind this military coup."

Saul watched with great interest as the TV showed images of his friend, Josh.

"This is General Josh Redmond. The violence that we are seeing around the country is, in fact, the result of a coordinated effort by active duty military, reserve military, and a volunteer militia of over 2 million citizens to oust President Abbas, his cabinet, and select members of Congress. The coup came about after a coalition was formed last year under my leadership with the help of key members of the clergy and Christian, Jewish, and American Muslim communities. I can confirm that the vice president and at least 20 members of Congress were killed early this morning during the first hour of the coup. I am proud to lead this elite group of Nationalists in combat. Our goal is to stop the tyranny of President Abbas and restore the democratic principles that have guided this country since its inception. I call on all patriotic Americans to join us in this struggle. With your help, our country can be great again. The Republic, established by our forefathers, will prevail. God bless you, God bless our Nationalists. And, God bless these United States of America."

As the station rejoined new programs in progress, Saul turned up the volume to better hear the latest news.

"I just received VAPTs from several people from our nation's Capital," Rakeem pauses as he listens through his earpiece. "These are unconfirmed reports, but it seems that most of the riots around the country are over. WTTG Fox News reports that military helicopters continue to circle the city, as tanks and light armored vehicles surround both The White House and Capitol Building. But according to sources, some key members of this rebellion have been arrested. Citizens are asked to abide by the curfew and to return to their homes. Peace has apparently been restored for now. These are just preliminary reports that have not yet been confirmed. Stay tuned to CNN as our reporting on the Civil War continues."

And we're off.

Rakeem took a deep breath as he composed himself during a commercial break.

Chapter 76

The 'Independence Day Massacre', as the media dubbed it, lasted seven days. Starting on the 8th day, July 11th, things quieted down considerably, with only minor scuffles and signs of civil disobedience. But martial law remained in effect. Checkpoints were in place and authorities rounded up dissidents and subversives who were on a *threat to national security list* developed over the past year. In the key battleground areas, houses were searched for weapons as people phoned a threat hot line; informing on their neighbors. Americans hated the Martial Law. Even though some of their liberties were curtailed under President Abbas, they still had more freedom than most countries. Under martial law all civil rights were suspended and military justice applied.

The climate in the country looked an awful lot like the Second Red Scare and the Black Scare, dark periods in history. The first, in the 1950s, was ushered in by Senator Joseph McCarthy who was on a crusade to stamp out Communism. The latter began in 2032 when Senator Ted Baxter, fearing the rise in Islamic extremism, launched a similar campaign against Muslims. In both instances, the senators were making accusations of disloyalty, subversion, and treason without proper regard for evidence. As in those cases, this situation found citizens turning on fellow citizens, making unfounded accusations, to direct scrutiny away from themselves and their families.

So the announcement that Martial Law was concluding on July 31st was greeted with great enthusiasm. The 8 pm curfew was eased to 11pm, a time that was much more agreeable to restaurants and movie theaters, both of which relied heavily on evening business. Club owners who relied on late night and early morning business were still dismayed but the American public, which had been feeling like captives in their homes, was feeling a little better.

The latest statement from the White House indicated that, while it would take years to completely repair the damaged infrastructure, progress was being made with air and ground transportation returning to normal. Adding to the increasing optimism of the citizenry was the announcement that shortly after the end of Martial Law, National Guardsmen would slowly be redeployed to their bases of origin with local, state, and federal authorities returning to their regular duties in law enforcement.

But while everything appeared to be settling down, with Americans returning to work and normal activities, tensions still ran high. Friends and loved ones were lost and there was only one person to blame. Americans, who typically had short attention spans, were not going to forget the carnage. The pain in their hearts would linger for years.

For Abbas, squashing this coup d'etat was a great victory. In hindsight, he no doubt went overboard by using foreign troops. But the president was thrilled that his administration had effectively been able to restore order and that his presidency was uninterrupted and had another historical moment that would add to his legacy, his glory, and the glory of Allah.

The ongoing investigation yielded significant results. Search and seizure ensured that thousands of weapons were confiscated and out of the hands of potential enemies. In DC alone hundreds of dissidents, including Demetri Kotsopouos had been arrested. His execution was carried out by firing squad on August 5th, one month to the day following his conviction for treason for his indefensible actions on July 4th when he "mercilessly, and with great malice," took the lives of three of the president's closest friends and supporters.

The average person understood that Kotsopouos' punishment fit his crime. However, the continued unrest in the country worried Abbas. People became outraged when friends and relatives were rounded up and charged with treason. To appease them, the president decided to temporarily stay the executions of those who had been convicted. *What difference would a few months make if it helped him restore order?*

Later that month, six field officers fearing charges of conspiracy and treason surrendered to the Secret Service. After two weeks of questioning, the administration had a clearer picture of their role in the failed coup and about the men to whom they reported.

The six were told that they might be brought up on lesser charges if they cooperated. As a result of their testimony those members of the Joint Chiefs involved in the insurrection were arrested and accused of multiple counts of sedition, conspiracy, and treason. Oddly, not only did Admiral Barrington escape prosecution but he received a promotion. The rest were being held in Leavenworth for what the president expected would be a speedy trial and execution. As proof that no one is above the law and that military justice is swift, all six of the cooperating officers, despite what they were promised, were convicted of treason and sentenced to death as well.

One thing that still bothered the president was the fact that the leader of the coup, retired General Josh Redmond, was still at large, and his whereabouts were unknown. He seemed to have vanished completely as a sweep of his home by the FBI and interviews with friends and neighbors proved fruitless. They were unable to uncover any evidence at the home, and there was neither evidence of foul play nor any indication of how, or to where, the Redmonds had escaped. While President Abbas secretly hoped that the Redmonds had committed suicide as an honorable way out of the mess they created, he knew deep down that this was wishful thinking on his part. No, his enemy was still around. But the president felt secure in his belief that, even if General Redmond was alive, it was unlikely that he would ever be heard from again, let alone have enough support for another attempt to unseat him.

By October 4th, just 3 months after the initial attacks, order had been fully restored and the local authorities had things under control. While the rebels had not gotten to him, Abbas was sure that there were cells that were not going to go away soon. The incidents of violence, though far fewer than they had been even a week ago, served as constant reminders that the republic was still in disarray. In fact, just down the street from The White House, a newly built mosque was blown apart. Forty Muslims, who were in the Mosque for noon services, were killed. Most states kept their National Guard units on high alert.

Maybe it was a false sense of security, but Abbas believed that the coup was over, the democracy had been restored, and he believed that it was time to move on. He felt the need to deliver a State of the Union Address. While the timing was unusual, the president felt that with all that had transpired; with all of the turmoil of the past few months, Americans needed to hear firsthand that the union had prevailed. Americans needed to be know that he, in no uncertain terms, was fully in control.

Chapter 77

It was 8:50 pm. Angela sat quietly in the day room watching TV. While a little out of the ordinary, given that this was only October, the president's State of the Union address would begin shortly. He had delivered one every month since the start of the coup attempt.

"I was a part of that," Angela absent-mindedly said out loud with pride as images of past fighting in the streets of the country's major metropolitan areas flashed across the screen. Surprisingly she was still alive having only recently been charged, tried, and convicted of treason.

A reporter for MSN was giving background information to the audience as if he thought everyone watching had been asleep for the past three months. *What a moron*, thought Angela. Next, images of armed guards and armored personnel carriers in the streets of Washington filled the screen just before the cameras shifted to the House of Representatives Chamber in the Capitol.

First, the deputy sergeant at arms addressed the speaker of the house and loudly announced the newly appointed vice president and members of the Senate, who entered and took their assigned seats.

Then he addressed the Speaker again and loudly announced, in order, the Dean of the Diplomatic Corps, The Chief Justice of the United States, and the Associate Justices, and the newly constituted Cabinet, each of whom entered and took their seats when called. The justices took the seats nearest to the speaker's rostrum and adjacent to the sections reserved for the cabinet and members of the Joint Chiefs.

The sergeant at arms stood just inside the doors, faced the speaker, and waited for the president to ready himself for his entrance into the chamber. Finally, just after 8 pm as

Abbas reached the door, the sergeant at arms announced "Mister Speaker, the President of the United States."

Angela watched, with tears in her eyes, as the president walked down the aisle to thunderous applause; shaking hands and kissing friend and foe alike. "He has to put on an act, like he's friends with everyone and they'll all work together in a spirit of cooperation," said Angela to no one in particular.

After handing copies of his speech to the speaker and vice president, the president prepared to make his address as the Speaker introduced him to the Representatives and Senators, stating: "Members of Congress, I have the high privilege and distinct honor of presenting to you the President of the United States."

"Mr. Speaker, Mr. Vice President, Members of Congress, fellow citizens:

"Three months ago, a civil war was fought on American soil for the first time in over 180 years. The casualties in this conflict were eclipsed only by those of the Civil War of the 1860s. Over 400,000 Americans lost their lives, and another half million were wounded over the course of just a few weeks. The cost of the damage to the infrastructure of our county runs in the trillions. There can be no price put on the destruction of monuments and national treasures; lost to our children and future generations. Many historic buildings that represented the early struggles of our founding fathers and that paid homage to many great Americans are gone. During the fighting Independence Hall in Philadelphia, Old State House and Faneuil Hall in Boston, Old Quaker Meeting House in Flushing Queens, and Tudor Place right here in Washington were destroyed. But the carnage went beyond our large eastern cities. Historic and religious buildings in small towns also were heavily damaged. The Mother Mosque of America in Cedar Rapids, Iowa, the oldest mosque in North America, was burned to the ground. Also, 1,000 mosques and over 600 churches and synagogues around the country were either destroyed or suffered significant damage."

"I'm extremely saddened that devastation of this magnitude had to occur. Traditionally ideological differences are settled through peaceful means in a country like ours. Apparently, that is not always possible; as evidenced by the utter disregard for the electoral process that some traitors have shown over the past few months."

"I'm pleased to report tonight that our union is strong. Over the past few months, we've worked hard at rebuilding the trust of the American people, rebuilding some of the key components of the infrastructure like roads and rail lines that were compromised, and restoring aspects of our government through key appointments and in some cases special elections. I'm happy to report that we have completed this part of our recovery and that our government is fully functional. The stock exchange and most financial institutions have been back in operation since July 14th. The hospitals, especially in our cities, while overcrowded are functioning well. Our economy, though sluggish early on, is making a recovery."

"We've accomplished a lot, my fellow Americans, but there is still much to do. I'm confident that with your help, we will achieve the goals that we've set forth."

"I'd be remiss if I did not recognize some of my loyalists killed during the uprising and thank some of the people who were by my side in bringing this conflict to its rightful conclusion."

"First off, I lost a very dear friend when Omar Khalid was assassinated. Then, former Vice President Syed Rashad, along with some key members of my administration and 20 members of Congress lost their lives in separate, but coordinated attacks shortly after fighting broke out on July 4th. We should all mourn these patriots and never forget them. Their deaths are a loss to the entire country. I, personally, will miss their invaluable countenance but most of all their friendship.

"I'd like to thank President Amjad Waseem of Syria and President Muhammad Tahan of Iran for their understanding and acceptance that the events that resulted in the deaths of some of their warriors were collateral damage that resulted from the coup attempt here in our country. They have both agreed to an armistice. As part of that treaty, all political prisoners held in the Middle East have been released. The United States has agreed to make reparations of $50 billion to compensate both countries for damages to their war planes, tanks, and military installations that our forces attacked in early July." "Included in this total was compensation to the families of the Syrians and Iranians who lost their lives on US soil. It is my hope that we have lasting peace and that our countries will remain strong allies."

"To my friends, allies, and the many Americans who have supported me in our quest for a more disciplined roots-based America, I pledge that we will not be deterred in achieving the goals that I set, over three years ago, when I took office. This insurgency serves as proof to the world that our country is strong and that even this major test could not shake our confidence or destroy our union. I promise you that I am more committed than ever to the future of our great nation and to ensuring that my vision of a greater America is realized."

"In closing, many of my enemies who staged the July 4th coup, including some of the rebel leaders and all of the Joint Chiefs, have been captured and are awaiting the long overdue death sentences that have finally been handed down by the courts for their treason. To those still at large, I say that you are all public enemies of the United States, war criminals to most of the world, and my personal enemies. I will not rest until we have captured and sentenced you for your heinous crimes. I will never forget my pledge."

"Thank you, may Allah bless you, and may He bless the United States of America."

Angela, still crying, was ushered from the day room back to her cell. All of the "so-called" traitors had been required to leave their small cubes for the sole purpose of seeing that their treachery had failed, and their incarceration, trials, and sentences were the result of their flawed thinking and actions. President Abbas had ordered the prisoners to watch the broadcast as punishment partly because he wanted to rub their failure in their faces but also because he wanted them to understand fully what his father had taught him years ago. Change doesn't come easily or without a price. The United States is still the strongest Democracy in existence. But in a Democracy, the only way to change the government is through the long and arduous task of voting. After all, isn't that how he got elected?

While their trials took longer than normal because of the recent turmoil, Angela, Nicky, Qasim, and the Joint Chiefs had all recently been convicted of treason and were awaiting execution. Death row, in the recently reopened Leavenworth Prison, was overcrowded now, but it would be less so in 22 days when their sentences were carried out. There would be no appeals.

At the closing of the speech, President Abbas left the speaker's platform and after shaking the hands of each member of his cabinet, walked down the aisle to loud and very jubilant applause. As when he entered, he stopped to shake the hands of friends and supporters who were standing as a show of respect and support. Tarif Mansour, who had written this famous speech, bowed with hands clasped before giving the president a kiss on the cheek.

Looking straight ahead, Abbas raised a fist and then pointed it right at the cameras.

As he reached the midpoint between the front and the back of the room, there was a loud explosion in front of him followed by several more in a matter of seconds. The columns that surrounded the chamber began to crumble. People started screaming as they tried to head toward the exit doors. Unfortunately, all of the doors were demolished and the upper level that housed visitors and the press corps began to topple.

Outside, the distant rumble of devastation pierced the ears of those nearby who bore witness to a cloud of dust flying around like a sandstorm in a desert. The entire south side of the Capitol building seemed to implode. Explosions were heard every second moving in a counterclockwise motion around The Capitol Building until the final and largest explosion occurred near the very top of the dome ensuring its complete collapse. The building was reduced to rubble in a matter of seconds.

Chapter 78

Aaron Rudzinsky sat anxiously in his Lincoln down the street from the residence of Secretary of Treasury, Thomas Hilton. Months ago when the planning had just started, and he and Josh were working toward the goal whereby Josh could wrestle the reins of power from President Abbas, Thomas Hilton and Lawrence Richter, weren't even in anyone's thoughts.

They had assumed that both of these men would be in attendance at all official functions, but it was learned earlier in the day that Hilton was the designated survivor so he would not be attending the president's speech this evening. Richter had announced earlier that he would be forced to miss the speech for personal reasons. No other explanation was given.

The problem was magnified when they realized that both men were in the line of succession. With all other successors removed, one of these seemingly staunch supporters of Abbas would assume the presidency. Swift action had to be taken to ensure that they would pose no threat.

General Redmond approved the plan that Aaron had presented earlier in the day.

At approximately 7 pm, Secretary Hilton got into his car for the short drive to his favorite restaurant where, unknown to anyone, he was to meet Larry Richter. He buckled his seat belt and turned on the ignition. A massive explosion left his car incinerated in his driveway.

Aaron sped off feeling pretty good about his day's work.

An hour earlier, Aaron had spied on Lawrence Richter from over 100 yards away through a pair of the latest Laser Rangefinders. Richter's wife and two children were away, visiting relatives in upstate New York. Richter was supposed to attend the president's speech but plans had changed when he received a call earlier in the day from Tom Hilton.

Aaron saw Richter going into the bathroom to shower. Time was of the essence as he didn't know how long Richter took to shower and dress. Aaron, wearing coveralls and driving a stolen Paul's Auto Repair Service truck, pulled into the driveway of the two story townhome in Potomac Hills, climbed underneath the Secretary's two-year-old Lexus, and made a small slit in the brake lines.

Forty minutes after leaving Hilton's residence Aaron was driving north on I-95 in Maryland. He loved listening to some of the greatest rock music ever streamed. While his Streamer was usually set to block news feeds, he removed the block to hear what was being said about tonight's events.

The feed reported the shocking news report about Hilton's death. That was followed by another report suspecting a link to the death of Mr. Richter, who had been killed when his 2046 Lexus SE failed to negotiate a dark winding curve on the George Washington Memorial Parkway in Virginia sending the car over a small embankment and into a large southern oak tree.

Aaron smiled. His father would not be proud of what he had done. He wouldn't expect it from the rabbi. But the general, being a man of action, would. Aaron had tied up the loose ends by killing two traitors and clearing the way for a return to the United States that he once loved. No, his father would be upset but he was confident that General Redmond would recognize these as heroic acts and Aaron as a true patriot.

Chapter 79

News reports of these terrorist attacks were instantaneous and often a mixture of fact and half-truths. One thing was certain; the face of America had just been altered again.

At 10:15 pm, The recently appointed Deputy Chief of Staff of the White House, Franklin Mills, briefed reporters and the country on National TV.

"As you know, there was an attack on the Capitol Building tonight," started Mills. "President Abbas, the vice president, the White House chief of staff, most of the cabinet, the newly appointed Joint Chiefs, the justices, and all but a few members of Congress were killed in the attack."

"There were only ten members of Congress who did not attend the address tonight. I have been in contact with each. They are in hiding at this moment. John Barrington, Interim Chair of the Joint Chiefs, was excused because of illness. Two members of the president's cabinet were not in attendance, but they too were killed in two separate incidents. Secretary of the Treasury, Thomas Hilton, purposely excused from attending the session, was killed when his car exploded in his driveway. Secretary of The Interior, Lawrence Richter was killed when the brakes on his car failed, sending the car over an embankment and into a large tree. Both men had been alone at the time. As you know, these men were in the line of succession to the presidency. Their deaths were neither accidental nor the result of some terrorist organization but the work of Nationalists who had staged a coup just a few short months ago. Retired Major General Josh Redmond, the leader of the Nationalists, has assumed the presidency on an interim basis and will speak to you now. I give you President Redmond."

With that introduction, General Josh Redmond of the US Army two-star variety stood before the cameras and spoke for the first time as president of the United States.

President Redmond assured the country that there was nothing for them to fear and that this was not an instance of coincidence or a terrorist attack on US soil, but the culmination of a plan that was put in place almost a year ago. He told the nation that he had selected a new vice president, recently retired Navy Admiral John Barrington, and that he had already assembled his cabinet and would be meeting with them shortly. He promised to speak to the nation in a couple of days to introduce the cabinet members and to discuss the status of the union at that time.

The military was under the command of his longtime friend and mentor, US Army Four-Star General Aloysius Barr, who had been briefed on the plans six months before the coup. Many of the key military brass had been supporters of the coup and those gentlemen were in place to maintain order. Those who had been loyal to the former regime had been assassinated earlier in the evening, the final piece to Americans reclaiming their country. While there was no sitting Congress at the moment, the nation should consider that nothing more than a temporary situation, no different than when they were in recess. Special elections would be held over the next few months to replace the deceased members of Congress. There would be a special presidential election in the future, but the date for that could not be set until the country was back on its feet. Until that time, the military would be in charge of the country with him at the helm and martial law would remain in effect.

The president then thanked what he called the "real allies of America." He singled out Canada for providing a refuge for himself and many of the patriots who were forced to flee the country after the first stage of the coup. He then mentioned what he called the best kept secret of the coup; the unwavering support that he received from the leaders of Israel, Great Britain, and France.

The president warned supporters of former President Abbas that all eyes were on them, and any attempts to vindicate his death or to usurp the new administration's authority would be dealt with harshly. He told Syria and Iran that he would not be bound by the unlawful terms of the prior administration's treaties and warned them to stay out of the affairs of the United States because further actions by them against this administration, or this country, would be considered acts of war.

Before wrapping up, the president announced that he was immediately commuting the sentences of Angela Marie DiPietro, Qasim Khalid, Nicky Gervasi, the former Joint Chiefs, and all others convicted of treason as a result of their actions on July 4th. While the prior administration considered these brave people to be traitors, history will bear witness to the fact that they were, in fact, the patriots that he claims them to be.

In his closing remarks, President Redmond asked the country to mourn those who gave their lives to ensure freedom for all. While she was not a part of this conspiracy, Redmond praised Carol Carson. It was her call to arms speech during her trial and the sacrifice of her life that made her a catalyst that transformed social unrest into revolution.

He praised Demetri Kotsopouos, who, by his actions on the morning of July 4th likely saved the lives of millions of Americans. He expressed deep regret over Demetri's execution for treason on August 5th. He then expressed his deepest sorrow for those, who history would consider "collateral damage" who were killed tonight inside of the Capitol building. He expressed his regrets that many had to lose their lives, especially White House Chief of Staff Tarif Mansour, members of the highest court, and the members of the press, but reiterated that there was just no other way to bring about the needed radical change in such a short time.

His last sentence only served to show the nation that he was in fact in charge as he ended with "Please keep my administration in your prayers. Thank you. May God bless you and may God bless these United States of America."

Chapter 80

Three days had passed since the final day of the regime of purported extremist Ahmad Abbas. President Redmond was preparing another presidential address. It was unusual for a president to address the nation twice in three days but these were far from ordinary times.

What should the president tell the American people?

Should he simply tell them that the ten members of Congress who did not attend Abbas' last State of the Union address had been supporters of his who were told not to attend? One, Senator Landry of New Jersey, had been an explosives expert under Josh in Afghanistan. He led the team which planted the devices that ultimately took down the entire Capitol building. As he had promised his old friend, he would die with that secret.

Should he pay homage to some really brave people by talking about the grassroots effort to take back the country and the hard work of persons like Angela, Tony, Nicky, Saul, Aaron, and Qasim? Should he tell of the bravery of Qasim's brother, Makim, who gave his life in support of the mission? Does anyone need to know that the sole purpose of assassinating the White House chief of staff the month before the coup was merely to get Abbas to move Tarif into the position of chief of staff so that Tarif could report on Abbas' actions?

Tears came to Redmond's eyes as he thought of the hundreds of thousands of people who had died during the first stage of the coup. Should he let the nation know that the rioting in the streets was a planned diversion? Would the American people forgive him for staging a ploy that ultimately cost so many lives?

He could never say it out loud, but one thing would haunt him the rest of his life. Once President Abbas had learned the basics of their plans, Redmond knew that the original plan had no chance of succeeding. A coup d'etat relied heavily on the element of surprise. It was in that context that Plan B became not a viable alternative but the final critical stage of the plan. He was the only one who knew that. It was the only way to ensure the element of surprise.

Reflecting again on the loss of life saddened Josh. He had anticipated that the number of casualties during the first stage would be minimal. And it would have been had Abbas not called his friends in Syria and Iran to ask them to send more troops for deployment along with those already at Ft Belvoir and Andrews AFB. Many of the 400,000 people who were killed were outright slaughtered by Syrian and Irani troops who were sent to the major cities before the protest marches even started. Redmond still wondered how Abbas knew about the riots in enough time to position the foreign troops at the right spots, at the right times, to squelch the riots and cause so much loss of life. Why hadn't Tarif known about Abbas' plan? Or did he, in fact, know about it?

Redmond didn't have the answers to the last few questions. But when it came time to make a decision about who he should warn about the Capitol bombing, he had decided that he could not trust Tarif with even the knowledge that there was a Plan B. So Tarif Mansour, who had been instrumental early on in providing much-needed intel, gave his life. Was he a martyr, a Judas Iscariot, or merely collateral damage?

Josh Redmond finally decided that it was simply time to move on. The heroes of this fight knew who they were, as did those who were such an important part of its success. They didn't get involved so that they would be praised. Receiving accolades was the farthest thing from their minds. No, thought Josh, simply getting on with their lives was all they had ever wanted and that, in itself, was their just rewards. Saul could go back to just being the spiritual leader of his synagogue. Though she had to face her future without Tony,

Angela would, at least, be able to dress as she wished and eventually begin a new career as the White House chief of staff. And, Qasim could go back to being a chemical engineer, taking pride in knowing that he and Makim, like their father, had stood up to fight for what was right.

So tonight President Redmond would focus on the future and the need to heal. His speech would be reconciliatory. He would ask the American people to judge Muslims, not on the basis of the former president and other extremists. He would highlight the brave efforts of Qasim and Makim Khalid and others like them; who came to this country for a better life. They were no longer immigrants but Americans who were willing to stand up for what was right.

Tonight he would tell the American people what they needed to hear. The union was once again strong. He would let them know that the government by the people and of the people was once again fully operational and truly "for the people." He would introduce his new cabinet and outline the plans he set in motion for the election of new members of Congress. Then he would announce his proposed changes to the constitution, including the reversal of the harsh executive orders of the former president and the imposition of term limits on Congress. He would also tell them about the five men and four women centrists who he would nominate to the Supreme Court; three Christians, two Muslims, three Jews and an Athiest. Finally, he would announce the date for a presidential election stating the obvious that he would be seeking the office of Commander in Chief. He would run as a member of the newly formed 'Nationalist Party of America.'

Josh hoped that, like war heroes of the past; Washington, Jackson, and Eisenhower, he too would be rewarded with his first elected four-year term. He secretly wondered if he would be fondly thought of throughout history as a man of principle who, like Thomas Jefferson; was a patriot above all else. Or would history prove unkind, remembering him as a traitor for his acts of sedition?

It didn't matter, as he was heading down his charted path. But Josh would never forget the recent history, mistakes that were made in the country, and he would ensure that he and his administration would not repeat those of the past. The future was at hand and tonight Josh would focus on that future. Americans deserved hope. America needed closure.

The End

CPSIA information can be obtained
at www.ICGtesting.com
Printed in the USA
LVOW12s1721221116

514096LV00003B/523/P

9 781537 558806